AWK-
WEIRD

AWK-WEIRD

AVERY FLYNN

Preview of *Loud Mouth* © 2019 by Avery Flynn

Entangled Publishing, LLC
2614 South Timberline Road
Suite 105, PMB 159
Fort Collins, CO 80525
rights@entangledpublishing.com

Amara is an imprint of Entangled Publishing, LLC.

Edited by Liz Pelletier
Cover illustration and design by Elizabeth Turner Stokes

Manufactured in the United States of America

First Edition October 2019

For all my weird, nerdy, never-say-the-right-thing sisters.
Normal really is highly overrated. Xoxo

Chapter One

Tess Gardner was just about all peopled out. But sadly, ditching her bestie's wedding wasn't an option.

Standing in the shadow of one of the potted palms along the edges of the Hayes Resort dining room, she sipped her wine and counted down the minutes until she could go up to her room, slip between the ridiculously high thread count sheets at the luxury hotel, and fall back into the book she was reading. They'd barely finished with dessert, and there would be more toasts and lots of dancing celebrating Lucy's wedding tomorrow.

It wasn't that Tess wasn't thrilled for Lucy and her soon-to-be husband, Frankie—she was. However, over the course of the past year, Tess had become a seventh wheel in their friend group. Every one of her three best friends had paired up. Now she was standing off to the side at a fancy lodge resort outside Harbor City watching Lucy dance with Frankie, Fallon laugh with Zach, and Gina kiss Ford.

It was amazing and awesome and completely awful all at the same time.

Her three best friends were moving on without her.

Oh, no one would actually say that out loud. In fact, her girls probably didn't even realize it was happening, but growing up like Tess had, being shuffled from relative to relative like an unwanted familial obligation had given her a sixth sense about not belonging.

Sure, there was still their weekly girls' night at Paint and Sip, but how much longer would that continue? Not long. So even as she knew she'd stand up as one of Lucy's bridesmaids tomorrow and be genuinely happy for her friends, she'd be resigning herself to the reality of the situation as well.

Everything was temporary. That's just how life worked.

Maybe she should get a cat or a dwarf pig or a goat or *something* to help fill the inevitable friend void. She could name it Kahn and then reenact the great Captain Kirk bellow of "Kahn!" whenever it was time to call it in for dinner. Or she could always go with Darth or Rey. A puppy named Boba Fetch would be pretty funny.

"Gouda and Edam are cities in what country?" one of the guys gathered around a nearby table asked.

A group of the Ice Knights hockey players whom Lucy worked with as a PR goddess had been sitting there for the past ten minutes playing some trivia app. So far, they'd been doing okay—well, the guy playing by himself against the four teams of two men each was—but it physically pained her to hear so many wrong answers hurled out.

This question was a prime example. The teams facing off against the lone man were going through every popular city in Italy and France as the app's timer *beep-beep*ed its way down to the limit.

"The Netherlands," she said quietly to herself as she watched Frankie spin Lucy around on the dance floor.

One of the players who was acting as the questioner, the one with the curly hair Lucy had introduced as Ian Petrov, called out "The Netherlands" as the answer and then asked the next question to pop up on the app. "What is another name for the star fruit?"

There was a moment of silence followed by grumbles along the lines of, *What the hell is a star fruit* and *Where are the sports questions?*

"Carambola." Tess sipped her wine as the information about the fruit scrolled through her head, one word after another, just like it had her entire life.

The yellow-green fruit originated in Sri Lanka and grew on a small tree that produced bell-shaped blooms that eventually became star fruit. She could go on with more facts and stats. Sometimes, she couldn't stop her brain. It had always been like this. Factoid after factoid getting downloaded onto a massive mental server that never seemed to fill up and always seemed to come out at the worst times.

Like now.

The Thor look-alike Ice Knights player, whom she hadn't met, must have caught her saying that last answer because he wasn't laughing at his friends like he'd been doing for the past ten minutes. Instead, he watched her, assessing her with a calculating gaze as cool as the ice blue of his eyes. Then he winked at her.

Pulse kicking into high gear, she whipped her head around so her gaze was back on the dance floor, if not her attention.

Shit. Shit. Shit.

The first rule of being the odd woman out was to not be so fucking obvious about it that strangers noticed. And yet, here she was lurking near a group of people she didn't know, answering all the trivia questions in a game they were playing without her like a supreme dork. And she'd gotten caught.

She pulled her phone out of her bag and glanced down at it, hoping it looked like she'd just gotten a text from someone.

Was it late enough that she could escape? How much more attention would she draw to herself if she sprinted away like her body was screaming at her to do?

More than an injured gazelle limping through the lion enclosure at the Harbor City Zoo.

Take deep breaths. Scroll through old texts from Gina, Lucy, and Fallon. Smile as if you aren't in a fight-or-flight panic moment right now. In a minute, you can calmly walk away without flagging yourself as being completely and utterly awk-weird.

"Perfecto, torpedo, and parejo are all shapes of what?" asked Ian, reading off the question from the app.

Before Tess could answer—in her head this time, because humiliation was not her kink—Thor's twin answered.

"Cigars," he said.

She didn't mean to look over at him. It just sort of happened. And because this was her life, which was filled with one uncomfortable situation after another, he was staring right at her. Unlike Tess, he didn't seem to have a single qualm about getting caught watching. The other men at the table groaned, and someone told him to fuck off. He shrugged away the curse and flipped the bird at his buddies, but his gaze never left hers.

Looking away now would be good, Tess. Go on. Turn your head. Turn it.

But she didn't. She couldn't. Maybe there was something in her wine pinning her to the spot.

Ian asked, "What was the first name of the real Chef Boyardee?"

Thor's twin raised an eyebrow, challenging her to answer.

"Hector," she said, meaning to do so only in a soft whisper, but the combination of the song ending, the wine, and the man who watched her as if she were the most fascinating person in the room made her voice louder than she intended.

"Holy shit, that's right," Ian said, swiveling his body around to look at her—a move replicated by everyone else at the table except for Thor's twin, who'd been staring at her the whole time. "How did you know that?"

How many times in her life had she been asked that? Too many to count, and unlike any of the trivia questions he'd been asking, she didn't have an answer. It was the way her brain had always worked, giving her an out when things got overwhelming or just plain shitty.

"Let's make this interesting," Thor's twin said. "Miss Chef Boyardee and me against all six of you, best out of three sets."

Wait, what? How had she gotten involved in this? She glanced around the room for backup. However, her girls were all preoccupied with the men they'd fallen for, and everyone at the other tables who she kind of knew—including the entire Hartigan family—was either dancing or sitting at one of the many tables around the parquet floor laughing and taking pictures. It was just her.

"What's on the line?" one of the other guys asked.

Thor's twin lifted up his glass of what looked like scotch on the rocks. "Losers cover the team bar tab for the weekend."

Another player Lucy had introduced her to, Alex Christensen, let out a low whistle. "Considering this is one of our few weeks off until the season ends, that bar tab will be substantial."

"Worried, Christensen?"

Alex snorted. "Just trying not to make that famously locked-up-tight wallet of yours cry."

"You won't because we aren't gonna lose." Thor's twin glanced over at her, everything about him screaming ultra-confident sex god, from his blond hair that brushed his shoulders to the dimple in his cheek to his not-of-this-world muscular forearms visible below his rolled-up sleeves.

"Right?"

She wasn't the kind of woman guys like Thor's twin talked to. She was the one in the corner in a fandom T-shirt with bookish earrings.

Okay, tonight she had on a dress, and her obnoxiously curly hair was pulled back instead of corkscrewing around her face and getting caught in her glasses, but still, she was not even close to being *that* woman.

"Everyone loses," she said, the words slipping out before she could stop them. Nerves and old habits made the possibility of stopping a random factoid from spilling out next to impossible. "Stephen King's *Carrie* was rejected thirty times before it was accepted."

"But we're gonna be number thirty-one." He stood up and pulled an empty chair out for her. "Come join the fun."

Peopling was never fun. It was fraught with danger and embarrassment and that sickly damp-palmed feeling that she was about to make a mistake, or more likely a million of them. Walking away was her best choice, but she didn't, and she had no idea what to think about that.

. . .

"Oh my God, Thor, how did you know that minimum wage was twenty-five cents an hour in 1938 but *not* that Lisbon is the capital of Portugal?"

Cole Phillips let the Thor comment go. When Tess had sat down at their table, there had been introductions all around, but she'd stuck with her nickname for him. Cole had given up on correcting her when she'd gotten ten questions in a row right. He knew better than to fuck with someone's process. As long as they won and he didn't end up footing what was going to be an epic bar tab, Tess could call him Scrumdiddlyumptious while spanking his ass if she wanted.

Still, his ego couldn't take that comment lying down—especially not after he'd watched his ex-girlfriend Marti sneak out an hour ago with the Wall Street type she'd been dating for the past month. Sure, his pride was dinged up about it, but it didn't bother him as much as he'd figured it would when he'd heard she was coming. Maybe change wasn't Satan on a pair of roller skates after all.

"Not everyone is such a trivia nerd that they're gonna know that Cincinnati was known at Pordo...Porso...Portopolis in the nineteenth century," he said, stumbling over the word.

"Porkopolis," she said with a giggle that was a little breezier than it had been a glass of wine ago. "Oink. Oink."

Damn, she was cute with her big eyes that her glasses didn't do a thing to hide. Even the curls that had slipped free from her pulled-back hair and the pale-blue dress cut like she was a pinup girl couldn't take away from the fact that Tess was the human equivalent of a cinnamon roll—sugar and spice and everything nice. If he was the kind of guy who did cute, he might be tempted.

But he didn't do cute.

Really, he only did one type of woman, and her name was Marti Peppers and she hated his guts. They'd been on-again, off-again since before he'd joined the league six years ago. They'd been off for the past six months, and this time it wasn't going back on again. She'd been explicitly clear on that. He'd given her his heart, and she'd given him, well, not a pen but about a dozen paintballs to the back and a single-finger salute.

Christensen turned to the other Ice Knights players who'd come upstate for the weekend for Lucy's wedding. "How are these two drunk assholes beating us?"

Tess let out a squawk of protest. "We're not drunk; we're happy."

He nodded in agreement. "What she said."

Okay, there were too many jagged pieces where his heart had been for him to be happy, but he definitely wasn't drunk. Slightly off-kilter? Yes. Blasted? No.

"Last question for the six," Ian said, using the fake announcer voice he used in the locker room to make everyone laugh. "If you chuckleheads miss, then team twosome gets a chance to steal. If they miss it, you win. Either way, I'm going to drink my weight in beer and you fools are covering the bill. Ready?"

The others nodded.

"In what country was Arthur Conan Doyle born?" Ian asked.

Svoboda cocked his head to the side. "Who?"

"The guy who wrote *Sherlock Holmes*," Christensen answered.

One of the rookies, Thibault, took a drink from his beer and said, "I thought that was a TV show."

"It was a book first," Christensen said, giving the rookie a don't-be-a-dumb-ass glare. "It's gotta be England. Holmes was the greatest English detective."

"Is that your final answer?" Ian asked and waited for the other man to nod yes. "Wrong!"

Everyone on the other side of the table groaned. Christensen sank down in his chair while the rookie tried—and failed—to keep a serves-you-right smirk off his face. Ian turned to Cole and Tess.

"He was…" Tess paused. "Can I confer with my partner for a second?"

Ian nodded.

She waved Cole closer, and he leaned half out of his chair so he'd be close enough for this little chat about who in the hell knew what because it wasn't like either of them didn't know Doyle was born in Scotland. She pivoted in her chair so her back was mostly turned away from the guys on the other side of the table to give them a modicum of privacy. The move gave him a perfect view of the top swells of her tits—or it would have if he'd looked. He did not. At least not for long.

"The league minimum salary is around three-quarters of a million dollars," she said, her voice low. "You make at least that, right?"

"More." A lot more, but he didn't need to put that out there.

"Oh," she said, surprise lifting her tone. "Are you a really good player?"

Maybe he was a little more than off-kilter, because he couldn't wrap his brain around the fact that she didn't know the answer to that. He had a billboard up in the middle of Harbor City's touristy hot spot, a contract with Under Armour, and was in the sports news pretty much all the time. "You know the league minimum but not if I'm any good at hockey?"

"People aren't really my thing." She played with the tail of the bow holding the straps of her dress in place. "And the other guys, some of them are rookies, so they make a lot less?"

If he hadn't been so distracted by the way she toyed with the bow, wondering if it was going to hold, he would have caught on to her plan sooner. "You're not thinking…"

She nodded. "I am."

His wallet screamed out in metaphorical protest, but how was he supposed to say no to that face? "You are a horrible influence."

"Nothing could be further from the truth." She smiled, showing off a dimple that could probably cause cavities. "I'm completely harmless."

He didn't believe that, not even for a second.

"You're sure?" she asked, turning serious.

When he nodded, her smile got even bigger, and it gave him the same buzz he'd gotten when they'd made the playoffs.

Turning back so she faced the table, Tess said in a loud, clear voice, "While I disagree, my partner insists he's right. Sir Arthur Conan Doyle was from Australia."

"Wrong," Ian said, smacking his palm down on the table for emphasis. "He was born in Scotland."

Cole couldn't believe it. She'd gotten him to pay the team bar tab *and* had thrown him under the bus. Australian? That wasn't even in the right hemisphere of the correct answer, and she knew it. There was definitely some tart to her sweetness.

While the other players erupted in high fives and smack talk, Cole wrapped his fingers around the arm of her chair and tugged it close. "That was not very nice."

"True," she said, not seeming the least bit sorry. "But look how happy you've made them."

Of course they were thrilled. The lucky bastards were going to be drinking on him all weekend—and he wasn't going to hear the end of it pretty much ever. In fact, Christensen had that look that always preceded enough shit-talking to fertilize every cornfield in Nebraska.

"But now *you* have to figure out a way to get me out of here without it looking like a retreat so I don't have to deal with all of that." He waved a hand at the celebratory dance moves Christensen and Svoboda were trying to pull off. "That would be cruel and unusual punishment on top of that bar bill."

She looked guilty for about three seconds, then said as she stood, "Well, we may have lost, but at least we don't have to dance or anything like that."

His fellow Ice Knights players clamped on to what she'd made to sound like a throwaway line that most definitely wasn't.

"Dance! Dance! Dance!" they chanted in unison.

Not laughing wasn't an option, so he gave in to what had lately been a foreign reaction. "What have you done?"

Given the fact that he'd had to almost yell to be heard over his idiot teammates, he wasn't surprised when instead of hollering back, she raised herself up on her tiptoes and leaned in close.

"Giving you an escape," she said, her lips nearly touching his ear. "Come on, once around the dance floor and we can go out through the conservatory doors with your fragile male ego mostly intact."

He glanced over at the door on the other side of the mostly packed dance floor. It would take some weaving and skill to get through the crowd without looking like they were running, but he was a guy used to moving the puck through a line of professional athletes paid highly to get it away by stick or by check, so this would be easy.

Grinning down at her, he grabbed her hand. "Good plan."

And it was, right up until they moved onto the dance floor and he had her in his arms. His steps were half a beat too slow but more due to his own inability to dance than the scotch. His hand spanned the small of her back, resting against the smooth silk of her skin exposed by the backless dress, and her head fit against the pocket of his shoulder, because of course it had changed to a slow song as soon as they stepped on the parquet.

He noticed everything about her as they swayed to the beat: the hitch of her breath when he brushed his thumb against her skin, the way she moved closer as they made their way across the floor, and the tease of her curly hair against his neck. All of it combined into a heady mix of anticipation and desire that had him searching for the door before he did something stupid like give in to the urge to kiss her in the middle of the dance floor.

Then she looked up at him, her full lips slightly parted and desire on full display in her eyes. Suddenly, doing something stupid seemed like a very good idea.

"On the count of three, we make a break for the door," he said, forcing the words to almost sound normal.

And what came after that? Hell if he couldn't wait to find out.

Chapter Two

Tess's pillow was tickling her nose as it moved up and down in a smooth, steady rhythm as if it was taking deep, steady breaths. That made no sense unless— Her heart paused and her lungs stopped functioning as she jackknifed into a sitting position, her eyes squeezed closed because looking meant seeing and that meant— She peeked.

Oh my God. It hadn't been a steaming-hot dream.

She'd had sex with Cole Phillips.

Cole.

Fucking.

Phillips.

Thor's twin himself.

Multiple times.

In the conservatory.

In the foyer of his massive hotel room.

Finally, in the ginormous bed that was only being half used because they had been curled up together until about ten seconds ago.

Oh my fucking God.

She had obviously lost her mind. Oh sure, she could blame the three glasses of wine or the wedding atmosphere for helping to lower her guard, but one of Lucy's clients? A professional athlete? A guy she'd just met?

Next to her, Cole started to move, his hand patting the bed for her. "It's too early to get up, Mar—" He jolted up.

Now both of them were sitting in bed, staring at each other with horror-filled eyes and breathing as hard as if they'd just gotten done outrunning a pack of zombies.

Good thing she was the type of woman who accepted that fate had it in for her. If not, she would have been painfully disabused of that notion as soon as the metaphorical light bulb went on over her head that the first guy she'd had sex with in nearly forever had woken up thinking she was someone else. That would have been some real ouch right there.

"Tess," she said, gathering the sheet close to her chest and scooting one butt cheek at a time over to the edge of the bed. "My name's Tess."

"Of course it is." Cole shoved his fingers through his hair, and it magically fell untangled to his shoulders like he was in some kind of shampoo commercial. "I just wasn't all the way awake."

That wasn't fair—his perfect morning hair, not what he said. A giant *whatever* on almost calling her someone else's name, because it wasn't like she had any delusions about who she was and who he was and what the hell had just happened. Nope. She was all about unvarnished truth regarding her interactions with all but a handful of people. It's why she loved trivia. Facts were simple, straightforward, and easily defined. People were very much not that. Ever. Which she knew more than anyone and why the bold truth that she'd fallen prey to the wedding curse felt even worse. Judging by the way Thor's twin's gaze was darting all over the hotel room, landing on every piece of furniture twice but not her a single time, he didn't get it.

"Don't freak out," she said as she lowered one foot to the floor and stood up, taking the sheet with her. "We got weddinged."

Of course he looked at her now, while she was trying to hold up the sheet with one hand and put on her panties she'd swiped off the carpet with the other. One-handed pantie put-on-ing was not easy for the uncoordinated like herself. Looking up at the ceiling and away from the man in the bed seemed to help, though, so that's what she did, using a standing-on-one-foot hop move followed by a quick yank up to get her undies in place.

"Weddinged? What does that mean?" Cole asked.

"We got caught up in the whatever of the happy occasion." She glanced down at him. That was a mistake. He was totally naked, but the blanket around his waist stopped her from getting the whole view in the morning light. "Then this happened."

"Weddinged." He added a little *huh* sound to the end of it, as if he was putting the new vocab word in a mental filing cabinet for use later.

"Exactly." She clutched the sheet to her chest as if he hadn't already seen, touched, and licked every bit of her, which she was not at all thinking about as she walked sideways to the chair where her dress had landed in the rush to get naked last night. "But hopefully it's still early enough that I can get back to my room without being seen."

He grabbed his phone off the bedside table. "It's ten."

"What?" An electric zap of panic shocked her right down to her toes. *Shit. No.*

Abandoning the sheet, she sprinted the rest of the way to the chair, grabbed her dress, and tugged it over her head as she hurried to the door. "I was supposed to be in Lucy's suite getting my hair done thirty minutes ago." She grabbed her purse, stuffed her bra inside it, and picked up her shoes from the floor by the door where she'd left them last night. "I gotta go."

"I'll see you later at the wedding."

Later? She had to face him again after this? *Oh, fuck me running.*

And since she had no idea what to say to that, she did what she always did and fell back on her friends the random factoids, whether she wanted to or not.

"Romans used to give newlyweds a special loaf of bread, and some grooms would break it over the bride's head, which is why we have wedding cakes now," she said.

Shut up, weird brain.

Cole chuckled. "I really hope Frankie doesn't try that with Lucy. I don't see it going over well."

She didn't disagree, but she didn't trust herself not to give a whole lecture on the history of that phrase, so she opted for brevity. "Bye."

And she all but ran from the room, down the nearby stairs, and to her floor. Setting a speed record, she showered, got dressed, grabbed her bridesmaid's dress, and hustled with still-damp curls to Lucy's suite. Her girls were all there. Lucy was getting her makeup done. Gina sat on a stool while a hairstylist pulled her hair into a complicated updo that seemed to be held together by hope and hairspray, but there were probably a million hairpins in there. Fallon sat in the corner, dress already on, hair pulled into a simple French braid as she watched hockey highlights on her phone.

"Look who finally arrived," Lucy said with a smile as she gave Tess an assessing once-over.

Tess jerked to a stop, biting the inside of her cheek to keep from spilling secrets or factoids. She did not want them to know what just went down. Cole would forget about her before the vows were said, and she was totally okay with that.

She knew how to deal with being forgotten about.

What she didn't know how to handle was her three best friends all looking at her like she was a king cake with a surprise hidden inside.

These women knew her. There was no way she'd hold up under an interrogation. Her best option might be to beg the makeup artist to do something drastic with her look so she'd have to stay perfectly still and couldn't move or talk or make eye contact. Was that possible outside of getting a *Mission Impossible*–type mask? Probably not. She was definitely screwed.

Gina let out a relieved sigh. "We were about to send the search party."

"That would be me," Fallon said, raising her hand.

"Sorry," Tess said, sitting down in the on-deck chair for the makeup artist. "I forgot to set an alarm."

"So it had nothing to do with sneaking off with Cole Phillips last night?" Lucy asked.

"We went into the conservatory for some quiet," Tess said, clasping her hands tight in her lap. "The DJ was loud."

"Poor Cole," Gina said between blasts of hairspray from the stylist. "That guy is in a rough way. Thanks for hanging out with him."

"How do you mean *rough*?" Not that she cared, but she *was* naturally curious. That was all.

Gina shook her head, much to her stylist's annoyance. "He's been dating and not dating Coach Peppers's daughter, Marti, for about a million years, and she finally called it off a while back. According to the online gossip, he's totally brokenhearted."

"Yeah," Lucy said before blotting her bright-red lipstick. "But will this one take?"

"That's the million-dollar question." Gina got down from the chair as the stylist checked her over from every direction.

"But she seems serious about it, even if he may not be ready to walk away. Oh, I hope it works out."

And that was Gina in a nutshell. No matter how she used to deny it before she met Ford, Gina was a total romantic at heart, and it was no surprise she'd become a wedding planner. She was all about the happily ever afters.

Tess? Not even close.

"Honestly, Tess, you're the best for keeping him from moping," Lucy said. "If anyone sees him doing it at the reception, especially when Marti is nearby, please send up flares. The guy needs all the friends he can get because he is a mess right now."

"He sure is playing like one," Fallon, the resident Ice Knights superfan, said. "He's distracted, and it shows on the ice."

"Not everyone gets a Lady Luck," Tess muttered.

Fallon rolled her eyes. "Don't even. Zach turning his game around had nothing to do with me."

"Well, either way, we Ice Knights fans salute you," Gina said.

Tess's brain was spinning. Things had just gone from her normal level of awk-weird to something approaching epic levels of oh-my-God-run-away awk-weird. She'd done something totally out of character for her and banged a guy she'd just met six ways from Sunday. Then—to make it even more uncomfortable—*he* was hung up on another chick, and they were all going to be at the wedding together.

There was no way this was going to be anything other than a disaster.

• • •

Cole was in hell, and they were playing the "Electric Slide."

There wasn't enough alcohol in the world for this—which

was good because he was still footing the tab for the team. Sure, there was an open bar, but everyone but the rookies thought it was funnier to go to the hotel bar and not the wedding reception bar for their drinks. Assholes. Sure, they weren't wrong, it was funnier, but they were still assholes. There was no way it could get worse.

"So." Petrov drew the single-syllable word out into at least four. "You disappeared with the curly-haired chick last night."

Obviously, Cole's previous declarative statement was now rendered false.

Sliding his attention away from the dance floor and over to the man sitting next to him, he saw the center had ditched his bow tie, and he had a glass of top-shelf single malt in his hand and a shit-eating grin on his face. This was going to be worse.

Cole shrugged. "It was a dance."

"Then a disappearance."

Followed by some damn good sex and—oh yeah—the totally awesome move of waking up and calling the woman he was in bed with by his ex's name. That had been a shit move even if remembering his own name when he first woke up was a challenge. He'd spent the past six months waiting for Marti to agree to give it another go—which she always did—and turning away every single opportunity to get it on with anyone else. Then he'd gotten weddinged. Something the quick-thinking center next to him wasn't going to let him forget, so he might as well dig in and get chippy about it.

"You have a point to make, Petrov?" Cole asked.

"Just an observation and a hell-yeah for finally moving on." Petrov clinked his glass against Cole's. "I haven't seen you with anyone in months, despite the efforts of some of our more creative fans."

"I don't need to move on from anything." Eventually

things would realign and go back to the way they had always been. Solid. Sure. Unchanging. Just the way he liked it. This was just a temporary glitch, not forever.

"You trying to tell me that nothing happened last night? Bullshit. I saw how you looked at her."

"Nothing important happened." Inwardly he cringed at what a dickhead he sounded like, but he kept that internal, covered under fourteen layers of ice. However, if he gave Petrov even a hint that it had been more, he'd never hear the end of it. "It was a nice time."

Three nice times. He'd gone around and searched his room until he'd found the two torn-open condom packets on the dresser top and the one stuffed into the pocket of his suit pants from the time in the conservatory, just to double-check his memory that they'd been three nice, protected times.

The other forward on his line, Alex Christensen, had packed Cole's wallet with condoms for, as he put it, "the premium opportunities a wedding offered." Cole had figured it for the hazing it was. Using them had never crossed his mind until Tess talked him into doing the one thing he never did voluntarily—lose. What in the world was going on?

"First Christensen lines my wallet with condoms, and now you're whispering in my ear about Tess," he mumbled to himself before looking up at the god-awful fresco on the ceiling of the reception room that had been painted with a Greek god theme, never mind that they had Icarus flying away from the sun instead of toward it.

"Maybe we all think it's time you tried a new path," Petrov said, completely missing that Cole's question had been rhetorical. "Ever think that maybe, even though Marti is one of the coolest chicks we know, you should just walk away after this breakup? It's been six months." He gestured toward the dance floor. "She seems to have moved on. Follow her lead. You've been ignoring the other women throwing themselves at you for months, but last night you fall in with Tess? Sounds to me like you're ready to move on."

Cole looked over toward the dance floor. He didn't have to search to find her. Marti was dancing with that Wall Street guy, who looked like he couldn't make up his mind between ogling her tits or stealing from a widows and orphans charity fund. Where had she found this prick? She was better than him.

"If I could have everyone's attention," the DJ said over the music, loud enough to clear the questions from Cole's head. "It's time for the garter and bouquet toss."

A chair was brought out to the dance floor and a laughing Lucy was led to it by the redheaded giant, Frankie, she'd married. As she sat down, Frankie whispered something in her ear that had the toughest, no-nonsense shark of a public relations crisis management guru blushing, and then he reached under her dress and pulled her lace garter down her leg.

"If we can get all the single men to line up at the far end of the dance floor and the single ladies at the opposite end here by me," the DJ said.

Cole had absolutely no intention of moving from his seat, but Christensen and Petrov each hooked an arm under his, hauled him up out of his seat, and force-marched him to where all the single dudes were milling about.

"I'm not catching that thing," Cole said, stuffing his hands deep in his pockets.

Christensen just grinned that never-lost-a-tooth miracle smile of his. "Don't worry, the plan is for us to catch it for you."

"You two are assholes," he said with a sigh.

Petrov lifted one shoulder in a lazy shrug. "Something you already knew to be true."

"One," the DJ said, starting the countdown.

Frankie twirled the garter around one finger and eyeballed the crowd of single guys. Cole took a step back deeper into the crowd, only to be shoved none too gently back to the front by a pair of his line mates who really needed to get a hobby or a girlfriend or both.

"Two."

Frankie pulled back on the garter like it was a slingshot and aimed at a part of the crowd farthest away from Cole. He looked over his shoulders at Christensen and Petrov and shot a smirk at them. The only way to keep him at the front was if they both stayed there blocking his path, but that left the entire rest of the crowd unguarded if they were going to snatch that garter out of midair for him as they'd planned. It was the curse of the double-team.

"Three."

At the last second, Frankie pivoted and shot the garter straight at Cole. It flew through the air like a puck zinging toward the goal. He didn't mean to reach up and grab the flying lace, but muscle memory was a helluva thing. The garter was in his hand before he realized he was reaching for it.

Motherfucker.

He shoved the damn thing into his pocket as fast as he could and ignored the self-satisfied laughter coming from the two chuckleheads behind him. Maybe no one noticed.

"And we have our bachelor winner," the DJ said. "Now, all the single ladies lined up on my side of the dance floor, get ready because here comes the bouquet!"

Lucy turned her back to the gaggle of women, did a couple of I'm-about-to-toss-it-but-didn't moves, and then—finally—let the bouquet go. It arced across the opening before smacking Tess hard in the face and then falling to the floor as everyone in the room let out a collective gasp.

"I'm all right," Tess said as she picked red rose petals out of her hair. "Tis only a flesh wound."

Old school Monty Python? He grinned despite his annoyance at the whole garter thing.

"Let's give a hand to our lucky guests who will get the dancing started," the DJ said, his shaking voice obviously an attempt to cover his laughter.

The fuck? A dance? No. This whole carrying-around-Lucy's-garter thing was weird enough without adding in a very public slow dance with the woman he'd gotten weddinged with last night.

He didn't move. Neither did Tess. Instead they both stood there on opposite sides of the dance floor, her looking just as horrified as he felt.

"Mr. Garter Belt and Ms. Bouquet to the Face." The DJ laughed at his own joke. "You're up."

"But I didn't catch it," Tess said, her voice going up at the last word.

No one seemed to be listening to her valid argument, though. Instead, her people were doing pretty much the same thing as his—shoving him out onto the dance floor as a slow song started playing. Last night, he'd curled an arm around her waist and pulled her close without a second thought. Not so much today. Without the high of the trivia game and the social lubrication of a few drinks, everything seemed to move slower with a higher level of awkward.

"I'm not gonna turn into a stalker," she said as she settled her left hand on his shoulder. "You don't have to worry."

Way to go, dumb-ass, you made her feel like shit. You should bottle that talent. "Who said I was worried?"

She looked up at him as they moved around the dance floor, filling up with other couples. "So you do that a lot and don't have weird stalker problems?"

"Do what?" How had he not noticed last night that she had one blue eye and one green? It was subtle, only a few shades different, and she was wearing glasses, adding in a protective layer between her and the world, but still he should have noticed. "You have heterochromia iridum."

"It's not uncommon," she said, narrowing her eyes at him. "More than two hundred thousand cases are diagnosed each year, but don't change the subject. I know you're still hung up on your ex. I have no delusions that last night was anything more than just us getting weddinged."

Her no-nonsense declaration hit with the sharp crack of a stick to the cheek. For reasons unknown, it burned, stung, and just might have drawn blood. Not that it mattered. It didn't. It wasn't like he was interested in her anyway.

He spun them around a little faster than the beat, needing to move. "Good to know."

After that, they both kept their mouths shut, which was for the best. Last night had been a fluke occurrence. His tomorrows were already planned right down to the alphabetized books on the shelves in his den, the breakfast he'd been having every day since he was ten, and the woman he was going to end up with—Marti. The woman who had always been there for him no matter what. They'd find their way back to each other. They always did.

"Did you know the garter toss originated in England and France because guests would try to tear off a piece of the bride's dress for good luck?" Tess asked, her grip on his shoulder a bit tenser than it had been before. "Grooms started flinging part of the bride's wedding outfit to calm the crowd and stop the wife from having a nervous breakdown at the idea of having her outfit ripped to shreds while she was wearing it."

"I didn't." He mentally shook off the unease that crept in whenever he thought about a possible change in his routine and dug for a wedding factoid of his own. Competitive? Him? Fuck yeah. "Did you know bouquets were originally garlic, herbs, and spices carried by the bride to ward off evil spirits?"

Tess cracked a smile for the first time since she'd gotten a face full of rosebuds. "I'll add that one to my list."

The tension seeped out of his shoulders, and even though he didn't mean to, he drew her in closer and they swayed to the last bars of the song. Moving on to something up-tempo, the DJ called to the crowd to put on their dancing shoes. Yeah, Cole definitely didn't own any of those and, judging by the way Tess just stood there and looked around at everyone else, she didn't, either. Finally, her gaze landed back on him.

"Good luck with her, your ex," Tess said, taking a step back out of his arms. "I hope it all works out."

Before he could say anything in response, Tess hustled away from him, disappearing into the crowd. Looking down, he spotted a couple of rose petals clinging, against the odds, to his tux lapel. He wasn't likely to see Tess ever again, but he still slipped the petals into his pocket as he walked off the dance floor, wondering what factoid she would be able to tell him about roses, the origin of the tuxedo, or the stats for the most popular wedding songs. He'd have to figure that information out for himself, though, because she was right. They had gotten weddinged. Really, what were the chances of ever running into Tess again? Zilch. Zero. Nada. And that was a good thing. Really.

So why was he staring at the spot where she'd disappeared instead of over at Marti and her idiot date like he usually would have been? Fuck if he knew. He was a hockey player, not Freud.

Chapter Three

One month later...

If there was anything Tess could count on in life, it was her period coming every twenty-eight days like a perfectly engineered clock made of cramps and Almond Joy cravings. Today was day twenty-nine, according to her tracking app, and she was sitting on the edge of the tub in her tiny bathroom not breathing and watching four home pregnancy tests lined up on the counter next to the sink while her kitten, Kahn, weaved around and in between her calves.

Were four tests overkill for what would no doubt be a negative result? Probably. They'd used condoms. Three of them. It had only been one night. More than likely it was just the stress of her asshole landlord uncle threatening to raise the rent on her flower shop and her apartment above it. Forever in Bloom was finally turning a healthy profit, and she had plans to use that extra cash to hire an accountant so she wouldn't be doing the books herself.

Kahn mewled and bit Tess's leg with his pointy little

teeth.

"Ow!" She massaged the spot right above her ankle to rub the sting out. "What was that for?"

The kitten, a puffball of black and white fur, just flicked his tail and stared up at Tess as if she'd somehow disappointed him by even having to ask the question. Kahn's teeth were no joke, and from the kneecaps down, she was starting to look like a pincushion.

Her phone buzzed as it vibrated against the counter, and she sat up straight, bite forgotten and nervous swirling in her belly remembered. If she'd been all in for the test result to come back one way or another, this experience might be different. Calmer? More hopeful? Instead, she was just a jumble of mixed-up emotions, ranging from please-let-it-be-yes to oh-my-fucking-God-no and everything in between.

Family was something she'd never really had until she met her girls Lucy, Fallon, and Gina. Her mom had seen her mostly as an inconvenience to be dropped off at various relatives' houses whenever possible for as long as possible. Those aunts and uncles never let her forget that she was an obligation and it was only because of their Christian duty that they welcomed her into their homes—even if that welcome was more of a tired tolerance.

But a baby? That would be creating her own family. She could make sure to do it right because she'd seen firsthand how it could be done wrong.

Doubt circled upward, twisting and distorting all of that hopefulness because what if she really wasn't meant to have a family? How many times did she have to learn that lesson? Even if she kept the baby—if there *was* a baby—did she really think she'd be enough as a single mom? Or would she just repeat every mistake that had been visited onto her?

Kahn took a swipe at her shin and narrowed his little eyes at her as if to say, *Just look already.*

"I thought the whole cats-rule-the-humans thing was an exaggeration," Tess said more to herself than the kitten and stood up so she could lean over and look at the pregnancy test result screens on each of the four sticks.

Plus.

She stared, blinking and uncomprehending.

Plus.

Her pulse skyrocketed.

Plus.

A lump—of excitement? anxiety? wonder?—formed in her throat.

Plus.

Before she kept forgetting to breathe, and now, it felt like she couldn't stop inhaling and exhaling air, but she was doing it so quickly that none of it was actually getting to her lungs. She pressed her fist to her belly, holding it firmly in place, and then jerked it away.

Baby.

There.

Okay, not really. And it wasn't a baby yet but a fetus so small an ultrasound tech would probably be able to circle something on a screen but to Tess it would be indecipherable. That didn't change the fact that this was happening. She was pregnant.

She plopped back down on the edge of the tub, her knees too weak to keep her upright, and focused on her breathing enough to actually slow the panicked hyperventilating thing she had going on and inhale a long, smooth breath through her nose and out her mouth. She repeated that five more times before she gave in to the constant whir of her brain and tried to process what she was going to do next. She had options.

It was too late for Plan B, but she could get an abortion.

She could have the baby but give it up for adoption.

Keep it and start her own family.

So which one was the right answer for her, right now, in this moment? Abortion made sense. Beyond her girls, she didn't have a support system. Was she really ready to be a single mom without one? Did she have the tools to do it right, or would she be continuing the family curse? She'd barely gotten to a point in her life where she felt qualified to have a pet. A baby needed and deserved so much more attention and love than she was sure she knew how to give.

Then there were the logistical issues. The demands of being a small business owner weren't conducive to going it alone on the parenting route. Who would cover the flower shop when she had to go to prenatal appointments? Could she afford health insurance for the both of them? What about day care? That was easily the cost of another car payment, if not more.

Standing up, she tried to still the thoughts running through her brain faster than she could grasp and then walked over to the bathroom mirror. She lifted her shirt, looking down at her stomach. The little pudge under her belly button had been there for years, so she expanded her abdomen to make it look bigger, rounder. That's what it could be in a few months.

But was she ready? Even with her doubts, she couldn't ignore that feeling that she was. She was staring down her thirtieth birthday, owned her own business, had an apartment, didn't have *that* much debt, and a family was pretty high up there on her want list. Most importantly of all, she *wasn't* her mother and never would be. This baby would know it was loved, had a place in the world, and was never an obligation. She couldn't fix her childhood by having this baby, but she could give this baby the childhood she'd wanted—that had to count for something.

It wouldn't be easy. Single momming was not for the faint of heart. Then again, neither was anything else she'd managed to do in her life, including working her own way through college, starting a business, and just living life on her own in general.

She could do this.

Glancing down at her belly, she rubbed her palm over it, one soothing circle followed by another and another.

She *would* do this.

She was having this baby.

Letting out a deep breath, her lips curled upward in a smile that didn't falter until two words entered her mind: *Cole Phillips.*

How in the hell am I going to tell him?

• • •

Paint and Sip nights with Lucy, Gina, and Fallon were sacred. She wouldn't miss it, not even with her brain not taking half a breath between shooting out pregnancy factoids at her.

"Placenta" is Latin for the word "cake."

The uterus expands more than five hundred times its usual size during the course of pregnancy.

Babies drink urine in the womb.

God, her brain really needed to shut the fuck up already.

"Perfect timing, Tess." Gina slipped her arm through Tess's as they walked through the door into the studio. "I am dying for a glass of wine. It has been *a week*. The bride from Harbor City is a delight but her soon-to-be husband the accountant? Oh my God. Total nightmare. Groomzilla galore."

"Tell me everything," Tess said.

And that's all it took to get Gina off and running on this Hank guy and how high-maintenance he was. It was a brilliant move. No one told hilarious demanding-client stories like Gina, and this would get them through at least the setup for tonight's painting. She was going to tell her girls about the pregnancy and enlist their help in tracking down Cole's number so she could tell him, but she wasn't ready yet. Instead, she listened to Gina describe the ten-minute voicemail Hank had left about the difference between the colors white shadow and eggshell mist as they sat down next to Lucy and Fallon.

"Have you seen this week's painting yet?" Lucy asked, nodding toward the front.

Larry, their instructor, stood next to a painting of a pie with a radioactive glow sitting on a windowsill with a view of a decrepit nuclear reactor. Someone must have been reading about Chernobyl or Three Mile Island.

"I don't know," Tess said. "I think including the skull and crossbones as an imprint on the pie crust is pretty genius."

"We need to get him to try some cheerier reading material just for a change of pace," Gina said as she poured four small plastic cups of red wine. "Last week was a cow being led into a slaughterhouse."

"Larry would find a way to make *Harold and the Purple Crayon* horrifying," Fallon said, accepting her cup from Gina. "The man has a gift—let him express it."

Gina made noises of agreement as she handed a second cup to Lucy and then turned to Tess, the cup filled nearly to the brim with cheap Merlot. For a second, all Tess could imagine was a little skull and crossbones etched into the plastic cup.

"I'm good," she said, waving off the drink.

Gina chuckled. "You know this high-quality product isn't available on just any grocery store shelf."

"Yeah," Lucy said, joining in on the joke. "You wouldn't want to turn this stuff down unless you're pregnant."

Tess blanched, her palm automatically going to her belly.

All three of her girls stared for a second, their jaws going slack with realization.

Tess nodded. "And I'm keeping it."

"You're pregnant!" Fallon practically shouted. "This is awesome."

If only it had been Gina saying it, there would have been hope that the two words would have been whispered. Everyone in Paint and Sip whipped around to stare at Tess. She smoothed her hand over her curls, all of which were frizzing from the light snow outside, and tried her best to melt into the background.

It's where she liked to be.

People forgot about her and, as she'd learned at a young age, it was always safer when she wasn't noticed. Being reminded of her presence had only made her relatives remember that she'd been foisted upon them in the first place. They'd start complaining loudly about the extra mouth and wondering with harsh regularity when her mother was going to come reclaim her.

That wasn't going to happen in the art studio, though. All the regulars, including her girls, were raising their cups in toast—even Larry, who almost looked like he might be smiling.

"Thanks," Tess said when they wouldn't stop staring at her as if waiting for confirmation of Fallon's exclamation. "I'll be one of the nearly forty percent of American women who are unmarried when they have babies."

All of the happy murmurings silenced, and Larry's hint of a grin disappeared as if she'd imagined it.

Way to go, Tess. Nothing like letting your awk-weird show in public.

"To Tess and the forty percenters," Gina said, holding up her cup.

Fallon, Gina, and Lucy wrapped their arms around her in a group hug that helped settle her. This feeling, the one that made her warm and content and at ease, was what she wanted the baby to grow up bathed in.

After the hug ended, Lucy held her by the shoulders and gave her the look that sent her misbehaving crisis communications clients into a flurry of I-will-never-fuck-up-again activity. "Who is the mystery man?"

"Yeah, who have you been hiding from us?" Gina asked, sitting down in front of her blank canvas, wine in hand and attention focused solely on Tess.

"Did you know a rhino's horn is made of hair?"

None of her girls even batted an eye. Damn it. There was something to be said for being able to throw people off their game by throwing random facts their way. It was amazing how often that worked. For someone like her who hated to people, it kept interactions blessedly contained and short.

"Nice try, Tess," Lucy said. "But we're here so often that Larry barely even shushes us anymore. Spill."

"Cole's the dad. We used three condoms, but something must have been wrong with them."

"He triple wrapped?" Fallon asked.

"At the same time?" Lucy looked up at the ceiling as if she was imagining the logistics of rolling one condom on top of another and then doing it again just to be sure. "I know he has this whole cleanliness thing, but that's just fucking weird."

"No," Tess managed to squeak out. Oh God, why was this embarrassing? These were her closest friends. They knew she had sex. "We did it three times the night before Lucy got married."

"In one night?" Gina did a quick series of quick happy claps. "No wonder you were late for hair and makeup."

"I'm impressed you were able to roll out of bed at all," Lucy said with a chuckle. "Good for you."

"Wait," Fallon said, using one of her paintbrushes as a pointer and directing it at Tess. "That was only a month ago.

How can you know you're pregnant? You could just be late."

"That's what I was hoping, but I took tests. They can tell even before you get your period now."

"Plural?" Lucy asked.

Tess nodded. "Four of them. They were all positive."

"Then I guess after Paint and Sip, I'll go get my uncle's shotgun he left me along with the house and we go have a little chat with Cole about his intentions." Gina squared her shoulders and arranged her brushes, prepping to paint the radioactive apocalypse. "The serial number was filed off it, but I'm sure that was just a Luca family quirk and not because it was probably used in the commission of a crime like Ford says. It'll be fine."

"He doesn't need to have intentions," Tess said, the words tumbling out of her as she tried to figure out how to explain the situation to her girls so they didn't form a vigilante posse. "I'm not trying to make Cole marry me. I barely know him and, anyway, I'm not sure I even *ever* want to be married. However, there's no way I'm going to keep this baby a secret. He deserves to know he's going to have a child."

"So we go along for moral support," Lucy said.

Yeah. That was not going to happen. "I'm sure that's how he'll see it, as opposed to oh, I don't know, the torch-bearing villagers after his head."

Gina *tsk-tsk*ed. "We're not that scary."

"Yeah we are," Fallon and Lucy said at the same time.

"I appreciate it, but this is something I need to do myself. All I need is his address." She turned to Fallon, who was engaged to one of Cole's fellow Ice Knights players, and Lucy, who kept the players out of hot water. "Can either of you get that for me?"

Lucy took out her phone and opened her contacts app. "Consider it done." She hit send.

Tess's phone buzzed in her pocket, alerting her that

Lucy's text went through. "Thanks, you guys are the best."

"We're your best friends," Fallon said, reaching over to give her a quick hug. "It's what we do."

"Well, that and buy a million teeny tiny baby clothes," Gina said with way too much excitement.

Lucy swiped Tess's wine cup. "And drink your wine now that you can't."

"More wine for us," Gina said with a giggle as she snagged the cup from Lucy.

Fallon, who never messed around when it came to a competition, did an oh-look move and then just took the cup from a distracted Gina and downed it before anyone could stop her.

They were all laughing hard enough that when Larry shushed them for the beginning of class, they could barely catch a breath. That was the thing with her girls—they always made things fun, even the hard things. Her phone buzzed in her pocket, alerting her for the second time that Lucy had texted Cole's info. Now all she had to do was figure out how to tell her baby's daddy that the stork was coming to town. That would be easy, right?

Hi, we haven't talked since that dance when I told you good luck with getting back together with your ex, but we're gonna have a baby. Surprise!

Oh yeah, this was going to go over like Forever in Bloom running out of roses on Valentine's Day.

Chapter Four

Consistency was the key to making Cole's world work.

Game day or not, he was usually up by seven and out the door by eight thirty, headed to the rink for treatments and the morning skate. After that, it was media availability, the team meeting, and lunch. Then he was either getting on a plane to go to another city for a road game the next day or—if it was a home-game day—back to his house for a pregame nap before heading back to the rink for on-ice warm-ups, a quick game of hacky sack to relax, and finally it would be time for puck drop.

That was his life, eighty-two games October through April with only four off days a month. And that didn't even count the additional games for the preseason that started in September or the postseason if the Ice Knights made it into the playoffs for three best-of-seven game rounds before a best-of-seven final series to win it all—the Stanley Cup. If that happened, his season wouldn't end until early June. On off days and between seasons, he followed the schedule as closely as possible with more film review, a few team barbecues, and the occasional trip to whatever construction work site across the western half of the United States his dad was working at that week.

Every day, game day or not, he followed the same routine so closely, Cole didn't even need to set an alarm. He just woke up when he was supposed to, went through his day as scheduled, and never, ever changed a thing except reporting to the rink during off-season. Why mess with what was working—especially when he knew all too well because of his constantly moving childhood what happened when chaos was introduced.

Nothing good.

And that was why he was at home on one of the few off days the team had this month watching game film on a loop so he could see in high-definition as he had his ass handed to him repeatedly thanks to the new offensive strategy Coach Peppers had insisted he try. It wasn't working. What he used to do, the way he moved across the ice, *that* worked. This new shit? He looked like a kid from the juniors trying to keep up with the big boys.

He ignored the buzz of his doorbell the first time. Petrov and Christensen had been tag-team texting him all morning. They could find someone else to be the fourth in their indoor golf simulator game. Golf was the worst. Was his opinion based at least partially on the fact that he sucked at it? Yes. He was a professional athlete who hated losing almost as much as he hated someone fucking with his routine. He was who he was, and he wasn't about to change.

At the second buzz, he got up and looked out the window. Neither Christensen's Mercedes-Benz coupe or Petrov's Range Rover was parked next to his black Dodge Hellcat. Instead it was a teal VW Bug with eyelashes attached to the headlights and a FLOWER POWER bumper sticker.

"Who in the fuck?"

That's when he saw her. Tess. He hadn't seen her since Lucy's wedding. She wasn't wearing a dress this time but instead a pair of jeans and a lime-green sweatshirt declaring BOOKMARKS ARE FOR QUITTERS—but there was no mistaking her. The woman walking back to her car was Tess Gardner, haunter of his stray thoughts for the past month.

He hustled for the front door and made it just as she was backing her car out. "Tess!"

She stopped and pulled back into the spot next to his car, but she didn't get out. Instead, she sat in the driver's seat, her hands at ten and two on the steering wheel as she stared at him with a mix of horror and determination, as if she was the only thing standing between the goal and Wayne Gretzky in his prime. She looked like a woman about to lose but refusing to give up anyway—that was *if* she could get out of the car.

He waited on his front porch, not wanting to spook her, but she'd obviously come looking for him. Why, he had no clue. When she didn't make a move for her door, he walked over to her car and got in on the passenger side.

For as ridiculous as he felt sitting in a car with eyelashes on its headlights, he could take it. "Hey there," he said. "Everything okay?"

"Did you know a baby turkey is called a poult?" she asked, her voice a little shaky as she kept her hands on the wheel while the car motor ran as if she was going to have to make a fast break for it.

Okay, she was nervous. He got that. If it was anyone else, he might worry that he was in the car with a possible stalker, but this was Tess. He barely knew her and could confirm she wasn't the hunt-you-down-and-stare-at-you type.

She continued. "And a young deer is called—"

"A fawn," he finished for her, worry starting to form a knot in his gut. "Tess, what's up?"

She opened her mouth, shut it, opened it again, and said,

"I'm pregnant."

"Congratulations," he said, going on autopilot as the manners his mom had drilled into him did their thing.

When she didn't say anything back, just stared at him, her eyes—one blue, one green—huge and round behind her glasses, realization came at him like an illegal check from behind and left his ears ringing. But it couldn't be him. Not *him*.

"We used a condom," he said, his heart slamming against his ribs.

Tess nodded. "Three of them."

"How could all *three* fail?" It didn't make sense. None of this made sense.

"Only one has to. Anyway, were they expired?" she asked, a quiet question that landed like a bomb in his brain.

That fucker Christensen.

Cole was going to kill him. Slowly. Then he'd bury the body where no one would ever find it. After that, he'd bury himself alive next to Christensen for not bothering to check the expiration dates on a trio of condoms given to him *as a joke*. He was an idiot. Not that this was the time to say those words out loud.

"The latex degrades after they expire and is more likely to tear," Tess said, her hands still at ten and two on the steering wheel, a jerky, desperate tightness in her words.

"Do you want to come inside?" There was just too much to unpack to do it in the car.

She shook her head and for once didn't hit him with a random factoid. Yeah, when Tess went trivia silent, things had to be serious.

"I'll support you no matter what you want to do," he said, meaning it. "Just let me know."

"I'm keeping the baby."

Okay, that was not the answer he'd been expecting. He

let out a slow breath that came from some deep spot way down in his lungs reserved for this-is-an-oh-shit-moment-but-I-can't-show-it. Had he been wrong about Tess? Was this a money grab and that's why she was keeping the baby? Was that why she could barely look at him and why her knuckles were turning white from her tight grip on the steering wheel?

It would be so much easier if it was, but that wasn't it. He couldn't explain how he understood that to be the truth—he just did. He sensed it deep down in his bones like he did the moment when a puck left his stick and he knew it was going to find the net no matter what the goalie did to block it.

"I just wanted to give you a heads-up," she continued. "That's all. You can go back inside now."

"What? That's it?" he asked, the words tumbling out of his mouth driven more by pure emotion and adrenaline than logic. "What if I want to be involved?"

"Do you?" she asked as if she already knew the answer and that it was one bound to disappoint her. "Really?"

"I don't know," he said, louder than he meant to in the tight confines of this car with a neon daisy air freshener hanging from the rearview mirror and immediately regretted it. The words, however, kept coming anyway. "This hasn't happened to me before. Do we get married? Do I cut you a check? Do I need to set up a paternity test? Do we get lawyers involved? What happens next?"

She finally let go of the wheel and pivoted in her seat to face him.

She lifted one finger. "No, I'm not marrying you." A second finger. "No, I don't need your money." Her third finger, which just happened to be her middle finger, all by itself. "Fuck you and your paternity test." Her fourth finger went up with the others. "If you want to, but my vote is no, we can come up with an agreement on our own. Plus, I can't afford an attorney." Her thumb joined the rest. "And the baby gestates inside my womb for the next eight months before being born. Then we have a child, which I will raise. You can visit as much as you want."

Visit? Visit!

Even though he'd grown up being uprooted every nine to ten months to move on to his dad's next job site, at least he'd been with his parents. They'd been a family. He wasn't about to just *visit* his own kid.

"I want to be more involved than just an occasional visit. I want to be its parent, too." He had no idea where this was coming from. Babies were not in his game plan. They weren't part of his routine. Still, the words kept coming, and he meant every one. "We'll parent this baby together."

He and Tess just stared at each other, both of them obviously wound up to a breaking point, as his declaration hung in the air between them along with an epic shit ton of uncertainty, anxiety, and a sliver of hope. None of it was part of his daily routine or his life schedule he had planned out right down to retirement. After that, it was like the old-time maps—a blank spot with "dragons be there" written in a fancy font.

"We have months to figure this all out," Tess said, turning away from him so she stared out the front windshield again. "I just came by to tell you."

Maybe he was supposed to be offended by that, put off. Instead, the abruptness of it only served to cut through the tension inside him, and he laughed. "You want me to get out of the car now so you can leave, don't you?"

She nodded, her death grip on the steering wheel back in place. "I'm gonna be a good mom."

That's when it hit him. Tess had to be as freaked out as he was right now. They'd used condoms. Three of them. Still... he looked down at her belly...they were going to have a baby.

He reached over and covered one of her hands with his.

"You'll be a great mom."

She let out a shaky breath. "Thanks."

The tightness in her shoulders seemed to evaporate, and she relaxed back against her seat. Their eyes locked, and for a moment, he couldn't help but be pulled by that initial something that had drawn him to her at the wedding. There was something about Tess that piqued his interest above the neck and below the belt. And they were having a baby. Together. Mysteriously, that didn't seem as scary as it had seemed only a few minutes before.

Of course, that's when Petrov's Range Rover pulled into his driveway. He and Christensen were not going to let the golf thing go.

"Sure you don't want to come inside?" he asked. "We don't have to tell them if you don't want."

Tess let out a brittle chuckle. "You tell who you want—your friends, family, Marti, whoever—but I'm not really up for peopling with strangers right now. Just remember the first three months can be a little iffy."

He was just processing how in the hell he was going to tell people—including the woman he was supposed to have kids with…eventually…someday—when her statement made his brain take a left turn sharp enough to leave the smell of burned rubber hanging in the air. "What do you mean?"

Her jaw tightened and she looked away from him again. "Miscarriages are common."

The urge to reach over and lay his palm flat against her stomach even though he knew it wouldn't protect the baby was nearly overwhelming. Life was chaos. He just had to figure out how to control it enough to protect this little guy or little girl for the next eighteen-plus years.

That would be easy. He just needed to make a couple of minor changes to his routine, that was all. Totally doable. A snap. Like taking a puck from a baby.

How hard could it be?

...

The fact that Cole wasn't in handcuffs or at the indoor golf simulator—or in handcuffs *at* the indoor golf simulator—was pretty amazing right now. Instead, he was sitting poolside behind his house with Petrov and Christensen, who had the mile-long stares of people who had fucked with the wrong guy.

"Shit, man," Christensen said. "I didn't think. I just grabbed them from the box in my closet and handed them out at the wedding as a joke. I didn't mean—" He blanched. "How many babies am I responsible for?"

"Only one we know of for sure," Petrov said. "You didn't use one, did you?"

Christensen glared at Petrov. "I'm in a dry spell."

"That's what they call being too much of a prick to get laid these days." Petrov grinned as he gave the other man shit. "Good to know."

Thankful for the two-man floor show that meant he didn't need to say six words when he was having trouble putting three together, Cole just sat back and stared at the retractable cover of his heated pool. It had an Ice Knights logo on it and had been a gift from the team when he'd hit a contractual goal milestone last season—well, they'd given him the cover and a one-million-dollar bonus.

"Have you told Marti yet?" Christensen asked.

Cole's brain—which had been barely functioning—stuttered to a full stop. He hadn't even thought about Marti until Christensen brought her up. What in the hell was wrong with him?

Marti was the woman he'd marry someday. They'd been each other's first just about everything and sure, they broke up more than they made up, but they'd always be there for each other, constants in each other's lives just like they'd always been since they were teens.

She'd said just that when they'd broken up the last time.

Being with her was part of his master plan; he had it in ink on his mental schedule. And he'd forgotten about her—utterly, completely, without even a trace—until just now.

"Told Marti?" Petrov tossed an empty water bottle at the other man. "One, he just found out literally an hour ago right before we got here that he was gonna be a daddy. When would he have had time to tell Marti? Two, why should he tell her? They're not together and haven't been for almost a year."

"Seven months," Cole said, the correction coming out more from habit than active thought.

Petrov shook his head. "Not that you're counting."

He didn't mean to. He just did. There were certain things he'd learned that he could count on in life as being always the same. The size of a hockey puck. The width of the goal. Marti. Three of the most important constants in his life.

"We're gonna get back together," he said, daring the other men to say another damn word about it.

If they noticed his fuck-you glare, they didn't react.

"Why? Because the idea of change freaks you out or because you actually want to be with Marti?" Petrov asked.

Cole crossed his arms over his chest and settled back against the cushion of the lounge chair, enjoying the sun if not the lack of warmth January provided. "I don't have a problem with change."

He did. He knew he did. Coach Peppers and anyone who reviewed the tape for the new plays would be very attuned to the fact that he did. He used the same moves, in the same order, in every game. Still, he wasn't going to give the first-line center the satisfaction.

"Really?" Petrov got up and moved the lounge chair he'd

been sitting on so it faced away from the pool. "Then leave the chair like this for the rest of the week."

"That's just dumb." Cole fought the urge to go over and force him to turn it back around. "Chairs that are around a pool are meant to be facing the pool."

"You have four other chairs for that," Christensen said, joining in by turning his away, too. "Sit in one of those if you want to look at the pool you only use in the mornings on Mondays, Wednesdays, and Fridays like you had to clock a limited-number-of-turns pass every time you used it."

He glared at the other men who made up the scoring side of the Ice Knights' first line. "Assholes."

They didn't bother to deny it. They just laughed, big, loud sounds that nearly blocked the telltale *thunk* of his bungee-cord supposedly-raccoon-proof lock hitting the side of his garbage can.

He was out of his chair and sprinting toward the back of the garage where the trash and recycling cans were lined up. He got there right in time to see the raccoon who had balls the size of a Zamboni to show up in the middle of the day to raid his garbage, balancing precariously on the edge of the can and reach inside for the remains of last night's stress baking. The little fucker took one look at Cole, shoved a huge helping of homemade honey rolls into his mouth, and took off. The move knocked over the trash can and sent debris spilling out.

"Trash panda," he yelled as it scurried away into the wooded area behind his house.

Christensen locked a hand around his arm, stopping him from giving chase. "They're nocturnal, man. He probably has rabies."

"No, he's just evil," Cole said. "He figured out that I empty the inside trash cans every day before lunch, so he goes and grabs his while it's still fresh. I got that stupid lock so he couldn't get in there."

"And he popped that lock like me back in my joyriding days," Petrov said with a chuckle as he looked at the unclipped fastener for the lock. "Maybe you need to experiment with taking your trash out at different times, and then the raccoon will leave you alone when you stop leaving him daily lunch."

It made sense. It was also a change. Cole flipped Petrov off for both reasons.

"I cannot wait to see how fatherhood fucks with that precious routine of yours," Petrov said.

"It won't."

Both men looked at him as if he'd been beaned in the head with a slap shot. Then they looked at each other and busted out laughing.

"Shut up and help me fix this," Cole grumbled as he went to work cleaning up the raccoon's mess.

What saved Christensen's and Petrov's lives at that moment was that they did help. Sure, they continued to break out into giggles like teenage girls at a slumber party—at least according to what he'd seen in the movies; he had never been to a slumber party—but they helped, all while keeping their mouths mostly shut as he told them exactly how minimal any changes to his routine were going to be.

"It's a baby, not Godzilla," he grumbled to himself.

And as the words came out of his mouth, he ignored the little voice inside his head telling him that he was an idiot because having a baby was going to change a lot. The question was, how much?

Chapter Five

Two weddings and a funeral meant that by the time Tess locked the front door to Forever in Bloom, walked to the unassuming white door set off to the side of the building, and climbed the stairs up to her apartment above the shop, she was so ready for a nap, she was practically snoring as she moved. The pregnancy books she downloaded said she might be a little more tired during the first trimester. In the past week, she'd discovered it was more like she'd been turned into a sleep zombie. By seven every night, she was drooling on her couch for at least a thirty-minute nap that was followed by a full night's sleep when she finally curled up into bed at eleven.

Tonight, she might just skip the nap and go straight to bed-for-the-night part. However, Kahn had other ideas. He started pouncing on her feet as soon as she walked through the door, a four-pound ball of kamikaze energy. It had been such a nutso day, she had left him upstairs with the forty million cat toys she'd gotten him for Christmas. Of course, he just played in the box the fake mini-tree had come in, which explained why it was still sitting on her coffee table even though it was almost mid-January. All the ornaments were scattered around the floor, no doubt the victim of a vicious kitten beatdown.

"Kahn," Tess said at half volume as she bent down to pet the little fluff ball. The top of his head was wet and so were his paws. "Have you been hanging out in the bathroom sink again?"

She really needed to follow up with her uncle—again—about the building's plumbing. Mr. Martinez upstairs had been in an intense battle with her uncle about the low water pressure; meanwhile she'd been dealing with leaky faucets that came and went.

Of course, she or Mr. Martinez would move if they could afford to rent another building in Waterbury's competitive rental market—thank you, Harbor City rich kids moving across the harbor for its working-class ambiance, that prices had gone through the roof. That meant their landlord was not only being a shithead about fixing things but was making noises about jacking up the rents on the two apartments in the building along with her flower shop on the ground level. That was *if* he didn't just sell the building outright. He was such an asshole—even if he was her uncle.

Kahn rubbed his wet little noggin against her shin and let out an I'm-hungry mewl.

"Yes, my overlord, I will feed you now."

A few minutes later, she was pouring cat food into his bowl and checking the kitchen sink for drips. There weren't any signs of a leaky faucet. It had to be the bathroom. Grabbing a wrench from the junk drawer—let's hear it for growing up in rental housing and learning at least some rudimentary plumbing skills—she headed for the bathroom to search for the leak. That sink was dry, though, too. The bathtub and shower were just as much a desert. She turned around in the tiny bathroom, her attention landing on the toilet. It was the only other option. But the lid was down and the cover over the tank hadn't been shoved aside.

What the hell?

Had Kahn learned to turn the faucet on and off? Was he house-training himself to use the toilet? Did he try to go swimming in his overpriced continuous-pour-water-bowl fountain?

"How did you get soaked, Kahn?"

The kitten didn't answer. Instead, he rubbed his fuzzy body against her legs as he did a figure eight between them, purring loudly enough that Mr. Martinez upstairs would have heard if he hadn't gone to Florida to visit the sun and his daughter—in that order, he'd told Tess with a chuckle before leaving yesterday morning.

"Whatever it is," she said as she bent down to pet the car engine in feline form, "don't do it again."

Kahn meowed his agreement and they crossed the narrow hall to her bedroom. Yes. Sleep. She'd just take a short nap, above the covers so she wouldn't fall into deep sleep, and then have dinner later.

Best. Plan. Ever.

And it was, right up until she fell back onto her bed, arms outstretched and eyes already closed, right into the middle of her soggy comforter. Cold wet soaked her from her shoulders to the top of her ass and a giant drop of water splattered against her forehead.

"What the fuck?" She jackknifed into a sitting position, face tilted upward toward the huge stain on her ceiling dripping what she really hoped was water directly onto her bed.

With catlike reflexes brought on by the serious ewww factor of mysterious liquid coming from her ceiling, she scurried off the bed and swiped her phone from the nightstand where she'd dropped it before falling onto the bed. Kahn stood there looking at her like she'd lain down on the wet bed despite his very clear warnings as she dialed her uncle. She wasn't shocked when her call went to voicemail. The man had been dodging her and Mr. Martinez's complaints for weeks. She hung up and called again, and again, and again until he finally picked up.

"I know, I know," her uncle Raymond said. "You're still mad about the water pressure."

"Oh no, now I'm mad about the leak in the ceiling right above my bed." Her bottom lip trembled. *Stupid fucking hormones.* She was pissed not sad and yet here she was starting to turn on the waterworks like she was mimicking the damn ceiling.

"Put a bucket down," he said, sounding totally unimpressed. "I told you the plumbers in this town were booked up."

The number of drips had gone from light morning traffic to the full-on hellscape of the bumper-to-bumper morning commute variety since she'd started this call, and it didn't show any signs of slowing. In fact, it was getting worse. She couldn't even call it drips anymore. It was a definite stream emptying onto her favorite place in the world right now, her bed!

A bucket? For that?

"The ceiling is starting to sag," she said, working hard to keep the damn hormonal quiver out of her voice. "We're not talking a little bit of water here."

"You ladies and your exaggerations."

Okay, she might kill her uncle. Surely the jury would take her side. Maybe she could get someone on Gina's questionable, probably mob-connected family tree to hide the body where no one would ever find it.

"I'm not exaggerating." Frustration stomped the tears that had been threatening into oblivion and she swiped the audio call over to video, pointing her phone up toward the ceiling that was definitely drooping now. "See?"

Uncle Raymond made a dismissive grunt. "It's barely a bubble."

"There's obviously a busted pipe," she said, gesturing toward the growing lump in the ceiling as if her uncle could see her. "You need to get a plumber here *right now*."

"I don't know who you think you are, but *you* don't tell *me* what I need to do." He took a deadly pause. "Ever."

Before she could say anything, a few chunks of the drywall board fell down onto her bed with a wet *thump* sound, and then a stream of water started pouring from the decayed steel pipe in the ceiling.

One time, when she'd been about eight, her mom had left Tess at her aunt Beatrice's house for a "short visit" that had lasted twelve weeks. She'd been there only a few days when she was pouring a glass of milk from the very full gallon jug and realized too late that she couldn't control the fast-moving flow. Milk poured over the top of the blue plastic cup, ran across the counter, and dripped off onto the floor. She'd been so horrified by the sight and what her aunt's reaction would be that she'd stood there frozen and just watched.

She found herself turning statue again as the water cascaded down onto her comforter covered in multicolored flowers, dread seeping into her as fast as the water flow. It splashed down, forming a small pool of water that turned the teal flowers into a dark turquoise before spreading across the surface and water falling off the side of the bed. Kahn made a surprised squeak of a meow and sprinted from the room.

"Holy shit," her uncle yelled, his voice booming in the room despite the fact that it was coming out of the tiny speaker on her phone. "Go turn the main water valve off before the whole place floods."

The idea of everything she owned drowning under the

overflow jolted her back to the here and now. "Where is it?"

"Utility closet by the hot water heater."

She was running toward it before the words were even all the way out of her uncle's mouth.

Ten minutes later, the gushing had stopped and she was dumping out the buckets she'd found to catch what drained out after she'd turned off the main valve. Then she moved on to stuffing her sopping wet comforter into the washing machine and hanging her sheets over the fire escape railing. She was contemplating if she could fit the mattress out her window to air out on the fire escape when her front door opened.

"You here, Tess?" Her uncle's bellow carried through the apartment and sent Kahn scurrying for cover.

She wouldn't kill her uncle. She wouldn't kill her uncle. She wouldn't kill her uncle. It wasn't the healthiest mantra, but it just might keep her out of jail.

"You know, by law you have to knock before you can come in," she said, walking into the living room.

Raymond jingled his huge key ring. "I have a key."

"It doesn't matter." How many times had she recited that landlord/tenant law to him? A million?

"I'm your uncle," he said with a shrug as if that changed anything.

Raymond was a big, burly guy with more hair on his chin than his head and a determined glint to his eyes anytime money was mentioned. He had that glint now as he stood next to the neighborhood's favorite plumber, her cousin Paul—who wasn't Raymond's kid but her aunt Louise's youngest. There were a lot of Gardners in the neighborhood, lots of relatives to get dropped with when she had been growing up. Most were actual relatives. Others were relatives in name only but had been treated as if they were for so long that they might as well have been. Either way, her stays with them had always been temporary and awkward.

Raymond lifted a bushy eyebrow in the intimidating way he had when she'd asked for a second roll at the dinner table when she'd stayed with him for a weekend that turned into two months when she was twelve. "You want Paul and me to go back out in the hall and then walk out of here or do you want us to take a look at whatever you did?"

Too bad she wasn't twelve and easily cowed anymore.

"I didn't do anything. It was the old steel plumbing pipes that are the problem."

"You're a plumber now?" Paul asked, brushing past her and going into the bedroom.

"No," she said, following after him and her uncle. "I have access to Google."

In the bedroom, Paul looked up at the hole in the ceiling and let out a low whistle. "You're gonna have to replace it, and I'll have to check the rest of the pipes unless you want to have this happen again. Those steel pipes you have up there are way more susceptible to corrosion and decay."

Tess turned a told-you-so smirk on her uncle, the landlord from hell.

"No water until I can fix it, and it'll be a few weeks," Paul said as he took out his phone and started scrolling through his calendar app. "I'm booked crazy with all the renovations those Harbor City newcomers are doing."

Tess's smirk flatlined. "No water? But I own the flower shop downstairs."

Her breaths started coming in short bursts that did nothing to fill her lungs. No water meant no flowers. Her heart raced. No flowers meant no customers. She wiped her suddenly clammy palms on her jeans. No customers meant no money. A blast of panic singed her from her toes to the roots of her curly hair. No money meant overdue bills and financial ruin. That could not happen. She had a baby to think about.

"It's on a different line, city zoning requirement for businesses versus residential." Paul gave her the curious what-is-going-weird-with-you-now stare that all her cousins had been giving her for her entire life. "You just need to find a new place to live until the work is done."

Her uncle and cousin both looked away. For some reason, the automatic denial of a safe spot seemed to settle her nerves. Let's hear it for the familiarity of familial rejection. Yeah. She wasn't going to be couch surfing with them. A few days in a hotel she could do no problem, but a few weeks when she didn't have rental insurance on the apartment, only business insurance on the shop? She'd have to find a way to make the money stretch—the idea blossomed quickly like a time-lapse video—unless...

"I can sleep on the couch in the shop's office and just use the bathroom down there," she said, relief making her lungs unclench enough to take in a full breath.

"That violates city zoning rules," her uncle said. "You'll get me hauled into court for letting someone live in a business."

Tess had no idea what all her uncle got up to, but it wasn't always squeaky clean and he took pains to keep anyone attached to the city as far away from his properties as possible. Probably because most of them were only a few steps up from being declared fire hazards. Still, it wasn't like she really wanted anyone to find out she was couch surfing in her office.

"It's temporary," she said. "No one will know."

Her uncle crossed his arms and shook his head, his jaw set in a stubborn line. "I'm not going to court for you when I finally have someone on the line to buy this busted-up building—as long as it's not literally under water. You're not staying here. Find somewhere else to live until Paul patches this up."

Great. So not only was her apartment uninhabitable, her uncle actually had someone lined up to buy the building—which more than likely meant higher rent prices for her apartment and her shop—and she had to find a place to live for the next few weeks. At least the news couldn't get worse. Right?

• • •

Cole wasn't hiding in the hallway. He didn't hide. He was a grown man, a professional hockey player, and now a giant chickenshit. Therefore, he was not hiding or skulking or anything else Ice Knights defenseman and team captain Zach Blackburn's eyes were accusing him of at this moment. Uh-uh.

Cole was being smart. Since Tess had all but kicked him out of her tiny car and driven away after informing him he was going to be a daddy, they hadn't talked, texted, or set eyes on each other. Now he was lurking—*not lurking*, hanging out, which was a totally normal thing to do—in the narrow hallway outside her apartment because she hadn't invited him over.

No one had. He'd been volun-told to get his ass to Waterbury.

A half hour ago, he'd been in the Ice Knights weight room doing alternate leg-weighted squats while Blackburn and Stuckey proved on the sprinting area that defensemen—even first-line defensemen—were never going to be mistaken for forwards when it came to speed. He was about to tell them both that, because then they'd just try and run faster and it would crack up fellow forward Christensen and center Petrov, when Blackburn's girlfriend, Fallon, had burst into the weight room.

There had been a rush of discussion about Tess and a

massive water leak and the fact that she had to move out of her apartment for at least two to three weeks. And when Fallon left to go help Tess pack up what she needed, Blackburn had told her he'd be along in about five minutes with help—not to help, *with* help. That's when Cole should have known.

"You're the help," Blackburn said, giving him a look that would have scared Cole back in the days when the team captain had been the most hated man in Harbor City for good reason. "Let's go."

And that's how Cole had ended up in Tess's hallway, where he was waiting to be invited in and *not* shifting nervously from foot to foot like a scaredy-cat.

Blackburn came out of the apartment with a neon-rainbow duffel bag and shoved it into Cole's arms. "So you're just going to let the woman who's having your baby camp out at my and Fallon's house for the next few weeks?"

Cole adjusted his grip on the bag. Had Tess asked to stay at his house? No. Had anyone suggested that Tess stay at his house? No. Had he even made it into her apartment yet to say hi? No. Was he a chickenshit? Yes.

Fuck.

"Your place is bigger than mine," Cole said, still arguing even though he knew he was one, wrong, and two, going to give in anyway. "You have guest rooms."

"Don't change the subject." Blackburn glared at him. "You're gonna let the woman pregnant with *your child* stay at our house rather than yours?"

Cole peeked inside Tess's apartment. It was like an explosion of disarray and color. Every single surface was covered in flowers or plants or knickknacks devoted to some fandom or another. Then there were the books. They were stacked up on the counters and the floor, and in one case there was an empty plastic water bottle balancing on the top of one tower.

And it wasn't that they'd been moved out of the bedroom because of the leak.

All of it had the lived-in look of something that had been there for weeks if not months.

Compare all of that to his house, where everything was always in its place, the color scheme throughout the entire four-thousand-square-foot space variations on eggshell white and tan with the occasional plant—fake, of course—to break up the visual plane. Yeah, the neon duffel was never going to mesh in his off-white world.

"She's Fallon's best friend." And he was a giant lame-ass.

Neither fact was wrong—something Tess would appreciate.

Blackburn? Not so much.

The defenseman clamped his molars together hard enough that the team dentist probably would need to make time for him on the schedule.

"Your baby," Blackburn said between clenched teeth.

"Hey, Zach, can you—" Tess came out of the apartment, struggling under the weight of a suitcase with a broken roller wheel, spotted Cole, and jolted to a stop. "Oh. You. Hi."

Cole should respond—say hi, wave, smile like a dumb-ass who forgot words. He *meant* to respond, but he couldn't. Instead, he reached out and took the suitcase she'd been struggling with off her hands. A very small part of his brain tried to work out what she'd stuffed it with, since the damn thing weighed about a million pounds, while the rest of him surrendered to one single thought: *She's so fucking hot.*

Evolved man? Yeah, definitely not him.

In his defense, it was hard to be when all he could take in was the way her jeans clung to her round hips, the pink of her full lips, and the way her T-shirt clung to her curves. *And she's pregnant with your kid—how about you not gawk at a mother that way, you asshole.*

Especially when thinking like that was what had gotten them in this situation in the first place. Hadn't his dick and Christensen's faulty condoms caused enough trouble already without him wondering if he and Tess could go find some stranger's rehearsal dinner so they could get weddinged again?

"We were just talking about how it made so much sense for you to stay with Phillips while your apartment is repaired," Blackburn said, sounding even more self-satisfied than the expression of I-know-exactly-what-you're-thinking plastered across his face, *if* that was possible.

Her cheeks paled and her chin trembled before she pressed her lips together hard enough that a little white line appeared around her mouth. "There's no need for that. I'm sure I could swing a hotel somehow. I don't want to impose on you and Fallon or *anyone* else."

His nuts deked to the side when she said *anyone* in *that* dismissive tone, but underneath there was more, as if she were deflecting. Whatever her reason, it still stung. She'd liked him plenty before. They had been cordial the other day. Now he was just some dude? Ouch.

"It's no imposition; it's just Phillips there." Blackburn slapped a heavy hand down hard on Cole's shoulder. "Really thought that this would give you two a chance to get to know each other a little better before the baby comes. Now, if you're annoyed by the thought of having to eat Corn Flakes across the table from this guy every morning, you shouldn't, because he'll be on the road every other week."

The team captain wasn't wrong. Hockey schedules were brutal. Three games a week on average, at least half of which were on the road for a total of eighty-two games a season. Cole fucking loved it. The travel he could do without, but the daily grind of either playing or gearing up for a game the next day? It was just the kind of consistency he lived for. But the point of it was, he was crazy fucking busy. If he and Tess played it right, she really could move in and there would be as little disruption to their schedules—whatever it was she filled hers with—as possible.

"I'm not sure it's a good idea," Tess said, her focus popping around like a ping-pong ball, landing everywhere but on him.

"It's a great idea," Fallon said as she joined them in the hall, holding up her phone, the screen of which displayed what looked like the mother of all group chats. "Gina and Lucy agree."

"I don't want to be an obligation," Tess said, her voice wavering a bit. "I can just stay at a hotel. There are some extended-stay ones not that far away."

Blackburn and Fallon both sent him do-something-you-asshole glares, but he barely noticed. He was too busy taking in the way Tess seemed to shrink back against the wall, as if by doing so, she could get the entire world to not notice she was there.

He knew that body language. Shit, he'd had to unlearn that shit with every new school he was enrolled in every six to nine months growing up. The other two didn't realize it; they were a matched pair of bulldogs who didn't have it in them to ever let go of an idea once they grabbed hold of it. If anyone was going to save Tess from their "helpful" bossing around, it would have to be him.

"It's no obligation. Really," he said, meaning it. "It'll let us get to know each other a little better before the baby comes and work out the co-parenting stuff. You'll have your own space, and it'll be strictly as friends. I have no ulterior motives."

And he didn't—or more correctly, he wouldn't. It was just the shock of seeing her again that had thrown him into hey-baby mode. "Baby" being the key word he needed to remember from now on.

He had no idea how he was going to tell his parents or Marti.

When he and Marti eventually got back together again—because they always did, right on schedule and according to routine—he *would* have to tell her. He hadn't been kidding about the co-parenting; he wouldn't just be the guy who contributed half the DNA and wrote an occasional check.

As long as he and Tess stayed away from weddings and remembered that what had happened had been a one-time (okay, three-time) event, then there was no reason why they couldn't make this co-parenting thing work. He just needed to make a few small alterations to his daily regimen. He probably wouldn't even notice.

"Are you sure?" Tess asked, her gaze finally stopping on him.

He nodded. "Absolutely. Anyway, it's only for a few weeks, so if I make you want to pull your hair out, you just have to remember that it won't be forever."

She pushed up her glasses and gave him a hard look. "Okay, but we need to get some things straight first."

"Hit me."

"This is just temporary. No funny business. No shotgun wedding. No more nights spent naked together—no offense, but this"—she gestured between the two of them—"was a one-time thing."

"We got weddinged," he said, repeating her words from that morning back at her.

"Exactly." She nodded, her chin-length curls bouncing. "Can you agree to my terms?"

He nodded, trying to unwind why the declaration of her conditions hit like a puck grazing his balls. Still, he couldn't blame her. It wasn't like this had been her plan, either.

"Good," she said, her brass-balls facade slipping just a bit when she let out a shaky breath. "Let's do it."

"Finally," Fallon said with a sigh. "If that had gone on any longer, I would have had to hit you both with a delay-of-game penalty." She dipped a half step back into the apartment and reemerged with a wriggling black and white kitten. "Now, Phillips, take Kahn."

He lowered the suitcase to the floor and took the kitten. It was tiny and soft and it had big eyes and teeny tiny teeth that—he winced—sank with expert efficiency into his thumb.

"Why am I holding a kitten?" he asked.

"That's Kahn," Tess said with all the love in her voice. "He's coming, too, but I don't have a cat carrier yet, so you'll have to hold him."

"No." He shook his head and tried to hand off Kahn to Blackburn or Fallon—both of who just grinned and refused. "No cats."

"I'm not abandoning Kahn," Tess said, her voice wobbling again. "I don't do that."

"It's just a cat." Okay, a really soft, small cat but still a cat. And his house was a no-animal zone—a rule that stupid trash panda raccoon kept ignoring.

"Exactly." Tess blinked quickly and inhaled a deep breath. "It's not like he's a crocodile. But watch out for his tee—" Satan's fur ball bit him again, this time the side of his palm. "Oops. Don't worry—he'll grow out of it."

"Really?" It sure as hell didn't feel like it.

"Probably not." She did that shaky-breath, fast-blinking thing again. "But I've got hope."

And he had a big L in the win/loss column right now because Kahn the Biter was coming home with them.

"As long as there's that." He adjusted his awkward hold on the evil animal that just ended with teeny tiny little spike claws embedded in his palm. "He doesn't scratch things up, right?"

"Nope." She let out a cough that sounded like it was more than that, but her face remained neutral. "That's totally a myth that cats do that."

"Good." He'd moved around too much growing up to have any pets, even a goldfish, so he couldn't call her out on what seemed like a straight-faced lie, so he didn't. "I'm glad to hear that."

Okay, he could make this work. He'd just set down the ground rules. It would be fine. Kahn picked that moment to bite Cole's thumb again. God, he hoped that wasn't a sign of what was to come.

Chapter Six

Kahn was missing.

Tess was barely awake the next morning and yet she was already in super-silent panic mode. Why quiet hysteria? Because Cole's house was a museum where every exhibit was dedicated to something the color of cold oatmeal. It was so clean, she could practically smell the bleach, and even the idea of speaking above a whisper seemed out of place and weird. So a kitten wandering around free to claw its way to satisfaction on what was probably a ten-thousand-dollar taupe-colored leather couch? Yeah, that was the kind of situation that definitely called for dying-to-pee-but-still-twenty-minutes-from-the-next-interstate-exit urgency.

"Kahn," she whisper-yelled, following the words with the soft click of her tongue against the roof of her mouth.

Usually those two sounds got him to respond, but this time nothing happened. She'd already checked under the bed, in the window seat overlooking the evergreen-tree-filled backyard, and in every nook and cranny in the bedroom and its attached bathroom. Kahn had disappeared—or more correctly, he'd wandered out beyond her room.

Fuck.

She should have known better. It wasn't that she'd *planned* to let her adorable little terror loose in the Louvre, but that was starting to feel like the story of her life lately.

She hadn't planned to get knocked up. She hadn't planned to have the ceiling above her bed collapse. She hadn't planned to move into Cole's very nice, way-too-fancy-to-touch-anything house. But here she was, even if her kitty was missing. There was a joke in there somewhere and if she wasn't about to drown in a cold sweat, she would have found it. Right now, though, she had to find Kahn.

She'd left her bedroom door open just a crack this morning when she'd come back from the kitchen with a mug of hot tea and a piece of toast slathered with raspberry jam. The idea being she'd snuggle and snack in bed for a little bit with Kahn before starting to actually wake up, since normally the first two hours of the day were a hazy mess for her. A morning person she most definitely was not—which explained why it took her a minute to notice the tiny raspberry-colored kitten paw prints leading out her bedroom door.

"Shit."

The last thing she wanted was to have to explain to Cole why there were jam paw prints all over his scary-mommy-level clean house.

She scrambled out of the room, her rainbow unicorn fuzzy slipper socks sending her sliding across the pristine and ultra-shiny hardwood floor as she tried to turn left into the hallway a little too fast. Hurrying to catch up with Kahn before he shredded the curtains or went to town on a toilet paper roll, she followed the paw prints. The purple splotches disappeared through the barely there opening of a door on the other end of the hall. Rushing forward, she pushed open the door and half slid, half speed walked inside before coming to a dead stop in the middle of Cole's bedroom.

Double fuck.

She hadn't realized this was his room. Last night, she'd been so exhausted after carrying in her stuff that she'd crashed almost immediately after he'd shown her the guest room. She hadn't even gotten a full tour of the house, just a nod that the kitchen was that way and the living room just past it. Now she was standing in the middle of a bedroom that was all white—seriously, the whole thing was like the inside of a jar of mayo—except for Cole and the purple imprints of Kahn's paws leaving a trail across the snowy expanse of the bedspread.

The paws led to Kahn, who'd made a little bed for himself in Cole's jaw-length blond hair that allowed the little fur ball to be curled up right next to Cole's face.

This was bad. This was really bad.

"Kahn," she said, her voice as loud as possible while still maybe not waking up the half-naked man she was most definitely *not* checking out. "Come here, kitty, kitty."

Neither cat nor man moved.

Triple to infinity shit.

She had to get Kahn out of here. And the paw prints? She'd figure out a way to fix that. Where there was a will, there was a Magic Eraser and a plan.

Tess tiptoed across the room, avoiding the paw prints on the floor so she wouldn't spread the jam, and made her way over to the side of the bed. The trick was going to be picking up the kitten without waking up Cole. She was gonna need a lot of luck and more than a little help from above to keep Kahn's kitten mouth closed.

Heart hammering in her chest, she did her best to pretend she was the heroine in some action-adventure spy movie having to avoid red laser lights and delicately reached out for the kitten. Her fingertips were just brushing fur when everything went to hell.

Kahn let out a meow of surprise and launched himself straight up in the air in that way only cats can do. He landed, no doubt claws extended, right in the middle of Cole's bare chest. That sent Cole jackknifing into a sitting position while letting out a yowl of pain, the motion dislodging the kitten, who did a midair flip and landed softly, paws first, on the floor. Kahn sent a hiss of disapproval at her—*her!*—and then zipped out of the room, leaving only a couple of purple paw prints in his wake.

Cole rubbed the red spot on his chest. "Why are you in my room?"

"Kitten retrieval." Did that sound breathy? She felt breathy. Her lungs had stopped working the moment her gaze locked onto his long, strong fingers massaging his muscular chest right over his pecs. Was it hot in here? It felt hot. "Kahn was purring."

He lifted a blond eyebrow, one side of his mouth quirking up before smoothing back into a line as if he was fighting back a smile. "Is that what the buzzing in my ear was?"

Okay, she might not have the best people skills—okay, *any* people skills—but she knew when someone was giving her shit, and Cole was most certainly doing that. She was about to call him on it and let him know exactly what she thought about it when he tossed back the covers, revealing that he slept only in a pair of black boxer briefs.

Deep breath, Tess. You will not look below the waistband. Doesn't matter if you've seen it before—and licked it and kissed it and sucked it and...

"Most scientists think purring starts in the cat's brain when a signal is sent to the laryngeal muscles," she blurted out, sounding every bit as panicked and totally awk-weird as she felt because the voice in her head that was supposed to be her conscience had gone total horndog on her. "They vibrate as much as one hundred and fifty vibrations per second. That makes the cat's vocal cords separate as the cat breathes, which is the purr we hear."

Cole stood up and stretched, his arms reaching outward, every muscle straining. "Fascinating."

"Are you mocking me?" Embarrassment burned its way across her skin for what she was saying about purring and what she was thinking about how forearms were really overrated and trying to remember what that V thing by a guy's hips was called.

"I'd never tease a woman in my bedroom like that." He gave her a slow up and down. "Especially not when she was only wearing an oversize T-shirt and nothing else."

"How can you tell I'm not wearing anything else?" Her brain processed her words the second *after* they left her mouth because of course that couldn't happen *before* she said it. Nope. Not always-says-the-wrong-thing her. "Never mind! Don't answer that."

One side of his mouth went up in a cocky grin, but it flatlined out when he looked down at his bed, his gaze following Kahn's bright tracks across the white comforter and out the door. Belly sinking, she knew what he was about to ask before he opened his mouth. If only she had a better answer.

Cole's sharp gaze turned back to Tess. "Why are there purple paw prints everywhere?"

• • •

About an hour later, Cole put away the mop and moved his comforter—now free from purple paw prints—from the oversize washer to the dryer. That relief at everything being in its place settled in him and his chest finally unclenched just like it always had when he unpacked the last moving box as a kid.

Sense of right restored, he followed the smell of heaven into the kitchen. Tess, who now had on jeans and a lime-green T-shirt from a superhero movie, was in front of the stove, singing off-key and dancing almost on beat along to the music coming out of her phone on the counter.

His gaze wasn't drawn to her ass immediately. He'd taken a whole two breaths in between walking into the kitchen and looking, which was pretty much a miracle, considering he'd been dreaming about Tess's ass—and the rest of her—all night. Having her right down the hall while adherent to the no-more-naked-together rule was going to be hell.

Get your shit together, Phillips. You got weddinged, not brain scrambled. She's in your kitchen, for God's sake.

Normally, the kitchen was off-limits to anyone but him. This was where he stress baked. He followed each recipe with precision, premeasuring each ingredient into little glass bowls and setting them on the counter in easy reach so he could add them as required.

Not Tess. The open egg carton was on the island. The bread was by the sink. There were spices and a bottle of vanilla spread out willy-nilly around the counters. It made his right nostril twitch, which was not a good look for anyone, let alone the guy whose attention got snagged—again—by Tess's perfect ass. Oh yeah, because if she turned around right now and saw him doing his best sneers-a-lot asshole face while he eyeballed her butt, she'd definitely bean him with the skillet.

Lucky for him, he managed to avert his attention before Tess turned around.

"I still can't believe you wouldn't at least let me mop up," she said as she flipped a slice of french toast in the pan.

Satan's favorite fur ball—sans purple paws—was curled up on the window seat. Kahn inched open one eye to glare at Cole before dismissing him with a flick of his tail.

Yeah, right back at you, buddy.

"I have a system to keeping this place clean," he said.

Tess turned to face him, her eyes big and round behind her glasses. "Are you trying to tell me that you don't have a service to do that for you?" She made a vague waving gesture at him. "I thought that's what all rich people did, and especially people like you." She mumbled something under her breath and fidgeted with the dish towel before saying in an embarrassed half squeak, "You know, a busy professional athlete."

"You mean spoiled jocks?" he teased.

Tess turned about sixteen shades of red, her gaze going down to her shoes as she seemed to physically shrink in front of him.

Way to go, asshole.

"I don't need cleaners," he said, hoping to be able to just push past the uncomfortable moment. "All I need is three hours and forty-two minutes once a week." Yes, he timed it. Yes, he had a bullet journal to track it. No, he was not going to tell her or anyone else about that. "It's when I catch up on my podcasts."

"Which ones do you listen to?" she asked as she took down a pair of plates from a cabinet and set them on the counter.

"Things like *Stuff You Should Know*."

"I *love* that one. The episode on how bar codes work was really cool." She put a couple of pieces of french toast on a plate along with some mixed berries and turkey bacon. "Want some?" She held out the plate toward him. "It's my specialty, made with secret ingredients and everything."

It smelled good—phenomenal really, like cookies in breakfast form—but he had his routine. "Nah, I have—"

"A usual?" She winked at him. "I noticed all the meal-prep containers in the fridge already."

"Exactly." He reached into the fridge for the prepacked breakfast he'd prepped the other day but didn't end up taking them out. The smell got to him. "Is there vanilla in the french toast?"

She held the plate out so it was practically under his nose. "Yes."

Giving in to temptation, he took the plate and grabbed a fork from the drawer. "So much for keeping your secret ingredient a secret."

She shrugged and smiled as if he hadn't broken her recipe code. "Whatever you say."

He used the side of his fork to cut off a bite and popped the french toast into his mouth. It was an explosion of flavor on his tongue. He inhaled four more bites. The eggs, the vanilla, the hearty thick bread, and something that made his mouth tingle. It was barely noticeable at first, but that undeniable buzzing against his lips continued until he couldn't ignore it.

"Is there cinnamon in there?" As if he didn't already know.

"You guessed it!" Tess took a bite of her french toast and closed her eyes in foodie bliss. "Sometimes I put in almond flavoring, but it seemed like a cinnamon kind of morning, don't you think?"

Heart hammering against his ribs and his jaw starting to feel like ants were marching across it, Cole threw open the cabinet over the sink, grabbed the Benadryl, popped out two tablets from the pack, and dry swallowed them.

"Are you okay?" Tess asked, rushing over with a glass of water. "Shit. Do you have an EpiPen? Do you need to go to the hospital? I could call Fallon—she's an ER nurse!"

"I'll be fine." This wasn't the first time it had happened and it probably wouldn't be the last. He had a process to deal with it.

"Are you sure?" Tess pressed the back of her hand to his

forehead as if he had a fever. "You didn't throw back that Benadryl like you were fine."

"It's a minor cinnamon allergy. I get hives, that's it." He pulled his phone out of his pocket because it was time to move on to step two. He started texting. "But I do have to tell the team doctor what happened—that's the routine outlined in the team rules."

"I swear, I'm not trying to kill you on purpose," Tess said, shoving her curly blond hair behind both ears. "Can I make you some cinnamon-free french toast to make up for it?"

Even if he was the kind of guy who liked to take risks, that probably wouldn't happen. As it was, this whole incident was pretty much the perfect reminder of why sticking to his routine was the best option.

"I'll just stick with my usual," he said, punctuating it with a smile now that his lips had stopped tingling. "Hard-boiled eggs, blueberries, bacon, and avocado toast."

Ten minutes later, he was smashing the avocado onto his toast while a slump-shouldered Tess shoved pieces of syrup-drenched french toast around her plate when his phone rang. Coach Peppers's face popped up on the screen. This was going to go about as well as the french toast.

"It's not that bad," Cole said in lieu of a greeting. "I'll be fine at practice and definitely for the next game."

"What, were you studying the new plays so hard, you forgot you're allergic to cinnamon?" Coach asked, his tone the usual mix of grit and annoyance. "Don't bother lying—we both know you've been avoiding the new system. The good news is you'll have extra time to learn it, because the doc wants you to miss practice today." Coach let out a frustrated huff of disgust. "The league is being more stringent about this kind of thing since Nelson had to retire because of his allergic reaction to the hockey equipment and Fesil ate chicken at a team dinner that had peanuts in it. And since tomorrow is an off day, I don't want to see you until the morning skate on game day."

"That's bullshit," Cole said, his body tightening as a blast of frustration shot through him. "Those cases were both extreme. I just had a few bites of french toast. I'm. Fine."

"Good to know," Coach said. "I'll see you when you're cleared."

Fuck. No. He didn't miss practices. Not unless he was missing a limb or something. This was hockey, not soccer. They played through the pain. Shit. He'd hit the ice after getting five stitches above his right eyebrow and scored more goals than any other game in his career. "That's not fair—"

Coach snorted. "Neither is life. Deal with it."

He hung up and Cole stared down at his phone, trying to figure out what had just happened. Hockey was his constant. No matter what town they lived in or how many times they'd moved that year, there was always a team—even if it was just pickup street hockey on a dead-end cul-de-sac.

Now everything in his life was in flux and he fucking hated it. All he wanted was his normal breakfast, to follow his usual schedule, and to skate his regular plays.

He dumped his breakfast back into the prep box and put it back into the fridge. "I should be on my run right now."

Tess looked up with a jerk, concern making the corners of her full mouth dip downward. "Is that safe, since you just had that reaction and took two Benadryl?"

"It's what I'm *supposed* to be doing." As opposed to getting distracted by Tess doing her ass-shimmy dance moves in his kitchen.

He had everything worked out. His career in hockey. His life with Marti—a second constant in his life after hockey. Shit, she was the reason there even was cinnamon in his kitchen cabinets. Change wasn't an option.

Now he was barred from today's practice, had knocked

up the wrong woman, and she'd almost poisoned him. It was just— He glanced over at Tess still sitting at the table by the big bay window. She was eating the last few bites of french toast with jerky movements, her whole body rigid and her eyes focused on anything but him—it was like watching a puppy who'd just been kicked, and it hit him right in the solar plexus.

Nice going, asshole. Do you feel better now that you made her feel like shit?

"Tess," he said, dragging his fingers through his hair. "I'm sorry."

"This is going to be a transition for both of us. No worries, though, I promise not to make anything else with cinnamon," she said with a forced smile as she stood up and walked with stiff steps to the sink, where she rinsed off her plate and put it in the dishwasher. "Well, I have to go open the shop. Don't worry, I'll make sure Kahn doesn't escape my room so you don't have to worry about kitten attacks." She paused, taking in a deep breath before letting it out. "And don't worry, we'll be out of here as soon as possible and you can get back to your normally scheduled life. I'll make sure you barely notice us until then. I don't want to be the crabgrass in your lawn."

And it was official. He was a giant dick. "You're not."

"That's sweet of you to say." She scooped up Kahn, who started purring almost immediately, and walked out of the kitchen.

Cole stood there in the middle of the white-on-white-on-white room, a feeling sinking in that he was missing something and not only did he not know how to find it, he didn't know what it was.

Chapter Seven

Who would have thought almost killing Cole wouldn't have been the worst part of Tess's day? Nope, that honor belonged to the momzilla of the bride standing in the middle of Forever in Bloom with that I'm-so-annoyed-my-Botox-might-malfunction look.

In the past thirty minutes, the soon-to-be bride, Christine, and her very involved mom, Valeria, had debated the five sample bouquets Tess had created for the big day. Of course, "debated" meant Christine had made her pick in twelve-point-two seconds while Valeria had spent the remaining time explaining over and over again that while none of the bouquets was really up to par, the one with the daisies was just the most awful choice.

"I know Christine asked for daisies and I totally warned her it was probably the wrong choice, but even she has to see it now that you've put together the sample bouquet," Valeria Henson said, her upper-crust Harbor City accent managing to reach levels of patronizing that Tess hadn't realized were possible. "It's not you—of course I'm sure you *tried*—but this is just all wrong."

The bouquet of white gerbera daisies, golden sunflowers, yellow roses, and pale asters mixed in with some gorgeous greenery—tied together with a thick ribbon of burlap—wasn't for every bride. It definitely wasn't for the woman whose high-end fashion labels had labels, but for her daughter, who looked like being uptown was the last thing she ever wanted? Yeah, the bouquet fit her relaxed vibe perfectly. Not that Christine was saying that. Instead, she just stared daggers at her mom's back and let out little huffs of frustration.

The ride over the bridge and back into Harbor City for these two was going to be awkward as hell. The secondhand embarrassment of even imagining what their trip home was going to be like had Tess reaching into the ever-present swirl of factoids in her head to pull out a few that could distract from the oh-my-God-people-are-the-worst uncomfortableness of the moment.

"Daisies were Freya's flower in Norse mythology," Tess blurted out. "She was the goddess of beauty and love. Today, daisies are sometimes given to new moms because Freya was also the goddess of fertility."

Valeria took a step back, managing to give her a look that was a mix of annoyance and confusion about whether Tess was mentally all there. It wasn't the first time she'd gotten that look from people. Hell, it was a big part of the reason why she limited her peopling as much as possible.

Tess braced herself for a stinging retort like her uncle Raymond was famous for delivering, but Valeria's eyes rounded and she spun around to face her daughter.

"I knew it," she said with an offended gasp. "*That's* why you're insisting on this country bumpkin bouquet. You just threw away all our plans and got pregnant by this totally inappropriate man. He's not part of our circle. He doesn't even belong to our club! How did this happen?"

Oh shit. Oh shit. Oh shit.

Tess gripped the bouquet tight enough that the scratchy burlap ribbon pricked her palms. If there was anything worse than having to deal with people, it was dealing with their messy emotions. It was just...*ugh*. Maybe they'd pull it in and wait until they got home to deal with the thornbush she'd accidentally tossed them into by—once again—saying the wrong thing.

"Well, young lady," Valeria said, her righteous demand for answers yanking Tess back into the hellscape of the here and now. "I raised you to always know your place. How did this happen?"

Christine uncurled herself from her chair situated between two hot-pink hibiscus trees, a dangerous gleam in her heavily lined eyes. "I fucked him, Mother. A lot. All over the beach house, the club cabana, and the penthouse." She took three steps toward Valeria, each move a warning. "From now on, when you walk into any room, you'll be wondering if I was on my knees sucking his cock in there, and the answer is yes. I did, and it was fabulous."

Valeria's only answer to that truth bomb was a sharp gasp.

Unable to stop the factoid flow brought on by so much raw emotion, Tess gushed onward. "Sunflowers symbolize adoration and longevity." She set the bouquet down on the counter with shaky hands as if this was just another normal day instead of a mother-daughter grudge match that would make MMA fighters back down because it was too vicious. "Asters are all about love and patience, but they used to be thought of as a magical flower and that you could drive away evil by burning them."

"Don't suppose you have a match?" Christine's question was directed at Tess but was 100 percent said for her mother's benefit.

Valeria let out an offended harrumph. "Well, if that's the way you feel about it, then you can pay for this wedding yourself."

Tess squeezed her eyes shut. Could she just sneak into the back or was that too chickenshit? *Which just happens to have been used figuratively for cowardice since at least 1929.* She held her mouth closed hard enough that her lips hurt. *Shut up, weirdo brain.* Also, to get to her office, she'd have to walk right through the mother-daughter war zone, and that wasn't happening.

Christine threw her hands up in frustration and let out a long and bone-deep groan. "I told you that Mason and I wanted to do that in the first place, but you insisted."

Ignoring her daughter, Valeria turned to Tess. "I want my money back."

Tess's gut twisted, dropped, and then dug down to the earth's mantle. Her profit margin was slim as it was. She couldn't afford that loss. "I'm sorry, but the deposit is nonrefundable."

Valeria lifted one eyebrow. "Do you really think you're any match for my attorneys?"

"You signed the agreement." And that declaration would have been a lot more powerful if it hadn't come out all shaky and nervous to match the panic zigging and zagging around inside her.

Personal confrontation with customers? Really not her thing.

"It doesn't matter." Valeria dismissed her concern with a shrug. "You'll have to deal with the time and expense of answering them anyway. Can you really afford to?"

Tess didn't need to do the mental calculation. She couldn't. "I can give you half the deposit."

"Wonderful," Valeria said with an icy smile before walking out of the flower shop without even a single glance back at her daughter.

Wow. That was… Yeah, it was something—and now she was out a customer and half a deposit. Mentally adding "find more dollars" to her to-do list already bursting with the regular workday tasks plus interviewing a new delivery person, Tess let out a sigh as she gathered up the five sample bouquets. Each of the bunches would go to the domestic violence shelter a few blocks away to brighten the place up as part of her community give-back program. Other display flowers and floral samples went to the funeral homes for those whose families couldn't afford any and a high school vocational program so budding horticulturalists could better study the flora.

"That really kinda screwed you over, didn't it?" Christine asked as she followed Tess to the cool display case.

Tess nodded, her round curls bouncing more jauntily than she felt. "Yeah." Really, what was the point of lying about it?

"I have another few years before I come into my trust, but I can afford at least equal the original deposit amount," Christine said. "Could we find flowers that would fit into that budget?"

Suddenly Tess was a lot more in sync with her curls bobbing up and down. "Definitely."

Christine smiled, ordered more like the burlap-tied bouquet for herself and her bridesmaids, said the rest of the flowers could be whatever would work with what was left in the budget, and paid the amount in full. Tess didn't know what to say so she—for once—kept the factoid part of her flustered brain quiet and just said thanks.

A few hours and waaaaaaaaay too much peopling later, Tess flipped the open sign to closed. It was Paint and Sip night. She may not be able to enjoy the clearance-rack wine and God knew what Larry would have them painting tonight, but at least she'd be with her girls.

Then she'd go home to Cole. Well, not home *to* him. He was just there. And so was she. And they'd be alone. And nothing would happen between them and that would be really, really good—*it would!* No matter how tempted she was, she wouldn't give in. That only happened at weddings.

. . .

Instead of sitting on his ass in his living room, Cole should be out on the ice. He should be skating until his lungs hurt and his thighs begged for mercy. It was that kind of day. Instead, he'd spent the whole day doing jack shit and now was staring at a book of hockey plays that made little to no use of his specific skill set.

He was fast.

He always knew the perfect spot on the ice.

He could practically become invisible to goalies.

But Peppers didn't want that anymore. He wanted something new. Peppers couched it as "additional skills" and "leveling up," but it all came down to more than minor adjustments and Cole fucking hated it.

He tossed the playbook down on the coffee table with more force than necessary and it slid off the side, landing with a soft *thud*, followed by a loud and pissed-off kitty yelp. The next thing Cole knew, Kahn was airborne, a length of white material stuck to one paw. He did some kind of midair spin move accompanied by a piss-poor hiss and then sprinted away at Mach speed, the white strip waving behind him like a flag.

"What the hell?" he grumbled as the kitten's tail disappeared behind one of the oversize tan leather chairs and for one spine-chilling second, all he could picture was Evil Kitty sinking his pointy little claws into the pristine leather. "You better not be thinking of taking revenge. It was an accident."

Sure, the cat was Satan's best friend, but that didn't mean Cole would throw that stupid playbook at him on purpose.

"Come on out from behind there."

Kahn didn't respond. *What were you expecting, Phillips, a well-reasoned dialogue?* No, because he knew better. Cats didn't respond to your call. They left nasty fur balls and hair everywhere—not to mention the lingering smell of a litter box—in their wake like a fuck-you flag to the humans who housed them, even if only temporarily. And they shredded things, which had to be why Kahn had something stuck to his back paw.

"Fuck me," he groaned.

Forget revenge, the kitten had taken a preemptive strike. The question was, what had the demon fur ball destroyed?

Getting up slowly, Cole kept his voice soft. "Here, kitty, kitty." He tiptoed over to the chair, feeling every bit like some inept cartoon villain. "I just want to see what you've managed to mangle, you sneaky little shit."

Okay, it wasn't the nicest thing to say, but it wasn't like the kitten could understand. It was all about the baby-talk tone he'd made sure to use. He peeked around the corner of the chair, ready to reach out and snatch the kitten, but the devil feline wasn't there.

He let out a deep breath and straightened up. What was worse than trying to sweet-talk a cat? Trying to sweet-talk nothing but air. He glanced up at the ceiling and shook his head. "You are an idiot, Phillips."

"I mean, I'm not gonna disagree," a man said, "but is there a specific reason this time?"

Cole whirled around, not even close to as skillfully as the cat had.

Petrov stood in his hallway holding what at one point in time had been a half dozen squares of toilet paper but now looked like someone had tried to turn it into streamers. Well, that was one question answered—what had been stuck to Kahn's paw—but not the other two in his head.

"What are you doing here and why are you holding those?" he asked.

"I picked the toilet paper up starting outside the front door and followed it here like some kind of TP bread trail," Petrov said. "Honestly, I figured it had to be a sign that your clean-freak ass had finally cracked."

"It was the cat."

Petrov's eyebrows practically disappeared into his hairline. "There's a cat here?"

He nodded, marching toward Tess's room. "*Her* cat."

"There's a dirty joke in there somewhere." And he was chuckling about it as they made their way down the hall.

"Shut up, Petrov."

Mercifully, he did, but that didn't mean he hung back as Cole followed the shredded Charmin to the partially open door of Tess's room. Once there, he hesitated, his hand hovering over the knob. All he had to do was nudge it open the rest of the way. She'd done the same thing to him and he'd been inside and asleep. She was at work. He was on the trail of that darn cat. That made it okay, right?

"You gonna stare or go in?" Petrov asked.

A man had to have boundaries.

No shotgun weddings. No getting it on together again. No wandering into her room and imagining her in there like some kind of creeper—which he was not. He'd barely thought about how she looked naked and spread out on a bed, her eyes half closed with pleasure, since she'd moved in.

Fuck.

He *was* a creeper.

"It's her room," he said. Reminder? Mantra? Plea? Yeah, it was pretty much all of that.

He was ready to walk away when Kahn let out a pitiful mewl.

Hell's Favorite Minion was probably trapped. He could've fallen into the toilet. *That would serve the little shit right.*

Cole had half a second of epic levels of satisfaction before guilt scratched at the back of his neck and his conscience whispered that Kahn might need help.

Letting out a groan he felt all the way down to the soles of his feet, Cole pushed Tess's door open wide and walked in. It smelled like her, flowery and light and cheerful, but that was the only sign that she was living there and would be for at least the next few weeks. The bone-colored comforter was pulled up with the matching cream and tan pillows on top. The walls—like in the rest of the house—were eggshell. The only thing that stuck out was Tess's brightly colored suitcase.

Well, that and the river of toilet paper running from the bathroom to the barely open door of the walk-in closet. A tiny paw slid out from underneath the door followed by a pathetic meow.

"Serves you right for taking blades to the toilet paper," Cole said as he swung the door open.

Kahn dashed out and used those spikes of his to climb straight up his jeans and T-shirt until the damn thing was close enough to rub the top of his fuzzy head against Cole's jaw.

Petrov shot him a smug grin. "I thought you didn't like cats…or dogs…or anything with fur or scales or feathers."

He grimaced as the kitten settled on his shoulder. "I don't."

Petrov didn't even have the decency to pretend not to laugh at that. "Whatever you say." Then he turned and looked around the room. "This is Tess's room?" He glanced into the empty closet. "She's not staying here?"

"Yeah, she is."

The other man crossed his arms over his chest and gave him a hard look. "And she's staying for longer than a weekend?"

"Two weeks at least."

"Then why is the closet empty?" he asked, the question being very much not a question. "That's not what chicks do. What's the deal with your lady not unpacking?"

"My lady?" He pet Kahn, not really meaning to but needing to do something with his hands—always his tell when he was trying to deflect. "What are you, a hundred?"

Petrov rolled his eyes. "Answer the question, Phillips."

"It's only been a few days," Cole said, the words sounding like a lame excuse even as they came out of his mouth. "Maybe she likes to wait."

He let out a snort of disbelief. "Unlikely."

"What, you know her so well?" Defensive? Him? Fuck yeah.

"You don't even know her. That's your problem."

"She's only going to be here for a few weeks." His brain was counting them down while his cock was trying to make them last. "What does it matter?"

"Because there is a baby, you dumb-ass," Petrov all but yelled at him. "Tess might only be in your guest room for a limited time, but she and that baby are in your life forever. That's one change you can't just ignore or try to strong-arm into going back to the old way of things. You're going to be a dad."

Yeah. That was the part Cole kept trying to ignore. It wasn't that he didn't accept the situation; it just seemed so unreal and far away. Of course, that didn't excuse him being an unwelcoming asshole.

"So I'll encourage her to unpack," he said.

"You're a fucking moron, Phillips." Petrov rolled his eyes. "If you can pull your head out of your ass, how about we go over those new plays that—believe it or not—are going to take your game up about a thousand notches. Not that you care about being the best or not losing your edge or anything."

Petrov stalked out of the room, his middle finger raised.

Cole returned the salute while the little engine that shed purred loud enough that Cole could almost block out the doubts kicking his metaphorical ass.

As much as it physically pained him to admit, Petrov was correct. He hadn't done anything to welcome Tess, he hadn't given Coach's new plays a chance, and his knee-jerk answer to anything new was always no.

Maybe he could give in a little to the changes—baby steps, nothing crazy like actually starting to like Fuzzy Beelzebub the Purring Impaler. After all, the cat was anchoring himself onto Cole's shoulder by embedding his claws into Cole's shirt and—a little bit—into his shoulder. The play clock was definitely ticking down on living with that. Oblivious to his future, Kahn rubbed his head against Cole's neck and purred louder.

He put a protective hand over the fur ball so he wouldn't fall off and headed toward the door. "I'll get her to unpack," he said, refusing to admit to himself that he was talking to a kitten. "But don't *you* go getting comfortable. This is still a no-pets, no-mess, no-change home. This is only a temporary adjustment."

• • •

It was after ten at night when Tess finally walked inside Cole's house still riding the nonalcoholic-sparkling-white-grape-juice high. Considering her sole delivery driver had just told her via text that he was quitting and not giving any notice, it was a miracle she was managing to feel pretty damn giddy. But that was the usual end result of a night with her girls.

The click of her disengaging the dead bolt on Cole's front door boomed in the quiet museum of a house. She held her breath, waiting, but no one called out. It wasn't like she was actually expecting him to be waiting up for her, but it wasn't three in the morning, either.

Shoving the unexplained sense of disappointment down deep into a dark hole, she carried her night's work down the hall and into the living room. Cole's fireplace mantel was depressingly bare, but not for much longer. Grinning like a woman up to no good—which, okay, she kinda was—Tess crossed over to the fireplace and set her latest Paint and Sip canvas on the mantel. She didn't notice Cole until she turned around and spotted him sitting in one of the chairs with Kahn at his feet attacking his shoelaces, but then she really took notice.

She'd never been a thigh woman, but she was when she looked at him sitting there in a T-shirt and basketball shorts that had inched upward, exposing thick and solid muscles promising that all sorts of exertions were not only possible but probable. Her pulse picked up speed and she forced herself to look higher. That was a mistake. It just put her attention firmly on the part of him that she knew for a fact was long, thick, and fucking magnificent. And the things he knew to do with it? Suddenly it was way too hot and she had on way too many layers of clothes.

Sweet saffron crocus, pull it together!

"Is that a werewolf riding a dinosaur in the middle of a lake?" He nodded toward the painting she'd put on the mantel as if he didn't notice her all but drooling at the sight of him.

"Bigfoot wrestling the Loch Ness Monster." She tilted her head to the side and squinted, using the move as cover to get herself under control so she didn't run across the room and jump into his lap. "But I could see where you got dinosaur. Nessy does have the whole apatosaurus look. Did you know that it wasn't until 1903 that scientists decided that the differences between a brontosaurus and apatosaurus were so small that they might as well be in the same genus?"

And there it was, the random factoid freak-out defense mechanism whenever she had to talk to anyone other than a select group of people she'd known forever. Great.

"I did not know that," he said, nothing in his tone reminding her of oh-you're-so-awk-weird reaction her outburst usually got from people. "But I do know that thing can't stay there."

"I know, Larry's ideas are a little out there, but this one was really fun to paint." She left off the part about the desperate need in here for some color. His house may be the place most of the color wheel had forgotten, but she didn't need to point that out. "It's so much better than the wilting lettuce when he was reading that book on food waste."

Cole got up and walked over beside her, his long legs closing the distance in only a few steps. They stood side by side, looking at the painting as if it was in a real museum instead of only being a few steps up from a velvet painting of dogs playing poker. Okay, Cole looked. She pretended to admire her work while steadying her breaths and concentrating really hard on not inching over so they were touching. She was the one who'd declared no more naked happy times. Why? Because she was obviously a giant idiot.

"What's he reading now?" Cole asked.

So distracted by the sight of his muscled forearms, the truth came out before she could overthink it. "Bigfoot erotica."

"That is not a real thing," he said, each word coming out with clear and perfect diction.

Oh God. All he was missing was a strand of pearls to clutch.

"It totally is." Man, not laughing out loud was really

hard when he made that shocked-virgin face. "Want me to recommend some titles?"

"No." He shook his head emphatically. "And now that painting really has to go because I will never *not* think of Bigfoot porn when I see it."

She raised herself up on her tiptoes and leaned in close to him as if she was one of those women who flirts in a way that doesn't involve random trivia—not that she was flirting because she most definitely would not do that with him. Look what had happened last time!

"Erotica and porn are not the same thing," she said, awed by her own brazenness. Yes, this was totally wanton behavior for her with full sentences minus factoids and everything. She had no idea who this woman who had taken over her mouth was, but she kinda liked her. "Although both can be pretty amazing."

Cole gulped. Audibly.

"It can't stay in the living room," he said after letting out a shaky breath.

"Sure." She gave him the same smile she gave her customers who insisted a purple dead nettle was actually a henbit. "Whatever you say."

"I gotta head in." His gaze went from the painting to her mouth before jerking up to look her straight in the eyes. "It's past my bedtime."

"You have a bedtime?"

Of course he did. It was probably the same time each night. That she was dead to the world within the same fifteen-minute time frame every night was something she had every intention of keeping to herself.

"I have a routine." His attention dipped back down to her mouth, and then he muttered something unintelligible under his breath.

For a second, he looked like he was about to say something

else but changed his mind and walked out of the living room. Tess watched him go—the view almost as good as watching him come closer—and then took down the painting, ready to carry it back to her room. That's when she got an idea. It wasn't a completely evil idea, but it was one she probably shouldn't implement.

Still...

Tess turned in the opposite direction from her bedroom and into the kitchen, Kahn trailing along behind her. Once there, she opened up the walk-in pantry and moved the protein powders (yes, plural) and more around so the painting was perfectly centered on the shelf. The bright, colorful, and totally bizarre painting would be front and center as soon as he opened the door.

Giggling quietly, she closed the door, already counting down to breakfast. Waiting until Cole woke up tomorrow and saw what she'd done was going to be hell.

Chapter Eight

Ice Knights players got four days a month off. Cole hated each and every one of them, so of course getting sidelined for his stupid allergic reaction couldn't have happened today—a regularly scheduled off day that he'd already planned for. No. Now he had an extra day of itching to get back on the ice. That meant one thing—stress baking.

Normally, this was the moment in his morning when he would have gotten up and headed for the shower. But the fuzz monster was back, lying curled up on Cole's pillow and tangled in his hair. Kahn's little pink nose was close enough that his breath tickled Cole's ear.

If I get up now, I'll wake him. Five more minutes won't hurt.

He'd just stay here in bed and list the pros and cons of a Bundt cake versus a pineapple upside-down cake. The first had glaze. The second had pineapple. The nutritionist was big on eating fruit and he had an organic pineapple in his kitchen. Really, who was he to argue with someone with a PhD in healthy eats?

Plan of action decided, he almost started to sit up, but Kahn was still there, snuggled against him. If the hell spawn got enough sleep, maybe he'd leave all the toilet paper alone today. That made sense. He'd stay here for a little while longer. It wasn't like the purr-o-matic could snooze for that much longer.

Cole wasn't giving in. He was compromising and giving Petrov and Christensen a big middle finger that he could make changes. The fact that his line mates wouldn't know about it—because there was no way he was admitting to anyone anything close to the fact that some people would think he was snuggling with a kitten—didn't matter.

And that's just what he was trying to convince himself of when he heard the unmistakable sound of Tess puking her guts up.

Kahn's beauty sleep didn't stand a chance. Cole was up out of bed and hurrying down the hall at breakneck speed. He made it all the way down the hall, through Tess's open bedroom door, and almost into her bathroom when his brain caught up with his actions. He hesitated outside the open door.

Hey, jackass, she probably doesn't want anyone to see her like this.

And if she's throwing up, she obviously needs help.

It was the second option that won out.

He peeked in. She sat on the edge of the tub, her eyes closed and her lips pursed. Her skin had that pasty just-threw-up sheen to it. He got one foot inside the door before the reality of the situation slammed into him like an illegal elbow to the head. *All right, you're here, Phillips. What the fuck do you do now?* He had no clue. Hug her? Call a doctor? Tell her it was better out than in?

Standing awkwardly in the door, half in and half out of her space, he asked, "You okay?"

"Oh yeah," she said, her voice rough and scratchy, before she stood up and grabbed her toothbrush. "There's nothing like heaving the absolutely nothing in my stomach every morning like clockwork."

Every morning? How had he missed that before?

Because ever since she told you that she's knocked up, you've been an asshole ignoring her as much as possible. Her moving in a few days ago made that harder, but you proved you were up to the challenge.

That asshole voice in his head was starting to sound a helluva lot like Petrov. And as much as he'd like to go bake the shit out of a pineapple upside-down cake to block out that fact, Tess needed him—or maybe he needed to do something, *anything*, to help so he'd feel less like the dick who fucked up her life plan by using expired condoms given to him as a gag gift.

"Should I call your doctor?" Because he sure as shit wasn't doing a damn thing to improve the situation.

"I just need to do this"—she put toothpaste on her brush—"and take another minute to catch my breath. Maybe some water."

Okay, that he could do. "I'll be right back."

By the time he'd returned from the kitchen with a glass of water and a handful of Saltines, she was just rinsing off her toothbrush. Kahn—the little jerk—was sitting on the closed toilet lid, eyeballing the toilet paper.

Cole didn't notice the way Tess's I'D RATHER BE SLEEPING shirt came to mid-thigh, giving him a great view of those legs she'd wrapped around his head when he'd gone down on her that night. And the hard tips of her nipples poking against the shirt? Yep, didn't even glance that way because his dick did not control him. He was an adult, not a horny teenager, and the woman had just had a very rough morning. So of course that meant it was totally out of the question to notice how the blue cotton material clung to her hips, or how her face had regained its color, or how the disarray of her blond curls gave her a just-fucked look.

And yet... Yeah, he was the jerk who noticed it all.

If he thought closing his eyes would help, he would, but the opposite had proven itself every night when he went to bed. His routine was to spend the last thirty minutes of the day going over plays. He was doing that, but they had nothing to do with the puck and everything to do with getting Tess to make that oh-my-God-I-can't-believe-I-just-came-that-hard face again. He was going to get calluses on his right hand with the rate he was going.

"Thanks," she said, taking the water he'd forgotten he was holding and drinking down a third of it in one take. "What a way to start what is going to be an absolutely crazy day."

"Things get that busy at a flower shop?" The words were out of his mouth before he could stop them.

Oh yeah, insult her business right after she's had a hell morning. Way to go.

"You have no idea," she said, not seeming to be insulted by his question. "I'm going in two hours early so I can get the billing and accounts out of the way before we open."

"You can't fit that in between customers?"

Yes. Tell her how to run her business. Every entrepreneur is dying for advice from a guy who hasn't ever even held a job that didn't involve lacing up skates.

Tess put away her toothbrush and squeezed by him out the bathroom door into her room. "Usually I do." She opened her suitcase lying on top of the bench at the end of the bed and took out some clothes—yes, including a purple pair of panties that he did not notice. "Today, however, I'll be making deliveries during the slow times because my driver quit last night without giving any warning."

"Is it good for you to be that active right now?"

And now you are a doctor. Never mind you barely passed biology and have spent exactly zero minutes with anyone who was pregnant besides her.

Could he staple his mouth shut? It would be preferable to the stupid things coming out now, since all his blood seemed to be headed in the opposite direction of his brain.

Tess rolled her eyes at him. "Women have been having babies for eternity under much more difficult conditions than this. We're not exactly fragile."

"Point taken." *Don't say it. Don't say it. Don't say it.* Of course, it was too late. He had a hated day off. She needed help. "I can do the deliveries today."

She let out a snort laugh and shook her head. "That's not gonna happen."

He raised an eyebrow in question.

"Come on," she said, crossing her arms just under her tits, which he did not even take a glance at. "You're an Ice Knights player in one of the most hockey-mad metro areas outside of Canada. You'll get recognized and mobbed."

"I'll wear a hat, pull my hair back." Why was he fighting to do this? He had plays to learn and a pineapple upside-down cake to bake. "No one will realize it's me."

"You don't have to do this," she said, her gaze dropping down to Kahn, who'd jumped into her open suitcase and curled up into a fluff ball. "I'm sure you have better things to do on an off day."

"I suck at off days." Not an overstatement.

She gave him an assessing look, tilting her head to one side and twirling one golden curl around a finger. "Too much unscheduled free time?"

"Pretty much."

Everything from her cocked-out hip to the disbelieving expression on her face screamed out that he was full of it.

"You're saying you're just dying for me to boss you around all day for minimum wage?"

"You don't have to pay me." The Ice Knights did that already. Money was not an issue.

"Really?" she asked, the single word all but calling him a liar. "What if part of the job is wearing a Bigfoot costume?"

He shrugged. "As long as I don't have to wrestle a dinosaur, I'm in."

She gave him an assessing look, then let out a long sigh. "We've got to be out the door in fifteen."

The half second of elation at having won—competitive, him? Always—fizzled out as soon as her timeline penetrated his brain.

"But that means I can't shave. I always shave." It was part of his routine.

There went that eyebrow of hers again.

"Fine," he grumbled, heading toward the door. He wasn't Christensen with his extensive hair prep, but fifteen minutes was still cutting it close. "I will skip shaving. I'll grab breakfast on our way out the door. What about you? Can I grab you something?"

"Nah, I'll just have crackers and seltzer water, but don't worry, I'll be good to have some real food at lunch." Her cheeks developed a sudden pink tinge. "And your breakfast isn't in the pantry, is it?"

"All my prepped stuff is in the fridge," he said, pausing halfway into the hall, his Spidey senses activated. "Why?"

She seemed to get really interested in Kahn lying in her suitcase, keeping her attention focused on the fur ball and not Cole.

"No reason," she said without looking up.

Yeah, that didn't sound right, but he now had fourteen minutes, and that didn't give him time to unwind whatever was going on—and there most definitely was something. Good thing they had all day at the shop together for him to figure it out. And lucky for him, that would give him something to think about beyond the fact that underneath her jeans, she was wearing lacy purple panties with pink polka dots.

. . .

Tess was triple-checking the morning flower deliveries manifest at the shop and doing her best not to notice the way Cole's perfect butt looked in those jeans because no good would come from eye fucking his ass at work. Or at home. Or when she was alone in the shower. She noticed anyway because oh my God how could she not?

She hadn't stopped noticing until he'd walked out the door, his signature almost-to-his-shoulders-length hair tucked under a grungy baseball hat, for the first round of morning deliveries. About fifteen minutes later, the texting started.

Cole: *I should have made a bet about not being recognized.*

Tess: *Who did you deliver to?*

Cole: *Some law office. Secretary did the happy cry thing when she read the card.*

Tess: *People love getting flowers.*

While the peopling parts of her days were always the most exhausting, it really was amazing to get to see people's reactions when they realized the flowers were for them. There were usually smiles, sometimes weepy tears, occasionally angry refusal (but that was pretty rare). Flowers meant something to people—love, friendship, a human connection. That couldn't be beat.

Cole: *So you still stand by your position?*

Tess: *That you'll get recognized? Without a doubt.*

Cole: *Bet on it?*

Tess: *I don't want you to take a sucker bet.*

She knew his delivery route and who he was about to meet.

Cole: *Too chicken to agree?*

Tess: *Does that actually work on anyone?*

Cole: *All the time.*

Okay, if that's the way he wanted to play it.

Tess: *Fine.*

Cole: *Stakes?*

Tess: *Loser buys dinner.*

Cole: *You're on.*

About twenty minutes later, after she'd just sold a dozen red roses (yawn) to a husband who obviously had fucked up something with his wife, the next text came in.

Cole: *So what am I buying for dinner?*

Tess: *You went to the hospital.*

Cole: *How did you know?*

Tess: *Chipsy is a massive Ice Knights fan. He knows*

things about you that you probably don't even know about yourself.

Chip Aronson—known as Chipsy to everyone—not only was an Ice Knights fan, he was a walking billboard for the team with an Ice Knights shirt, sweater, tie, lapel pin, or socks for every day of the year. The man wasn't a fan, he was an eighty-year-old fanatic.

Cole: *I barely got to the information desk before he had his camera ready.*

Tess: *Like I said, sucker bet.*

After that, the texts came in sporadically, but her social media notifications went nuts. Her Forever in Bloom Insta account was pretty much dedicated to weird facts about all things plant-based and only had a handful of followers. She posted pics of a new tulip arrangement with a snippet about how in Holland, tulips used to be more valuable than gold or did an artsy shot of the steamed broccoli she'd made for dinner and included a tidbit about how the vegetable is actually a flower.

However, according to her notifications, the number of followers was increasing exponentially, and it wasn't because she'd posted about how sunflowers are supervillains of the flower world because they produce a toxic substance that kills other flowers around them. Her counts had increased because Chipsy from the hospital's information desk had tagged the Ice Knights in his selfie with Cole, and it was getting reposted everywhere after the team had shared it.

Tess clicked on one of the notifications. A pic opened on her phone showing Cole in the same white Forever in Bloom T-shirt she was wearing. He was holding a flower arrangement while standing next to a woman who looked like she was about to dump whoever had sent the pansies in favor of the hockey forward.

Tess couldn't blame her. Even if she hadn't had the pleasure of seeing what was under his tee, there was just something about being able to zoom in on his biceps peeking out from under his sleeve. Did that make her a bad person? Or just horny? Both? Well, she couldn't do anything about it, so it didn't matter.

They'd had one night and a soon-to-be baby between them. No connection. No relationship. It was just the way she wanted it when it came to Cole Phillips. She wasn't about to be the woman who'd trapped her man by getting pregnant. She knew firsthand the pain of being that kid. There was nothing like growing up knowing you were only a means to an end even before ever being born.

The bell above the door rang, and an older woman dressed in head-to-toe sunshine yellow with rose-gold hair strolled in. Tess's sour mood evaporated. It would be next to impossible not to while facing Charla Evans, the matriarch of Mulberry Street. Charla owned one of the buildings two doors down and lived on the top floor—the entire top floor—with at least a dozen tropical fish, enough plants to make her own oxygen supply for a year, and her poet of a husband who wrote monthly odes to her beauty that he posted on the neighborhood message board.

"Mrs. Evans, I wasn't expecting you this morning."

"I hope you don't mind, but when I saw the notification that George—that's what I'm going to call my newest addition—was here, I had to come right away in hopes of having it delivered today. Now where is my little fella?"

Her "little fella" was actually a Hawaiian dwarf umbrella tree currently hanging out in the inventory sunroom. The plant clocked in at about thirty pounds counting the tray of pebbles, ceramic pot, premium soil, and the actual tree.

"My delivery man will be back in a few minutes, but let me go grab George so you can admire him, and then when Cole gets back, he can carry it to your place."

"Really, I was hoping to admire both," the older woman said with a dramatic sigh. "But I can wait to see this Mr. Hockey who keeps popping up on social media."

"I didn't realize you were an Ice Knights fan."

Charla gave her a wink. "I'm not."

Okay, then. Not wanting to get drawn any deeper down that particular rabbit hole, Tess excused herself and went into the back to get George. The mini-tree that looked more like a bush at the moment and had to be balanced just right or else the water in the humidity bed (which she called "pebble beach" in her head because it was just a tray filled with pebbles and water) would spill out over the edge. Picking it up, she adjusted for the fact that the front, which was closest to her, was heavier because of the placement of the ceramic pot. She'd need to warn Charla about that.

She was about to start walking toward the front when the door leading to the alley parking opened up and Cole walked through. No doubt because his cover had been blown, the grimy baseball cap was gone, allowing his hair to fall down, brushing the tips of his shoulders. Long hair wasn't usually her thing. But on Thor's twin? Yeah, it was totally becoming her thing.

Hello, patron saint of single moms. If you could hit me with a lightning bolt of oh-honey-no right about now, that would be great.

"Whatcha got there?" he asked, strutting in and heading straight toward her.

Tess froze. Her brain, the part that ran a business, did complicated math in her head, and remembered almost every random factoid she'd ever heard, went on vacation. "A plant."

"Here, let me." He reached to take the oversize bonsai-type tree.

Normally, she would have gladly given it up for him to carry, but in that moment with him so close in the oxygen-rich environment of the mini-hothouse inventory room that reminded her a little too much of the conservatory from their night together, she couldn't do it. She just knew deep inside her that this man was dangerous. Not that he'd hurt her—well, not on purpose—but that he had access to some secret spot inside her that no one had seen before. It was unsettling.

"No, that's okay, I got—" And that's the exact moment when she didn't anymore.

She tilted the back side higher than the front enough that a stream of water from the tray spilled out, soaking her shirt in a line that went right across her boobs. Of course.

"Oh crap," he said, taking the dwarf umbrella tree and setting it back down in its original spot. He turned back to her, his gaze dipping down to her chest. "I'm sorry I—"

Whatever else Cole was going to say remained a mystery because he went totally silent. She didn't have to guess why. White shirt plus water plus thin lacy bralette equals total embarrassment—especially when her nipples had gone into full headlight mode. She'd like to think that had happened because of the splash of cool water. That would be a lie, though. It was all Cole.

Nice going, Tess.

"Did you know a fifteen-year French study showed that women who skipped wearing a bra had a yearly seven-millimeter lift in their nipples?" The words rolled out without her even considering them. *Shut up, Tess.* "And their breasts were firmer and didn't show as many stretch marks?"

He yanked his gaze up to her face, the right side of his mouth twitching. "I did not know that."

"Not wearing a bra is believed to encourage the development of the muscles under the breasts, which can lead to better posture. Plus, some women report that not wearing a bra can alleviate back pain because of the increased muscles." *Close your mouth, Tess.* "The study didn't look at women over thirty-five, though, so who knows if it was just a free-boob French doctor's onetime results or if big corporate bra is squashing other studies to keep women's boobs under wraps." There. That was it. She was not going to talk about bras anymore. "I need to take off my shirt."

Oh my God. What is wrong with me?

Cole went very still, the vein in his temple pulsing, as he kept his attention focused solely on her face. "Okay."

The air in the sunny room went from a pleasant humidity to strip-off-your-clothes-and-run-naked hot. The image of seeing Cole in his bed the other morning, his strong, muscular chest and abs, rushed to the forefront. Her hormones let out a resounding cheer of yes-let's-do-him-again and it took everything she had not to rush him right there and then. But she couldn't—wouldn't—do that. Neither of them meant to be in this situation. They could both be adults about it, and that meant safe and smart boundaries. She would not ever let this baby think for even a minute that he or she was just a means to trap a man with money.

Reality firmly acknowledged and brain back online, she said in her most boss-lady voice, "Please take the tree to Mrs. Evans out front and then carry it to her apartment two buildings down."

"You got it, boss." Cole grinned at her. "And don't worry, I'll take care of reservations for dinner tonight."

"Dinner?" Oh shit. She'd totally forgotten about that. And really she had every reason to because it was just talk… weird flirting…competitive banter…not reality.

"Never let it be said that I welched on a bet." He leaned in close, dipping his head down so his lips were practically touching hers. "You. Me. Dinner. It's a date."

Then he took a step back and with one flirty wink, he picked up the dwarf umbrella tree and carried it out front, leaving her to stare after him and that perfect ass of his. Yeah, that was the kind of view that wasn't about to make her nipples settle down anytime soon.

Fuck, Tess, get yourself under control. Yeah, good luck to her with that because she couldn't shake the feeling it was only going to get worse. How in the hell was she going to make it through dinner?

Chapter Nine

Tess hadn't been hiding in her office since she'd flipped the flower shop's sign from open to closed. She was doing very necessary paper shuffling and cleaning off her desk because a clean and tidy environment equaled a clean and tidy mind. Wasn't that how the saying went? Or was it idle hands led to feeling up the guy in her flower shop who had knocked her up and was completely off-limits? Yeah, that second one definitely sounded more likely.

That bet had been a really stupid idea—shocker, which was exactly what she'd told Gina when her friend had texted earlier.

Gina: *Ohhhh! Fingers crossed for a love connection at dinner.*

Tess: *Not gonna happen.*

Gina: *Why not?*

Tess: *Because we both know this whole thing was*

an accident and nothing is going to come of getting weddinged with Cole but a cute baby. Anyway, there's Marti.

Gina: *Maybe this is the time they don't get back together.*

Yeah, that was pretty much beyond doubtful. According to Lucy and Fallon, Cole and Marti were in an on-again, off-again loop, so Tess figured it was only a matter of time. And even without that part of it, staying with Cole was just one more temporary placement for Tess. Soon enough her apartment repairs would be finished and she'd go home and Cole would go on with his life the way it was before Lucy's wedding. History always repeated itself and she would be smart enough to learn from it and protect herself and the baby.

"Need some help in there?" Cole asked from the front of the shop.

Her pulse went all jiggly-jaggly. "Nah, I'm good," she said, clutching a stack of soon-to-be-due invoices to her chest. "I'm on my way out."

She shoved the bills into her top drawer, grabbed her purse, and headed out to the front of the shop, desperate to keep her head straight. "Did you know—"

"Nope," he interrupted her. "That's not gonna work tonight."

She jolted to a stop, her brain going into panic factoid override mode. "Tonight was written as two words until the eighteenth century."

"No factoids." He closed the distance between them, coming to a stop only a few inches from her.

They weren't touching. Sure, she was practically bathing in his hot-guy pheromones, but there wasn't any physical contact. Just her being her usual dork self, spouting off factoids while Cole stood close enough to make her pulse increase to the oh-my-God-kiss-me rate.

His gaze dropped to her mouth. "I know what you're doing."

"Sharing knowledge?" That didn't even sound truthful to her own ears.

"You're using it as a defense mechanism and to stay in your comfort zone as much as possible." That dimple of his appeared in his cheek as he smiled down at her.

Smarting at the direct hit that did nothing to ease the heady ache building from being this close to him, she struck out. "Sort of like you and your routines?"

His dimple disappeared. "No." His jaw set. "Yes." He let out a harrumph and shoved his hands through his hair. "Shit. Let's just go get some food."

She hesitated for a second but then pushed up her glasses, straightened her shoulders, and looked him straight in the eye. "Fine, no factoids, but I get to pick where we eat, and it has to be somewhere you've never been before."

The look of horror on his face was almost enough to take the sting out of his observation about her hiding behind the factoids.

Cole grimaced. "I'm kind of a picky eater."

"This is my shocked face," she said, pointing at herself while managing not to point out that researchers classified selective eaters into one of three categories.

And that's how they ended up at a mom-and-pop Peruvian restaurant sharing a round of starters—sea bass ceviche and a shredded chicken in a nutty creamy sauce called *ají de gallina* that Cole was devouring despite having looked at it at first as if it was possibly poisoned—before their waiter brought their main course of roasted chicken to the table.

"Will they think I'm weird if I lick my plate clean?" Cole asked. "This sauce is fantastic."

"It's the *ají amarillo*; they are the best peppers." It had a medium-size kick of berry/fruity spice that was so amazing. "It's one of the so-called holy trinity of Peruvian ingredients. The others are—"

Cole scooted his chair over until he was close enough that their thighs were touching, the sizzle of being this near to him effectively short-circuiting her brain. The rest of what she'd been about to tell him died on her tongue.

He slung an arm across the back of her chair, his fingertips brushing her shoulder. "Are you factoiding me?"

"That's not a real word." Of that she was 100 percent sure, even if her shaky voice didn't back her up on that.

"How long have you been doing it?"

She took in a deep breath. It was like the world had been switched into portrait mode with him in focus and everything else going blurry. The air around them was heavy with anticipation—not about her answer but about them and this constant pull between them. It made it hard for her to breathe, and she had to sit up, putting some space between her and his sinewy arm draped across the back of the chair.

Cole seemed to understand how overwhelming he was because he pulled back, adjusted his chair so it was turned toward hers but not touching.

"As long as I can remember." Riffling through her memories, she tried to pull out the one that would be the first but came up empty. "It can be a bit much for people."

"Friends gave you a hard time?"

"My cousins weren't always great about it." And that was being generous. For someone with as many cousins as she did who she grew up with, they made sure to keep their distance at school and at home. No playdates. No hanging out. Just that weirdo-don't-talk-to-me glare on the bus. "I didn't have many friends growing up."

"Why not?"

"As my aunt Haven once said, I'm an acquired taste and usually best in small doses." That would explain why her mother never let more than a few months go before dropping her off at another relative's house so she could go out and explore her inner self.

"Your aunt seems like a bitch," Cole said, sounding as if he felt it all the way down to his toes.

"She was just overwhelmed." Tess flinched as the memories came rushing back, the old hurt resurfacing with a solid *thwack*. "It wasn't easy to take in one more kid when she already had six to feed and keep track of while my uncle was on the road for work as a long-haul trucker."

Cole cocked his head to the side, confusion etched into his expression. "Why did she have to take you—"

Thankfully, however, the rest of his question she wasn't even close to wanting to answer got lost in the commotion when the restaurant's background music changed with an abrupt squeal of feedback to polka. Then an older guy wearing sunglasses, a rainbow wig, and an orange T-shirt with LAUGH IT UP written on it walked through the door, blowing on a whistle that cut through any remaining chatter in the restaurant.

"Oh my God," she said, turning to Cole, a giggly burst of happiness washing the ugliness of the past back into the shadows. "I've never seen Jules in person before. He's a Waterbury legend."

"Who is he and are the owners about to call the cops?" He looked around, tensing as if he was expecting trouble.

Oh, the poor sweet man. He had no clue what the world was like outside of his controlled environment. He was so in for a shock.

"No way." She shook her head, trying to melt into her chair so Jules might miss seeing her and calling her out to participate. "He's famous around here for staging these candid-camera/pranked-your-ride type of gags."

While one of the waiters stood and gawked, no doubt more than a little in awe, Jules walked into the middle of the restaurant, commanding everyone's attention.

"Tonight," Jules said in a ridiculously unidentifiable accent that sounded more than a little like the mom's from *Schitt's Creek*, "we all must dance for our dinners."

He clapped his hands and half the people who'd been sitting at tables like regular customers whipped off their full-length winter coats, revealing chicken costumes they were wearing underneath. Then the first polka strains of "The Chicken Dance" started to play over the speakers.

"Everyone, get up and let loose!" Jules yelled above the now-blaring music.

Cole, along with all the other non-costumed diners, jumped up out of his seat. "Come on."

Tess didn't just stay in her chair, she was frozen, the horror of actually mixing it up and being in the eye of attention freezing her to her seat. "No way."

"Live a little," he said, holding out his hand for her to take. "You know the chicken dance."

Heart racing, palms sweaty, and the apps swirling around in her stomach, she clamped her jaw closed to keep the "hell no" or the random factoid from passing her lips. Cole's finger under her chin tipped her face upward so she couldn't avoid looking at him. The mockery or annoyance that experience had taught her to expect wasn't there. It was just him looking at her as if she was really there and he wanted her to be. The shock of it was enough for her to take his hand and join in the fray.

"Don't worry," he whispered in her ear, "I'll be right there with you."

Feeling like a gawky teenager, she went through the chicken beak hand motions, flapping her arms like wings, doing the twist, and finally clapping on the beat along with the rest of the diners.

Jules grabbed an older woman out of the crowd and she ended up starting the line as everyone followed her through the restaurant, weaving in and out of tables as "The Chicken Dance" played on.

By the time the recorded accordion blasted its last note, she and Cole were laughing, and when he picked her up and swung her around, she didn't object. She just put her arms around his neck and brought her face near his, her lips so close that she'd barely have to move to kiss him. "Tempting" didn't even begin to describe how badly she wanted to follow through with the urge, but that wasn't smart. Theirs was a temporary arrangement, and she had to think long-term for her baby.

"You better let me go," she said, even though she really didn't want to.

Something dark and dangerous in the most thrilling of ways passed across his face, but he didn't voice it. Really, she'd probably imagined it, because he sat her down and put as much space between them as possible, considering they were standing right beside their two-person table. His jaw squared with tension, he glared down at the floor.

Way to fuck up that moment, Tess. Temporary, remember?

By the time she sat back down in her chair, the people in chicken suits had pulled long coats over their costumes and were following Jules out of the restaurant in a line as if he was the Pied Piper of Pollo. A not-so-small part of Tess wished she could join them, slink away from what would be an uncomfortable dinner thanks to her almost kissing Cole.

Usually it was some stupid thing she said that made things weird, not something she did. Not this time. Nope, tonight she'd driven them on the express lane to Awkwardville because of pregnancy horndog side effect that left her panties wet and her pheromones out of whack. And maybe if she kept telling herself that, she might just start to believe it.

. . .

Cole gripped the passenger seat with his ass cheeks and tensed his thighs as Tess took a corner at Mach Three. Ever since they'd left the restaurant, it was like she was a woman on a fast break and heading straight for the goal.

"Are you late for something?" he asked as she turned onto his street.

"Just ready for bed." She let out a little gasp as if she hadn't meant to say that out loud. "For sleep," she said, her voice higher than normal. "To go to bed by myself and go to sleep. Alone. All by myself."

Well, that told him. He didn't mean to smile at her obvious discomfort, but her verbal explosion was just kind of…"cute" was the only word that came to mind. It was very Tess, a little weird, completely genuine, and always surprising.

Tess slowed to a stop at a red light and sighed. "Maybe tonight I'll actually get some."

Instantly on guard, he tensed. "You haven't been sleeping?" That wasn't good—especially not with the baby on the way, her general health, and meeting the demands of her work.

"New places are like that." She shrugged and drove forward when the light turned green. "I think I went the entire sixth grade on three hours of sleep a night."

She said it with a light little laugh at the end, but he wasn't fooled. As the team trainers had pounded through his thick skull, sleep—or a lack of it—could have a huge impact on performance, mood, and health, which was why he had a schedule and a routine for getting his Zs.

"I have a technique to help with that," he said as he

prayed gravity would continue to work when she accelerated through another turn onto his street.

"Is it orgasms?" Tess asked. "Research shows that sex before bed can make your sleep better because of all the endorphins released." Her grip on the steering wheel went white-knuckle and she let out, "Oh my God. Forget I said that; just erase it from your memory forever."

That was not going to happen. Ever. He already had enough problems not thinking about Tess and orgasms in the same heartbeat as it was and that wasn't going to change. However, while he was an asshole, he wasn't so much of one that he'd rub that in her face. Instead, he kept his gaze on the road instead of her.

"Right," he said as soon as he could trust his voice. "Because we've got rules."

"Exactly." She slowed down as they approached their— *his*—house. "This is just temporary—at least everything but the baby." She pulled in and parked her car next to his in the driveway. "Time for bed." She squeezed her eyes shut and turned the engine off with more force than necessary. "Alone. Bed. Alone. Sleep. Oh my God. Did you know—" She stopped talking and brought her hand to her mouth before shaking her head and getting out of the car.

Trying to ignore the way her curls bounced while she marched to his front door or how her ass filled out her jeans, Cole walked behind her up the stairs. He wasn't ready for the night to end, which was weird. Usually unless there was sex involved, he wanted to be in bed—alone—and mentally prepping for the next day in, he glanced at his watch, twelve minutes. But tonight, he didn't feel the need for that routine. Too bad he had no clue what to do about it.

He didn't have a standard play for flirting with the soon-to-be mom of his kid who wanted nothing to do with him beyond co-parenting. So he unlocked the door and held it open for Tess with a little more force than necessary, all that frustration needing to go somewhere.

She started to walk inside but paused only a few inches from him. "All the trivia is like a reflex; sometimes it comes out before I can stop it or realize it's happening. I'm sorry—I know it's annoying."

"We all have habits and routines," he teased. "Even you."

One side of her mouth curled up and she turned to him, bringing her even closer and making his entire body burn with anticipation—of what he knew wasn't going to happen. She'd been more than clear on that.

"Et tu, Brute?" Tess asked with a sexy pout as she leaned in and rose up on her toes, bringing her almost eye to eye with him and definitely mouth to mouth. "You'd call me out like that?"

Those were not flirty words. They weren't a come-on. They weren't oh-baby-fuck-me-against-the-doorframe. Were they? Was flirting via trivia gems and Latin phrases a thing? No. It couldn't be. He just wanted it to be. And even knowing the truth of it, being this close to her was like a lightning bolt of lust straight to his dick. And while the logical part of his brain knew she didn't mean it to hit like that, the rest of him had very different ideas.

"You know," he said, trying to sound cool as he stole her defense mechanism, "according to Plutarch, Caesar never said that. When he spotted Brutus while the whole stabbing was all going down, he just pulled his toga over his head."

"And Shakespeare probably wasn't the first to use the phrase in a dramatic play," she said, one-upping him in what to her was probably just a trivia face-off and not some kind of bizarre mating ritual.

"You just cheated." Damn, why did he sound like he'd just gotten done doing goal-to-goal sprints on the ice? "No factoids, remember?"

"You're a bad influence," she said with a chuckle and turned and walked into the house.

"I can live with that." God, he'd love to live with that in a whole other way that involved no clothes and enough orgasms for the best night sleep ever.

"Good night, Cole," Tess said as she ducked into her room, Kahn appearing out of nowhere and following along behind, and closed the door, leaving him alone out in the hall.

Like the fool he was, he stood there in the open doorway and watched, half hoping she'd come back out. She wasn't going to. He knew that. She'd been clear on the rules and he'd agreed to them. Of course, that was before, and now he wanted to change the game.

Chapter Ten

Morning skate before a game always felt good. There was nothing but anticipation and possibility accompanied by the sound of blades on ice and the puck flying though the cool air. But after two days off? It was like Cole's birthday, Christmas, and Halloween where all the neighbors gave out full-size bars of candy rolled into one. And he couldn't wait to get out there onto the ice.

"Oh look," Christensen said as soon as Cole crossed the threshold into the locker room. "The flower delivery guy is here."

Helping out Tess yesterday had gone viral in a good way for the team, so unlike what had happened to Stuckey, Cole wouldn't be forced into a public dating effort orchestrated by his mom to clean up his image. Of course, Stuckey had ended up falling for his date and they were currently in cohabitational bliss with that horse of a dog of hers, but that wasn't the point.

What was the point?

Fuck if he knew beyond the fact that he was going to get

a metric ton of shit from the guys about it today. That would be worth it if he'd actually managed to accomplish his goal yesterday. He hadn't.

So much for trying to build that connection—the friendly connection, not the horny one that was going to give him calluses on his hand—and making her feel more at home. There was a reason why he stuck to his routine, and it was because he didn't suck at it.

"I expected roses from my many admirers," Christensen went on. "And all I got was an empty-handed poor man's superhero."

Petrov pulled his practice jersey over his head. "Thor's a demigod."

"What the fuck is a demigod?" Christensen asked. "Thor is the god of thunder, not a demigod."

"Marvel fucked him up," Petrov said, crossing his arms in front of his chest. "He was really a warrior badass with red hair and a beard, not some blond pretty boy with space magic."

At that, everyone in the locker room shut the fuck up. Saying that to Christiansen was like calling someone's kid ugly. It just wasn't done—at least not out loud.

Christensen loved two things in the world—women and Marvel movies. He had the damn things memorized, was at the first showing whenever possible, and had even made an obnoxiously big donation to a charity to get to attend a showing with a Q&A session with the cast. Even for one of his and Petrov's usual petty bitch sessions before a game—yes, Cole wasn't the only one with a routine—Petrov was taking it over to the more serious side of things than just letting out some game-day nerves.

"You don't talk shit about Marvel," Christensen said, squaring up in front of Petrov, who was pretty much his brother in all ways but blood, considering how often they bickered, bantered, and hung out to the point of being practically inseparable. "Say that again and we're going."

"You want to get knocked on your ass because Thor is a demigod who happens to be called the god of thunder?" Petrov took a step closer, a go-ahead-and-do-it smirk on his face. "Fine. I can make that happen."

"Hey, Itch and Stitch, stop your usual game-day slap fight. Everyone knows Loki is the only Asgardian worth having a beer with," Ice Knights captain Zach Blackburn said, his voice at a normal volume because he was so much of a scary badass that he didn't need to yell. "Anyway, I want to hear more about Phillips's new side hustle."

Cole shrugged and started dressing for practice. "I was doing Tess a favor."

"Were you now?" Christensen asked as he tossed an unopened bottle of water to Petrov, their practically-at-blows fight already forgotten as per usual. "How very like you to change your routine."

Cole flipped off Christensen, who just grinned back at him.

"First she moves in and now you're working in her flower shop," Petrov said. "That sounds like the beginning of a dirty joke."

He and Christensen high-fived like the pair of knuckleheads they were.

Before Cole could set them straight—maybe with a well-placed smack to the back of both their heads, mom-style—Coach Peppers stalked into the locker room holding a steaming mug that was no doubt more milk and sugar than coffee.

"If all of you are done with your knitting-circle gossip," Coach said, staring the men down, "how about you get on the ice, because we are not going to let LA skate all over us tonight. Phillips, you ready to show me you figured out the new plays?"

"Yes, Coach." He'd run through the moves some more last night after Tess had gone to bed, telling himself that it was all muscle memory. Once he built that, then the rest would come naturally.

Yeah, right.

"Good." Peppers took a sip of his too-sugary-for-words concoction. "I expect to be impressed."

And that's just what he'd be. The pregame morning skates were usually easier affairs than a regular practice, so they'd have everything to give at game time, but Cole had something to prove, and there was nothing he loved more than a challenge.

• • •

Forever in Bloom was only open until noon on Mondays because they were usually so slow that it justified closing up shop and allowing Tess to take one whole glorious afternoon off. After yesterday's viral deliveries, though, "busy" didn't even begin to describe it. Most of the folks were lookie-loos, hoping to see Cole, but they ended up buying small arrangements, too. The high point of the day, though, was when Mrs. Evans's great grandson, Ellis, showed up and applied for the delivery driver's position. He was majoring in horticulture at Watson University in Harbor City and was the perfect fit. She hired him on the spot.

So when Tess finally got home—well, not home but to Cole's house—she couldn't help but let out a relieved sigh that ended on a surprised yelp thanks to Kahn's favorite new game called pounce that always ended with the kitten gnawing on her shoelaces.

Cole hurried out of the kitchen into the hall. "You okay?"

"Just under attack." She scooped up Kahn, who did a

face nuzzle that ended with a light bite on her chin.

"He got me, too," Cole said. "Now he keeps eyeballing the vase on the island."

"What vase?" If there was one thing Cole's house did not have besides bright colors, it was knickknacks of any kind. The man's surfaces were barren.

Cole's cheeks flushed and ducked back into the kitchen. "Some guy selling flowers at the stoplight suckered me," he hollered from the other room. "I figured you'd think they'd add some color to the place."

She put a squirming Kahn down and followed Cole's voice into the kitchen. Light streamed in through the large windows, making the stainless steel appliances glitter and warming the taupe hue on the walls. But that wasn't what caught her eye. It was the explosion of deep-purple lilacs mixed with green and white popcorn viburnum blooms and yellow black-eyed Susans. They shouldn't have gone together—there was a lot going on with everything fighting to be the focus—but they did.

She couldn't help but smile. "They're gorgeous."

"It was either these or the roses."

"This was a much better choice." She wrinkled her nose. "Roses might pay the bills, but there are just too many other amazing flowers out there to default to what's expected."

He chuckled. "Note to self: No roses for Tess."

Oh God. Nothing quite like sounding like a flower snob when he'd been nice enough to bring home flowers. *Way to go, Tess.* Why couldn't she be normal around him? Sure, she wasn't exactly normal around anyone, but with Cole it was different. She actually wanted him to see her and not her defense mechanisms.

"Don't make that face. I wanted to get them," he said, leaning one hip against the kitchen island and crossing his arms over his broad chest. "Maybe you'll unpack now?"

"You noticed that, huh?" She smiled. "Well, it's only temporary, so I didn't see the point. I grew up unpacking so many suitcases and then packing them back up again that I just kind of got in the habit of keeping everything in there." She looked down at the counter, noticing the flour, cocoa, and sugar in premeasured bowls all perfectly lined up. "What's going on here?"

"Pregame ritual."

"I thought you guys just took naps." Okay, so she'd done some reading up on hockey. Pregame naps were literally part of the team schedule.

"Well, there's that, too, but first there is stress baking." He walked over to the cupboard near the stove and took out a glass bowl. "I make something before every game, and most of it usually ends up in the team box. Marti clued me in on the fact that everyone in there indulges in some emotional eating during the tense parts of the game. Plus, I always make sure to save some of whatever I make and eat it after the game if we win. Want to help?"

"That won't mess with your routine?" It was only partially a joke. The man seriously stuck to his routine.

"I'm learning to be flexible." He winked at her.

Uh-huh. She'd believe that when she saw it. "Let me change out of this, and I'll be back."

Okay, up until a minute ago, her only plans for the afternoon were binge-watching *Schitt's Creek* and—more than likely—taking a nap on the couch. Now she was doing something she never did. Baking. Scratch that, she was doing two things—she was unpacking. As soon as she got to her room, she opened up one of the empty dresser drawers and transferred her T-shirts over from her suitcase.

If Cole could learn to be more flexible, she could make herself unpack. The rest could wait until later, but this was a start. Heart beating a little faster, she changed her clothes and went into the bathroom to wash up. That's when she saw it. The Paint and Sip Bigfoot painting was on the wall above the decorative towels where a very beige abstract print had been before.

Her surprised laugh filled the large bathroom, bouncing off the white tile up to the high ceiling. The smart-ass. She'd meant to get the painting last night, but she'd been so tired after the crazy day at work that she'd forgotten. So this was how he was going to play it, huh?

"Game on, Cole Phillips."

Leaving the painting hanging on her wall, she hustled back to the kitchen. He watched her as if he expected her to mention it, but she wasn't about to give him the satisfaction. Nope. She was already plotting where to hang the painting next. Instead, she asked what she could do to help with the cupcakes and they were off, baking side by side.

"So you moved around a lot as a kid? That's why you don't like to unpack?" He poured the dry ingredients into a bowl and started to whisk them together. "I know how that story goes."

Oh yeah, she'd bet a month of her flower shop's receipts that he didn't know how hers went. "Tell me."

Cole rolled his neck, the conversation obviously not part of his usual chitchat even if he had started it. "My dad works construction; he has a specialized skill set and that means he travels the country doing jobs."

She cracked the eggs against the clear glass bowl all the wet ingredients would go into. "Are you sure that's not code for a hit man?"

He laughed, the sound warming her right down to her bright-purple toenails. She tried to shove the feeling away, knowing just how dangerous it was, but it wouldn't go anywhere. Cole Phillips was getting to her, and she kinda liked it.

Girl, you are so fucked.

"Considering the fact that my dad catches spiders and puts them out into the yard instead of squashing them, I'm pretty confident that he's not offing anyone."

She poured in the milk and other wet ingredients he had prepped into her bowl. "Did you like moving around?"

"I learned to live with it," he said with a shrug.

It didn't take a brain surgeon to know how he'd done that. All she had to do was take a look around his house or remember his never-changing schedule. "Now that *is* code for something."

He gave her a light hip check as he snagged her bowl and poured its contents into a well he'd made in the middle of his dry ingredients. "You calling me out on my routines?"

"Do they make you feel more in control?" she asked as she watched him mix the ingredients together, mentally recording the way the muscles in his forearms moved—really that kind of sexy should be illegal—for later on when she wouldn't get to see him do it in person anymore.

"I hadn't thought about it like that but yeah, it makes that itchy feeling creeping up the back of my neck go away. I like knowing where things are and that they'll be there tomorrow and the day after. That and the people who've known me forever—like Coach Peppers and Marti—they're my constants."

Marti. Perfect girlfriend Marti. He hadn't mentioned her much around Tess, but she was there anyway, along with Lucy's words from the wedding about how they always ended up back together.

"Change is uncomfortable," she said, scooping up a bit of cupcake frosting with her finger and sucking it off. "But sometimes it happens just when you need it."

His eyes darkened as he watched her lick the last of the frosting from her finger. "Thinking about the baby?"

"Of course." Because it couldn't be the fact that a little nugget of hope was growing along with their little peanut.

If there was anyone out there who should know better than to hope for a happily ever after, it was her—but here she was with Cole, baking cupcakes together and wondering if this was what her life could be like. The little teasing touches, the air of anticipation making her heart beat faster, the sense that this could be real if only she was brave enough to go after what she wanted for once in her life instead of resigning herself to the fact that everything was temporary. It was a heady, dangerous thing, and she'd thought she was only gonna help him make cupcakes.

Cole cleared his throat, his body tense and hard, then started to pour the batter into the cupcake tins. "So why did you move around so much growing up?"

All those light and bubbly feelings went flat in an instant. "It's a long story no one really wants to hear."

He looked up at her and for a second, the world stopped moving. "I do."

She gripped the counter, white-knuckling it, tethering herself to reality when all she wanted to do was float away on the fantasy of him. "Next time."

"I'm holding you to that," he said as he slid the filled cupcake tins into the oven.

While they baked, she washed the dishes and he dried and put them away. By the time the timer went off, she was stifling her early-afternoon post-lunch yawns.

"So what now?" she asked when he took the cupcakes out of the oven and put them on a cooling rack.

"We nap while they cool, then I frost them and leave for the rink."

"*We* nap?" Of course she'd get caught up on that one word because napping was pretty much the last thing she thought about when it came to Cole Phillips and a bed.

He flipped the tea towel he'd used in place of an oven mitt over one shoulder and gave her a slow up-and-down. The move should not have been sexy. It should not have made little bubbles of anticipation pop like champagne in her chest. It should not make her catch her breath while her mind played a mini-movie about what happened last time she and Cole slept together.

Good Lord. If she didn't watch it, she'd be clutching the countertop to keep herself upright and calling for her smelling salts.

He snorted. "You've yawned five times in the past six minutes. Pretty sure you could use a snooze."

"I'll just sit in the living room and binge some Netflix." That would be much safer.

"Your body is saying you need your rest, not couch cramps," he said, his palm going to the small of her back as he led her out of the kitchen. "What you need is a real stretch out. I have a system."

Somehow, she wasn't sure how they ended up just inside his bedroom. There was a whole room full of furniture but she only noticed the California king.

"Which side do you sleep on?" he asked.

"The right." The answer was out before she could even think.

"Perfect." He grinned at her. "I'm a left sleeper."

"So we're doing it together." Doing it? *Doing it? Oh my God*. She needed someone to save her from herself. "You know what I mean. We're sleeping together." Heat burned her cheeks and blood rushed in her ears. She was so smooth. It was a nap. Just a nap. He wasn't interested in her—they'd just gotten weddinged. He wanted Marti. There was nothing to this—for him, anyway. "I'm just gonna shut up now."

"Good thing being quiet is part of the routine. Now, come on." He flopped down on top of the covers on the left side of the bed. "Kahn is going to somehow magically know that I've gone to sleep and then try to strangle me before you tiptoe in and retrieve him anyway, so you might as well stay."

This was not a good idea. It was a bad idea—a little bit of the feel-good kind of bad and a lot of the bad-decision kind of bad. Yet she strolled right over to the bed anyway and lay down. The bed was huge, so there was enough room between them for at least two more people.

She let out a shaky breath and stared at the ceiling because looking over at Cole seemed too close to the feel-good kind of a bad idea. "What now?"

"Close your eyes."

Okay, it made sense. Lessons in perfect napping would include closing her eyes. She could do this. So why was she scared? Not of him but of what she'd picture as soon as her lids came down. It wouldn't be Cole as he was now in workout pants and an Ice Knights T-shirt. Nope. She'd be picturing the muscled expanse of his bare chest, because taking a nap with Cole Phillips was pretty much anything but innocent for her.

"Go through your body from your toes to your eyebrows," he said, his voice deepening and slowing as if he was already halfway asleep. "Concentrate on that one spot, then move on to the next one."

She did, and when she got to her fingertips and realized that his were so close, she went with whatever in her gut was telling her to reach out. She curled her pinkie around his. She didn't make it very much farther up her body. The sound of Cole's deep breaths along with the heat from his body lulled her into sleep.

It could have been a year or five minutes later when she woke up, disoriented if refreshed and in a little bit of pain because Kahn was playing pounce with her curls and yanking them.

"Have a good nap?" Cole asked, sounding farther away than the next pillow over.

Detangling Kahn from her hair, she sat up. Cole stood at the end of the bed in a navy suit that included a vest. It highlighted the athlete's perfection of his body and the dark blue of his eyes. He'd left his jaw-length blond hair down, tucking it behind his ears in a way that only seemed to emphasize the squareness of his jaw. Sweet begonias, the way he looked right now was definitely going into the fantasy bank.

"You're changed." *Oh yeah. Great opening line, Captain Obvious.* "You look great."

"Thanks, the tie was a gift from Mar—a friend." He rubbed the back of his neck and glanced down at the floor. "There's a frosted chocolate cupcake in the fridge for after the game."

Normally, the idea of a double-fudge anything would make her mouth water, but that was so far from what she was hungry for at the moment that it barely registered.

"Good luck," she said, the words coming out breathy and sleep-roughened.

"I don't need it." He gave her a sexy smirk that should be illegal. "I have a system."

And with that, he was out the door, leaving her still in his bed, not wanting to leave. *You better fix that.* She did. Not because she wanted to but because it would be really embarrassing if he came back and caught her smelling his pillows, the ones he no doubt had slept on with his more-than-likely-to-be-girlfriend-again, Marti. Tess let out a sigh.

Girl, you are so screwed right now.

• • •

Still riding the high of a three-nothing win, Cole parked in his driveway hours after the game ended—thank you, post-game interviews and traffic crossing the bridge from Harbor City back home to Waterbury. There was a chocolate cupcake and a giant glass of milk with his name on it waiting for him, but he'd make sure to grab two forks so Tess could have some, too.

When he closed the front door, though, the only one waiting for him was Kahn. The kitten swished his tail and licked what looked like a milk mustache from his tiny snout.

He scooped up the devil's favorite fuzz ball and started walking toward the living room. "Where's our Tess?"

Not that she was *his* Tess. She most definitely was not, which was exactly why that nap this afternoon had been a mistake. There was a power dynamic involved in having her here at his house, and the last thing he wanted was for her to feel like he was taking advantage of that. She didn't owe him a damn thing—especially not sleeping in his bed—and he sure as hell didn't want her to feel like she did. Before moving in, she'd set out her guidelines and he was going to respect them.

So when he found her in the living room, curled up on one end of the couch using the armrest as a pillow, he didn't wake her up. Instead, he stood there in the doorway, watching the game highlights play out on the screen. She must have fallen asleep watching the game. *His* game. He was halfway to her before he realized it, and that's when he noticed the blanket pulled up to her chin was the one Christensen and Petrov had given him as a gag gift for moving in. It had a giant picture of him on it, but pulled tight around Tess, it looked like she was wearing his jersey.

Fuck. That was hot.

Despite knowing he should just let her be, he scooped her up off the couch. The blanket fell away, revealing a different oversize sleep shirt from the other day. This one was neon blue and said PEW PEW in the Star Wars font. Her fuzzy socks pulled up to nearly her knees had light sabers all over them. According to conventional wisdom, it was not a sexy outfit. His cock didn't seem to care, thickening against his thigh when she let out a quiet sigh that tickled his neck.

Tess didn't open her eyes but snuggled her head against his chest. He didn't do this. Women didn't stay overnight at his house. He wasn't the kind of touchy-feely guy who took care of other people. His entire life had been about making sure that he was using his time and energy as efficiently as possible to make it to the NHL. Everything else was just a temporary good time—except for Marti.

Realization sucker punched him on the jaw.

That was the first time in days he'd even thought about the woman he'd planned on being his forever. Up until this moment, he'd figured they'd get back together just like they always did because that's what they did—it was their routine. But right now, right here with Tess in his arms and that damn cat of hers winding a figure eight around his ankles? Marti felt like his past, one he'd remember with a smile, but definitely not part of his future. Not anymore.

He had no fucking clue what to do with that little reality check.

"Good game," Tess said, the words seeming to barely make it out of her mouth as she hooked her arm around his. "Tried to stay up, but growing a baby is exhausting."

"Let's get you and the peanut to bed."

And as much as he wanted to turn right in the hall and take her back to his bed like he had this afternoon, he couldn't. A blue line had been painted onto the ice. Crossing it didn't just mean going into the opposing team's territory, it meant skating out into uncharted territory and that wasn't what a man who lived and died by the schedule did. So he turned left and tucked Tess into her own bed.

"Wait," she said, her eyes half closed with sleep. "Thank you."

"For what?" He wasn't fishing. He had no clue and thinking while she was in his arms was kinda hard.

"For yesterday at the shop. For tonight. I know Kahn and I have messed with how you like to do things. Thank you for making room for us until my apartment is ready."

She sat up and brushed her soft, full mouth against his in a kiss so brief, it shouldn't have stopped his world—but it did. Gliding the pad of her thumb across his bottom lip, a vulnerable bittersweet half smile came on her face as she watched him with the wary resignation of someone who'd been kicked by life one too many times. "I'm sorry. I shouldn't have done that. I know you have your constants. It won't happen again."

Cole could barely breathe. Thinking wasn't even a possibility. Whatever alarm bells there were warning of the danger ahead were muted by the overwhelming roar of lust rushing through him, stringing him tight and hard at the mercy of the one woman he couldn't have and shouldn't want.

"Good night, Cole." She lay down and pulled her covers up to her chin. "Congrats on the win tonight."

He might have mumbled "thank you" as he made his way to the door. He could have sung "Jingle Bells." He had no fucking clue. All he knew was that as he turned off the light switch and walked out into the hall, he had no idea what in the hell had just happened to make everything feel different.

Chapter Eleven

Kahn was missing again. Well, not *missing*. Tess knew exactly where he was when she woke up kitty-free in her own bed the next morning. The kitten had to be in Cole's room. It was where he went every morning for some predawn cuddle time. Part of her couldn't blame him. The other part of her dreaded having the delicate sense of connection she had with Cole severed because her cat had a crush on a man who wanted nothing to do with animals, let alone kittens.

She knew firsthand how easy it was to mess up a precarious living situation. When she was ten and her one-week summer stay with her second cousins had stretched into three, a spilled cup of grape Kool-Aid on the newly installed cream carpet had resulted in a quick hustle to another relative's house until her mom finally made it back from a road trip with her latest boyfriend.

And all that ugly was the last thing she was going to expend the emotional energy on this morning. She had more important things to deal with, specifically how to get Kahn away from the guy she had shamelessly kissed last night, which was the absolute last thing she should have done. It was second in embarrassment only to all the things she wanted to do to him and had dreamed about in high-def detail last night.

It had to be the pregnancy hormones. According to the pregnancy app she'd downloaded, her sex drive wasn't supposed to increase until the second trimester because of a powerful lust cocktail of increased estrogen and progesterone with a garnish of more blood flow to her lady bits.

Of course, science had probably never studied the effect on desire from living with a sexy-as-sin professional hockey player as a factor. That—it turned out—trumped morning sickness, pregnancy exhaustion, and her better judgment, which explained why she was lurking outside Cole's open door while he slept inside with Kahn draped across his neck like a fur scarf.

Your cat's going to try to strangle me...

Okay, it had sounded like he'd been joking last night, but who really knew? Her uncle Ted sounded like he was kidding before he'd started throwing plates against the wall the one time she'd stayed for a week with him, Aunt Chrissy, and their three kids. The best course of action was to tiptoe into Cole's room, retrieve Kahn, and get out of there without waking him up. It was a travel day. Morning skate followed by a plane ride to Minneapolis and a central US road trip until the end of the week. It was amazing how much hockey knowledge a person could pick up reading Harbor City Ice Knights obsessed website The Biscuit.

Holding her breath, she got right up next to the bed—keeping her eyes locked on the kitten and not the rise and fall of Cole's magnificent chest, or his hard-etched abs, or the way his mouth softened in sleep, or how freakin' long his eyelashes were across his cheeks, or— *Oh my God, Tess, dial down the stalker a little bit, all right?!*

She was just reaching for Kahn when everything happened at once. Cole's blue eyes snapped open. The cat jumped a million miles straight up in the air and sprinted out the door. She jolted back, letting out a startled squeal, and tripped over her own feet. The only thing that saved her from going down on her ass was Cole's strong arm wrapped around her waist and yanking her in the opposite direction—toward his bed. She landed mostly on him, managing to wrap her hands around the ironwork of his headboard before she pushed a still-covered-with-her-sleep-shirt boob into his face.

"Morning, Tess," he said, his hand moving from holding onto her waist to resting lightly on the outside of her thigh.

He said it like she always ended up with her breasts inches from his mouth every morning. Practically straddling him, one hand on his headboard and her sleep shirt hiked up around her waist, she tried her best to think of anything in the world to say at that moment.

"Hi, Cole."

Fucking brilliant.

She sat back so she wasn't in danger of smothering him with her tits. It wasn't until she completed the move that she realized what a mistake she'd made. There was no mistaking the hard, thick length of him pressed against the center of her panties. Her body rejoiced. Her brain went into full meltdown. Her mouth went into overdrive.

"Pregnant women experience greater sensitivity in their breasts and vulva because of increased blood flow—often that means more pleasurable sex." *Time to shut up now, Tess.* "There's also increased natural lubrication and the woman's clit becomes more sensitive." *I need Gorilla Glue for my mouth.* "Masturbation during pregnancy can be a great tension reliever and orgasms can be a welcome break from the less fun parts of pregnancy, such as morning sickness."

And she was going to wash away on a wave from Typhoon

You're a Dumb-ass. Her cheeks were burning and her chest was the kind of tight that came with putting on a two-sizes-too-small sports bra.

"Are you masturbating a lot?" he asked, his voice rough from just waking up and something more.

"Define 'a lot.'" She really needed to find a doctor who could install a filter between her brain and her mouth.

"Christ, Tess." He lifted his other hand so both were palm down on her thighs, not pressing, not teasing, just there, steady and constant. "Let me help."

Unable to stop herself, she rocked her hips, sliding her quickly dampening still-pantie-covered core against him. "It's not a good idea."

"Not at all." He tightened his grip, holding her close as she rubbed against him.

"I don't care."

And that was the truth of it—and it wasn't just the hormones. There was something about Cole that had nothing to do with how he looked—although let's get real, it didn't hurt—that touched her in a place she hadn't realized was there. That's why they'd had that night at the wedding, it was why she'd agreed to move in, and it was why she was where she was right now instead of halfway across the room.

"Can I help you, Tess?" His hand glided over her skin, dipping under the hem of her sleep shirt and coming to rest near the edge of her panties, the rough pads of his thumbs teasing the inside of her thighs. "Offer a little relief?"

It was almost too much, the sensations, the want, the have-to-have. Her clit was aching for more than the friction of rubbing against him. She needed more, and it was silencing all the you-shouldn'ts and be-carefuls that constantly swirled around in her head.

She trailed her hands across his chest, the springy curls dusting the top of his pecs tickling her fingers. "You'd do that for me?"

He arched his hips up off the bed with just the right amount of desperate force. "Believe me, you would not be the only one benefitting."

"Are you jerking off a lot?" She traced the hard edges of his abs as she tugged her lip between her teeth, needing the reminder not to move too fast.

He sucked in a breath, and his eyes flicked shut for a moment. "All the fucking time since you got here." He moved against her, the tips of his fingers pressing into the fleshy part of her hips. "Tess. Please. Tell me what you want."

Letting go of all the doubts, she reached for the bottom of her sleep shirt and pulled it off. "You."

His gaze moved over her as solid as a touch, from her mouth to the curve of her breasts to the not-very-apparent dip of her waist to her navy striped panties with the little anchors on them as she moved against him, desperate for the kind of wet friction she couldn't get as long as they were both dressed.

"I want to taste you first." His words came out harsh, needy. "I want to see this super-sensitive clit of yours, lick it, suck on it, feel you come on my face. Then I want to feel you riding my cock, taking as much of me as you need. Do you want that?"

It took her a second to realize he meant that as an actual question, not a rhetorical one because who in the hell said no to that coming from Cole Phillips?

"Oh my God, yes," she said, recalling the rest only as a last-ditch effort to remember her place in all of this— temporary. "But this doesn't change anything. It's for relief only."

One side of his mouth tilted upward even as his hands were leaving a trail of wanton desire as he brought them up to her waist. "Medicinal fucking?"

"Exactly."

She'd barely gotten the word out before she was on her back, her legs straight up in the air and Cole working her panties off.

Then there were no more words, not from either of them, because the moment his tongue circled her aching clit, they weren't necessary. They had their own language of touch and feel and pleasure. His hands slipped underneath her ass and he lifted her higher, changing the angle as he feasted on her pussy. Every lick, every slow lap around her clit, around her opening, left her panting and begging for more. And when he added his fingers to the mix, teasing her as he tongued her wet folds, it was more than she could take. Her orgasm started as a buzzing in her thighs that exploded upward and outward, making her entire body bow as she cried out so much sooner than she'd ever expected.

"The websites did not lie," she said, trying to catch her breath. "That was crazy fast."

Cole looked up from between her splayed legs, his mouth still wet with her. "Good thing we aren't done yet."

• • •

There was nothing more in the world that Cole wanted to do at that moment than to be buried deep in Tess as she squeezed his cock when she came for a second time, but two things stopped him. One, she was pregnant and, while he knew on one level that he wouldn't harm the kid, he'd never fucked anyone in this situation before and it was a little disconcerting. Two, he didn't have a condom. Rising up so he was over her, he looked down at her and the knowing look she gave him as he tried to figure out how to broach the subject.

"If you are waiting because you don't have any protection," Tess said, tracing his jawline with her full lips, "I think the U.S.S. *Knocked Up* already sailed."

"What about other stuff?"

"I'm clean." She nipped his collarbone before kissing the spot with her sweet mouth. "You?"

"Yes." Damn, it was hard to think with her talented mouth on him, teasing him until his cock was aching. "You're the only one I've had sex with in the past six months since…"

"Marti," she finished for him, her tone carefully neutral.

It was still a gut punch.

"Don't tense up, Cole," Tess said, lying back, her gaze moving away from his face. "It's not like we're anything but temporary."

Cole couldn't explain it, couldn't deconstruct the whys, but that one statement made him clamp his jaw shut to the point where his molars might be in jeopardy. And because he didn't have the words to explain what he was feeling, let alone what he was going to do about it. So he'd do the one thing he could. Show her.

He eased back a bit so that his face was level with her tits as he continued to prop himself up on his forearms above her. "You said these were sensitive."

She nodded. "Yes."

"So when I do this, is it too much?" He dipped his head down and flicked his tongue over the hard tip of her nipple.

She let out a shaky sigh. "No."

"And this?" He grazed his teeth over it, nipping lightly.

The soft moan of "fuck yes" and the way she let her head fall back answered that.

"What about this?" He sucked the sensitive bud into his mouth as he cupped her tit, teasing her with his touch.

"That is fucking fantastic."

He took his time going from one breast to the other, touching her, letting the morning scruff on his jaw rub about her, and toying with her until she was writhing on the bed, nothing but heady sighs and desperate moans. Then he went lower, kissing his way down to the apex of her thighs where she was still slick and soft from coming. He licked her, needing another fix of her pleasure, knowing it wouldn't be enough and that he wasn't sure it ever would be.

Temporary.

The word was like an annoying drumbeat somewhere down below the surface of his consciousness, fighting its way to the surface. But he wouldn't let it get there. Not now. This moment was about Tess.

Turning onto his back, he brought her with him so she was astride him again. Yes, he couldn't hurt the baby, he wasn't that delusional about it, but he still wanted her to take control, to get what she needed, what she wanted.

"Set the pace," he said, his voice hoarse from want. "I'll do my best to follow."

Tess lifted her hips but paused with his cock practically at her slick entrance. "What if I want you to take control, to fuck me like you did at the wedding—until I can't think anymore?"

That had been the night that had started it all. It had gone from kiss to touch to him on his knees with his head under her skirt in less time than it took to kill a major penalty. And it hadn't stopped there. They'd been insatiable, frantic, and raw with each other. No preset routines. No carefully thought-out plans. And she wanted more of that? Oh, he could definitely go there.

He cupped the back of her head and pulled her down for a demanding kiss that left her with a dazed expression as she sat back up.

"If that's what you want," he said, "then lower that sweet pussy of yours down and ride my cock so I can watch your tits and see myself slide in and out of you."

For a second, she didn't say anything, didn't move. *Fuck*.

He'd crossed the line. This was why he always followed the script, held back, and—most importantly—kept his mouth shut. Except when it came to Tess. That unregulated side of him always seemed to make an appearance with her. He was about to offer an apology, go back to his usual bedroom routine, but then Tess got this look in her eyes that sent a shiver straight to his balls.

"I want it just like that." She reached down to where they were nearly joined and wrapped her hands tight around his dick. "I want that wild, no-holds-barred, I'd-do-just-about-anything-to-fuck-you-right-now that we had that night. I don't want easy and slow." She jacked him one, two, three times until pre-cum covered the tip of his cock. "I want this."

She lowered herself onto his cock, her warmth surrounding him as she took him in all the way. Then she started moving against him, riding him hard and fast, chasing that sense of completion, that toe-curling blast of pleasure that took them out of the moment and out of themselves. Again and again, he watched his cock move in and out of her as she undulated her hips. God, she was going to kill him with this, and he wouldn't be complaining.

"That's it, Tess." He was already on the edge, fighting to last with her. "Damn, you feel so good."

He cupped her tits, rolling her nipples between his thumb and finger, tugging on them until she cried out, telling him to keep going. Then she dropped her hand to where they were joined and started working her clit with her fingers as she fucked him. Jesus. He didn't know where to look, and it felt so good, he wasn't sure he could see anyway.

"I'm gonna come, Cole," she said, letting her head fall back. "I want to feel you with me."

Since he was holding on by a thread at this point and his balls were curled up tight to his body already, that wasn't going to be a problem.

"Let me feel you come, Tess."

Her fingers went into hyper-speed mode as her hips bucked and he teased her nipples before she came, her slick walls squeezing him tight as her orgasm hit. He lifted up and drove into her, coming so hard, it was like he was falling and flying at the same time. And when she collapsed on his chest, he curled an arm around her and held her tight against him as they came down.

They were both still trying to catch their breath when his phone buzzed on the nightstand. He ignored it, but the calls didn't stop, so he snatched it up from the surface, not swiping accept call until he recognized Petrov's number on the screen.

"What," he answered.

"I'm in your driveway," the center said. "Are you running late? Shit. I have to tell Christensen. You'll never hear the end of it."

"Ten minutes." He hung up and let out a sigh. Great. Not only did he not want to leave Tess, he sure as hell didn't want to have to deal with the shit-talking twins Petrov and Christensen for the next week. "I gotta go."

"Sure." Tess nodded, unwrapping herself from around him and grabbing his sheet. "Road trip, right?"

"I'll be home in four days," he said, watching her get out of bed and wrap the sheet around herself.

"Who knows," she said, smiling a little too brightly as she headed for the door. "Maybe we'll get lucky and my plumbing will be fixed by then, so you'll get to come home to your old house. You've been so sweet to let me stay with you."

After what they'd just done, he was sweet? *What the fuck?* This wasn't how this was supposed to go. Sure, he had no idea what should happen next, but it sure as hell wasn't her calling him "sweet" and hurrying to get out of his room.

Tess paused at the door. "I'll get out of your way; I know

you have to hurry."

And then she was gone, taking his sheet with her as Kahn chased her from behind, jumping onto the tail of her makeshift robe and going along for the ride, while all Cole could do was stand there like an asshole who had no clue what was going to happen next.

Chapter Twelve

"So, uh, hi. This is Cole, which you probably knew already because of caller ID."

Shop quiet for the first time that afternoon, Tess listened to the message as she created an arrangement featuring pansies and violets for a customer.

"I'm just leaving you a voicemail like some weird stalkery person or your grandma, which I am not. Obviously." He let out an uncomfortable groan. "Texting just seemed rude after this morning. You're probably in the middle of making a flower arrangement or talking people out of buying roses."

Not a lie. The woman who'd called about the last-minute arrangements had wondered out loud about going the traditional route for her girlfriend and getting roses. Thank God Tess had been able to persuade her into something a little less pedestrian.

"Anyway, we're wheels up on the flight in a couple of minutes and I just wanted to touch base to say...um...yeah... to say...this morning was great. No! That's not what I wanted to say."

What the hell? The sex had been pretty fucking fantastic, if more than likely a bad decision on her part.

"I mean yeah, it was amazing, but I'm not just calling only because of that. I mean, you were clear on boundaries. I'm not going to cross those. I just—"

The voices in the background got louder before being muffled as if Cole had put his hand over the phone.

"Christ, Petrov, can I have five minutes alone? I shut myself in the massage room for a reason." Cole mumbled something Tess couldn't make out. "Sorry, okay, I'm gonna hang up now because I've fucked up this whole voicemail and I have no idea how to recall it or nuke it. Jesus. This is why I should have texted. Okay. Bye."

The voicemail ended right as she finished her arrangement and that satisfaction of a job well done was the only reason her cheeks were hurting from smiling so hard. Really. It was.

• • •

The game in Phoenix had been brutal, but the sweetest thing after winning against one of the dirtiest teams in the league was the little red circle with the number one in it near the telephone icon on his phone.

Score.

"Hey, it's Tess. That was some voicemail."

Cole wasn't smiling like a fool. He wasn't. The idiots on his line just kept pointing at him and laughing while Blackburn just shook his head in what looked like sympathy.

"Did you know a company called Televoice International is the one that came up with the term 'voicemail'?" The speed of Tess's words increased as if they just had to burst out of her. "They trademarked it and everything, but then everyone started using it and now it's just a generic term, sort of like Kleenex. Although Kleenex is still a used brand name.

Speaking of which, did you know Kleenex were originally invented as a cold cream and makeup remover and not to blow your nose? Crazy, right? So you're playing right now."

She watched his game? He rubbed a towel across his still-wet-from-the-post-game-shower hair and grinned. *Hell yes.*

"I don't know who eleven is on the other team, but I don't think it's right that he just slammed into you like that. Isn't that against the rules? And I'm not really watching you like some obsessed fan or anything. I just turned on the TV and your game was on. How did you do that? It's like being at a hotel and the TV always turns on to the channel advertising the hotel spa."

Tess paused, and the unmistakable revving-engine sound of Kahn appreciating however she was petting him came over the line. Yeah, Cole could relate. The woman had fantastically talented hands.

"And that's pretty much all I have to say and probably more than I should," she said, her words coming out in a rush again. "I'm just gonna hang up now and hope you never listen to this and the voice-to-text function that previews voicemails for you malfunctions."

If he had to track down a software developer and threaten to toss him down in front of the Zamboni going at full speed—which still wasn't fast—he'd make sure that the deletion of that message would never happen.

• • •

Tess was still fuming about the less-than-helpful conversation she'd had with her uncle, the landlord from hell, about her apartment—no, it wouldn't be habitable for a while and no, he didn't have an estimated date—when she noticed the voicemail alert on her phone. It was hell waiting to listen to it until she'd hustled her new delivery driver out the door with a morning's worth of flowers and the last customer picking up a bouquet left, but it couldn't be helped. She wanted to savor the sound of Cole's tempting-as-warm-honey voice and bask in the sizzling awareness that made her heart beat faster when she heard it.

Weird? Yes. It was her, after all. No one expected normal from Tess Gardner, especially not herself.

"Damn," Cole said, his voice rough as if he'd woken up early to make the call. "I was hoping to catch you before you went to work. First, yes, that hit was totally legal. It's a check and it's part of hockey. That's why we wear the pads. Not to one-up your Kleenex and voicemail trivia, but did you know that George Merritt of the Winnipeg Victorias was the first goalie to wear leg pads? He strapped on cricket pads for the 1896 Stanley Cup challenge game."

She had *not* known that, and she filed it away along with the mental image she had of Cole lying in bed, shirtless with the sheet riding low on his hips, his hand gliding down to disappear beneath it as his eyes closed and— *Holy crap, Tess. That's not a factoid; that's a fantasy, and they most definitely do not get filed together!*

"Do you play bar trivia?" Cole asked. "You really need to join a league. Maybe we should start one. Between the two of us, we're better than Wikipedia. Another game tonight and then it's a travel day out to—" The *thunk-thunk-thunk* of someone banging on a door stopped him mid-word. "Calm the fuck down, Christensen; I'm coming." He grumbled a string of curses. "Sorry about that. I gotta go. Maybe we'll get to connect before the game."

Tess stared down at her phone. She would not play it again. She would not. Nope. Not gonna— She hit the play button.

• • •

Losing sucked. It hammered Cole right between the eyeballs and ate its way into his brain, leaving nothing but doubts about his skills and his ability to make the changes for these new plays. Not to mention it really pissed him off. He wasn't alone in that. After the ass-kicking the Ice Knights had gotten in Minneapolis, the team bus had been silent and hostile on the way back to the hotel. It wasn't until he got back to his room that he finally checked his phone and the vise holding his balls in a tight grip loosened up.

"Imagine that, we're voicemailing again." Tess's voice came through like a glitter rainbow, which made no sense, but there it was. "So about your bed. Kahn is annoyed you're gone and did a very cat thing and peed on it."

And he'd thought the fur balls getting yacked up and claw marks on his furniture were what he needed to be concerned about.

"Don't worry! I washed it, but I figured you should know. The good news is the doctor doesn't think it's medical and because the automatic cat litter cleaner is working as advertised, so it's not a problem with a too-full litter box. The vet thinks it's because of separation anxiety. Basically, he misses you and is trying to mingle his scent with yours."

That was bizarre and gross and kinda sweet all in one. Lying back in the hotel bed, Cole flipped off his shoes and laid the phone down on his chest on speakerphone, the volume set loud enough that it was almost like having Tess in the room.

Who in the hell are you and what have you done with Cole Phillips?

"I'm taking Kahn with me to work today and tomorrow so you don't have to worry about him doing it again," Tess continued. "It's Paint and Sip night with the girls, so I won't be around before the game. And then I'm meeting with my uncle and the plumber early tomorrow about my apartment.

He tried to blow me off with a bunch of nonanswers last time we talked, and I'm bringing my lease agreement this time so he can see exactly what the penalties will be if he doesn't stop dragging his feet on this. Fingers crossed that gets everything moving, and then I'll be out of your hair and you won't have to worry about Kahn peeing on your bed again. Voicemail you later."

When the message stopped playing, he just stared up at the hotel-room ceiling. He didn't give a shit about the kitten peeing in his bed. All he cared about was the fact that she was one, having to deal with her jackhole of a landlord by herself—not that she wasn't capable, but he was a team player and she was on his team—and two, that she still wanted to leave. Both gave him heartburn. One had him grinding his teeth together in frustration.

• • •

Tess stared at the new voicemail icon, her stomach doing an oh-fuck gurgling thing. Up until now, each time the notification popped up, she'd hit play with a stupid grin on her face. Now? It was like touching a radioactive tuna-fish can. She'd been ignoring the notification all day. Still, whatever he said couldn't be worse than the scream fest followed by a *put your things in a bag you're leaving immediately* after she'd cleaned her cousin's goldfish tank and then had added untreated tap water to the bowl, not realizing the harm she was doing, and had killed Fishy.

Tess held her breath, sat in her parked car in the driveway of Cole's house, turned down the live broadcast of the Ice Knights game on the radio, and hit play.

"I'm going to pretend I never heard that the evilest cat to ever evil peed on my bed." Cole's voice played over her car speakers, filling it with his warmth instead of the censure she'd been expecting. "As for the apartment situation, I was serious about you staying as long as you want. It's no big deal. Plenty of space."

No. Big. Deal. She was trying to process that when she realized her cheeks were wet, which was really bizarre because she wasn't a crier—happy or otherwise. Stupid hormones.

"We're leaving for Denver right after the game. Did you know it's one of the few cities with seven professional sports teams? That's the kind of knowledge I would bring to a trivia team."

As Cole continued, she could practically see him pacing as he went. He'd probably been fully dressed when he'd left the message, but for some reason in her mind, he was pacing around with only a towel slung around his hips, his hair still wet from a shower, and that towel wasn't going to stay in place for long.

From crying to mental Cole porn in thirty seconds— hormones, you need to calm the fuck down.

"You can count on me for that kind of information along with Latin translations, baking tips, and military history," Cole said. "Oh yeah, and world geography. Really, you should think about it. Maybe we can give it a try when I get back. See how many points we can rack up. And just out of curiosity, are you going to pick up the phone at all or are we just voicemailing it while I'm gone?"

Fuck. She'd been hoping he hadn't noticed that. Time to fess up or keep dodging?

• • •

Cole popped his AirPods in, somewhat blocking out the cheers and fuck yeahs of his teammates celebrating a comeback win against the Wolves. He'd been having a decent game and then when everything was looking like a done deal, Coach had called out for his new plays. It had felt like skating through molasses with a hot pepper stuffed up one nostril. The rest of the team had risen, and he'd slumped. The stink eye Coach had given him? Totally deserved.

He hit play on the voicemail Tess had left during the game.

"Voicemailing could be our thing...uh...crap... Okay, that sounded less weird in my head, which should have been a clue that it was going to sound awkward as hell in real life." Her chipper voice plowed forward, each word coming practically on top of the other. "We don't need a thing, since we're not really a *we*, but if we were, this could be it and... Oh my God."

While she took in an audible breath and let it out, so did he, but Cole was probably doing it for a different reason as he slunk back against the team jet's seat. They weren't a *we*. She was right. Still, it annoyed him, which was stupid because it wasn't like he was looking for Tess to be part of his *we*. He'd always figured that would be Marti. She was the other half of his we; it was just all jumbled right now with her because they were in a down cycle. It always went up again. Was there something wrong with being a *we* with him?

"Okay, did you know that some guy tinkering around with military and aircraft equipment in 1949 is the father of modern ultrasounds and that at nine weeks, a fetus is the size of a grape? So that's what I'll be seeing on Friday. If you wanted to come, you could, and then we could check out the pub trivia at Marino's Bar and Grill. I mean, you'll be back by then but no pressure. So yeah. That's all I got. Bye."

Cole stared at his phone, nothing but white noise in his ears. Ultrasound? There was real and then there was going-to-have-an-ultrasound real.

He was having a baby.

• • •

Tess was noshing on a BLT on rye when she finally had five minutes in the shop alone to listen to Cole's message after her mad dash to Forever in Bloom when she woke up in the cold-sweat panic of missing her alarm clock. Well, "alone" was relative. Kahn was currently purring his fuzzy little ass off in an attempt to get another bite of bacon. She hit play on the message he must have left in the wee hours of the morning.

"Hell yes I want to go to the appointment tomorrow." The genuine enthusiasm in his voice made her heart do the cha-cha slide. "A grape? Really? That's so small. And if you're up for trivia after, Marino's sounds great. Text me the doctor's address and I'll meet you there. Speaking of texting, did you know the first text said 'Merry Christmas'? And I have no clue where to go from that. All I know is that I've left more voicemails for you than anyone else ever. There's a factoid for you. See you tomorrow."

And tomorrow's appointment was actually today. Four hours to be exact. She rubbed her belly, not sure if she was more nervous about seeing the baby or Cole.

Chapter Thirteen

Cole was late. He hated being late but especially for this. He vaulted up the stairs to Tess's doctor's office two at a time and hurried into suite 244. All the women in the crowded waiting room and the bored receptionist looked up when he strode in—none of them was Tess.

Fuck. Fuck. Fuckity fuck.

"You looking for someone?" the receptionist asked, her gaze already back on her computer screen.

"Tess Gardner," he said, keeping his voice barely above a whisper in the silent room.

"She's already gone back," she said, still not looking up, her fingers flying across her keyboard. "Hold on and one of the nurses will walk you to the ultrasound room."

Cole looked around while he waited, too nervous to sit down in one of the chairs even if there'd been one available. That's how he clocked the woman in the corner doing a not-so-subtle job of taking a creeper shot.

Shit.

Yanking down the brim of the ball cap he'd worn in

hopes of disguising himself, he did his best to shrink back into the corner. However, at six foot three and the only dude in the room, he wasn't exactly blending.

He'd have to let the team PR guru, Lucy, know. The press would have a field day figuring out why he was here, who he was with, and everything about Tess. He wasn't about to let that happen. She hadn't signed up for that kind of scrutiny any more than she'd asked him to use expired condoms.

Way to just totally fuck up someone else's life plan, Phillips.

The door to the hallway leading to the exam rooms opened up and a guy in scrubs with baby rattles all over them peeked out. "Tess Gar—"

"That's me," Cole said, rushing forward before the guy could announce Tess's full name to Ms. Nosy and the rest of the room.

They went straight to the door at the end of the hallway, where Mr. Rattle Scrubs knocked, waited for Tess's "come in," and opened the door for Cole to walk in first.

Tess was lying down on an exam bed, her bottom half covered with one of those paper sheet things. She was gnawing on her bottom lip, her eyes huge behind her glasses.

"Sorry I'm late," he said as he loitered in the doorway, not sure where to go or what to do. "Traffic coming in from across the bridge was a nightmare."

"More than three hundred thousand cars go over the bridge every day," she said. "It's the only fourteen-lane suspension bridge in the world."

He walked toward her, stopping at the foot of the exam table. "And I would have done commuter battle with all three hundred thousand to get here for this."

She gave him a little nod, and some of the tension in his body loosened.

"If we're ready to do this, then you should go stand over

there near Tess's head. There's a chair if you want to sit down, or you can stand," Mr. Rattle Scrubs said. "Then I'll dim the lights and we'll get started."

Cole did what he was told, reaching down and taking Tess's hand in his, giving her a reassuring squeeze even as his own nerves were going crazy. She gave him the smallest of smiles and squeezed back.

At first the black-and-white screen on the ultrasound machine just looked like a barren planet, but then a small black circle appeared with a little alien-looking blob inside it. The tech clicked the mouse a few times and made some noncommittal *uh-huh* noises while Tess's grip on his hand got tighter and tighter.

"That's your little peanut right there, and that"—a *whoosh-whoosh* sound came from the machine—"is their heartbeat."

Cole plopped down into the chair beside the exam table. He hadn't meant to, but his legs just stopped working while his body felt like he was floating and falling at the same time.

They were having a baby.

He'd known it before, but now it was as if he *knew it* in a whole different way. Bringing Tess's hand up to his mouth, he kissed her knuckles. Their gazes locked, and when he saw her huge grin, something shifted inside him. It was as if absolute joy and terror had shoved aside his well-ordered routine and declared a new sheriff was in town.

• • •

The rest of the appointment after seeing the baby was a bit of a blur. It was almost like she'd just driven home by instinct and adrenaline. Emotions too high for trivia, she'd begged off going to Marino's and had beaten him home. She was coming out of her room when she heard him talking in the kitchen.

"Yes, Mom, I know this is unexpected, but it's good news. Really. And no, you can't tell anyone else yet. Tess and I need to talk about when she wants to let people know."

Oh God. She hadn't even thought about other people wanting to know about the baby. Everyone she cared about, her girls, already knew. And her mom? Last they'd talked, she was living her best single life with some guy in Vegas, and that had been a year ago. The rest of her family was here in Waterbury but they…well, they weren't close in a family way. But Cole? He had family and friends and a whole life full of people who'd want to know.

"No, Dad, there is no reason for a prenup. One, she doesn't want to get married and two, this wasn't something she planned as a way to trap me into marriage. Tess isn't like that." He paused. "Yes, I know that about her even if I haven't known her that long."

Her stomach sank. Like mother, like daughter? Isn't that what everyone would think when they found out?

"Look, I called because I wanted you to know you're going to be grandparents, not for a lecture on responsibilities," Cole went on. "I'm well aware of what those are and I'm taking care of it."

He may not have called her and the baby an obligation, but that's what her brain translated it to. They would be tolerated and dealt with, not loved. That was just the way her life seemed to work out. And now she wanted to slink back to her room and have a good cry. She was just beginning to backpedal down the hall when Cole strode out of the kitchen and into the hallway, the phone still pressed to his ear.

"I love you, too," he said, his gaze going to her before dropping to the floor. "Talk to you later."

He hung up, and they just stood there in the hall staring at each other with the entire situation filling the space between them like an overgrown thorny bush.

"They're surprised, but they'll turn around," he said, shoving his fingers through his hair. "What did your parents say?"

"It's just my mom, and I haven't talked to her in a year. We're..." She paused—how in the hell did she even begin to explain it? "Well, it's complicated."

He just lifted an eyebrow. "I think it's time for you to tell me about growing up. Don't think I didn't realize you were dodging."

"It's a shitty story," she said, her chest already tightening.

"Okay, you don't have to tell me if you don't want," he said, pulling her into his arms.

The truth was, though, that she did. For the first time, she wanted someone else to understand—correction, not someone but Cole. She wanted Cole to know.

She'd meant to spill her story slowly, but it was like the whole factoid-spewing thing, except this time it was about her life instead of the minutiae of coffee-bean farming. Out came her entire sordid growing-up history about being shuffled from relative's house to relative's house until her mom got bored with her current obsession (new boyfriend, yoga, underwater basket weaving, whatever) and came home to claim her temporarily before the whole cycle started again a few months later.

"It would always begin with me saying something that came out wrong or asking a question I shouldn't—like if this time the guy was going to stick around or if it was wrong to make me go tell the cop at the front door that my mom's latest boyfriend wasn't home even though he was hiding in the hall closet."

That's when all the factoid stuff had started. It was safer to spew random trivia or just keep her mouth shut. Usually it meant a longer time between involuntary visits to the extended family.

"I learned it was best not to say anything of importance, period."

Everything she usually kept under a mountain of it's-not-really-a-big-deal denial that she'd never really told to Lucy, Gina, and Fallon—at least not in detail—came pouring out of her. She told him everything while moving back and forth across his neutrals-only hallway, and by the time she was done and there weren't any words left, she was wrung out like a wet dishrag.

"Your mom and your family are idiots not to realize how lucky they were to have you in their lives." He scooped up Kahn, who'd wandered out into the hall, and gave her a hard look. "You need bread."

Of all the things he could have said at that moment, that was pretty much not even on the list of possibilities. "What?"

"It's comforting, and I have whole-wheat flour and a great recipe." He nuzzled the kitten he professed to dislike and turned toward the kitchen. "Come on. You relax and I'll bake for you."

"You don't have to do that," she said, panic starting to bubble up inside her again. "I don't want to put you out."

He snorted—*snorted*—at her. "Have you realized how often you say stuff like that? Believe me, I'm well aware of what I have to do and don't have to do. This is something I want to do for you."

She didn't know how to react to that, couldn't quite process what it meant, so she went with it. And as she sat at the kitchen table with her peach herbal tea a few minutes later, Cole rolled up his sleeves—showing off those forearms of his that should be illegal—and started making bread.

He premeasured all the ingredients, cleaned off his already pristine counter, and went to work. She'd never considered baking erotic before and it may just have been the pregnancy hormones talking, but it was hot as hell. There was just something about seeing Cole work the dough with his hands, kneading it and shaping it, that had her clutching her mug tighter than necessary.

"You heard me talking to my parents," he said before pushing the heel of his palm into the ball of dough.

"A little." If she'd been Pinocchio, her nose would have been a mile long after those two words.

"You know how we moved around a lot when I was a kid?" He dropped the ball of dough into a bowl and covered it with a tea towel. "It sucked, but it was our life, and my parents tried to make it better by signing me up for the closest hockey league so I'd have that as a constant."

He went about setting the timer, rinsing off the prep dishes, and putting them in the dishwasher. Each move was efficient and practiced, as if he'd done it a thousand times, which he probably had, considering he'd never consulted a recipe card or baking app while making the bread.

"It helped, but the one thing I wanted more than anything was for things to stay the same. When the opportunity came to play for Coach Peppers with the Ice Knights, it was like finally coming back to the comfort zone I'd made growing up. Marti was here. A few of the other guys I'd played juniors with were here. It was the right spot and I knew it."

She could picture him, a little lost boy loved but without a sense of home. Here she'd been teasing him about his routine and museum of a house where nothing was out of place while the whole time it had been for a reason. She wasn't the only one still fighting those childhood insecurities.

The urge to put her mug down and walk over to him, to wrap her arms around him and tell him that he was home now, hit her right in the chest. But she stayed where she was because he didn't want to be home with her. He wanted to be home with Marti—Lucy had warned her at the wedding that he only wanted her—and instead was here with Tess because, as he told his parents, he knew his responsibilities.

"Change is hard," she said, needing to break the silence that had fallen between them.

Cole looked up at her, an intensity in his blue eyes that nearly jolted her. "I'm learning that sometimes it's worth it, though."

Anticipation sizzled across her skin, heating her up and leaving her wanting for something—she had no idea what beyond the fact that it began and ended with Cole. "Why did you tell me about you growing up?"

He shrugged his broad shoulders, not coming any closer but not needing to. She was fucking overwhelmed by him. The need to run closer and away battling it out inside her, gluing her to her chair, her hands wrapped around the half-drunk cup of herbal tea.

"It only seemed fair for both of us to unpack our baggage, since we're in this together," he said.

"Friendly teammates," she said, the words coming out like a squeak.

He stalked closer, stopping across the table from her, every move controlled but on the verge of breaking free. "Something like that."

But the look he gave her at that moment was anything but platonic. It was hot and wanting and dangerous. It was the kind of look that sent a warm wave of desire through her, that stole her breath and set off her you're-in-danger-girl warning sirens.

"Did you know Mark Twain was the first author to give a manuscript that had been typed to his publisher?" she asked, her nerves getting the best of her.

And there she is, the Tess Gardner guaranteed to make people take a distancing step back. Nice to see you again.

"Nope." He took the mug from her grasp, his fingers brushing hers and sending a jolt of oh-my-God-yes through her, and set it aside. "Did you know that Alexander Graham Bell invited him to invest in the telephone and he turned it down?"

She clasped her hands together, desperate not to give in to the urge to climb over the table and rip off his shirt. "Bell invented the world's fastest speedboat in 1919."

"How fast did it go?" he asked, his gaze moving over her, slow as a teasing touch.

Was the oven on? It was getting so hot in here. "Almost seventy-one miles per hour."

"Is this how you flirt with everyone, or do I just make you nervous, Tess?"

"Who said I was nervous?" *You mean besides reality?*

There was that knowing smirk, the sexy one that made a mockery of panties and good intentions. "Mark Twain and Alexander Graham Bell's speedboat."

"I have to go." She stood up so fast, her chair screeched on the tile floor. "It's girls' night with Lucy, Gina, and Fallon."

"Chickens aren't totally flightless; they can fly enough to get over fences," he said, crossing his arms over his chest.

The move drew her eyes back to his exposed forearms and her mouth went dry. "I did know that one."

He stepped to the side, giving her plenty of room to walk by him. She didn't trust herself, though, and went the long way around the table. And then she made like a chicken and got the hell out of there before she did something she shouldn't—again—even though she couldn't shake the voice in her head telling her it was exactly what she needed to do.

Chapter Fourteen

Tess had managed to avoid seeing Cole—if not thinking about him—for a whole day thanks to wedding-season business, but that break for her overworked libido was over now. The Ice Knights arena was rocking as Tess and Fallon walked down to the seats right at the glass that had been Fallon's since she became the team's—and more specifically Zach Blackburn's—Lady Luck. Tonight wasn't Tess's first Ice Knights game. She'd been to several, but never as somebody with more than a tentative connection to anyone on the team. Nerves strung tight, she sat down next to Fallon and watched Cole skate around the ice, taking practice shots and talking to other players.

She'd been watching him play on TV. Hockey was fast, rough, and trying to keep track of that stupid puck was nearly impossible, but she'd had fun. This wasn't fun. It was twist-her-gut-up-like-a-carnival-balloon levels of anxiety. On the screen, it all seemed distant and safe. Up here against the glass, the chill of the rink making the tip of her nose cold and the chippy *swish* sound of blades on the ice in her ears, it all seemed too real.

Tess rubbed her palm over her belly. "There is no way this is a good idea."

"Why?" Fallon asked. "You've been to games with me."

"That was before." Before she'd met Cole. Before she'd gotten pregnant. Before she'd started to think of him at weird times of the day—like every time she inhaled.

"So what's changed besides your bun in the oven?" Fallon, dressed in her team jersey with Zach's number on it, a pair of jeans, and her ever-present Chucks, tightened her ponytail, her eyes never leaving her defenseman boyfriend on the ice. "I mean, it's not like you guys are a couple or anything."

"Exactly." And it would be *awesome* if her lady bits could remember that.

"And you don't even like Cole," her bestie continued, "so really, you're just here for my moral support while Zach shuts down any scoring opportunity the Rage may get."

It was the lack of a diatribe against the Ice Knights' most hated rivals, the Cajun Rage of New Orleans, that tipped Tess off that maybe her friend wasn't as neutral as she was playing at. Well, that and the shit-eating grin Fallon had just turned on her friend that all but hollered, *I think you like him; you want to bang him.*

Fallon was many things—an ER nurse, a passable skateboarder, and one of the best takes-no-shit friends Tess could ever have. What she wasn't was subtle. At all. Ever.

Tess rolled her eyes. "You know subterfuge is really not your strength."

"Thank God, even trying was killing me." Fallon let out a full laugh and turned back to the ice. "So you surprise Cole by showing up at the game and then maybe you two hook up again and—" In the middle of all this, Fallon looked over at Tess, and whatever she saw on her face must have surprised her. She stopped talking mid-word, her eyes widened, and she let out a gasp. "Oh shit. You fucked him."

"Shhhhhhhhhh." Face on fire, Tess looked around at the people sitting nearby, but thank God, with the sound system pumping and everyone yelling at the Rage players to let them know just how very badly they sucked, no one seemed to have heard. "It was a fluke because of the pregnancy hormones."

Fallon twisted the end of her ponytail around her fingers, her face a little too neutral for her, who had an opinion about everything and wasn't afraid of sharing it. "Sounds totally reasonable; after all, everyone knows how you're the kind of woman who just flits from bed to bed having orgasms until you're too exhausted to tell your best friends that"—she exhaled and the facade dropped, revealing total and complete glee—"*you're banging Cole Phillips.*"

"Shhhhhhhhh." Tess waved her hands downward in the international sign for *lower your damn volume*. "My God, Fallon. You do not have an inside voice."

"That is one hundred percent fact." Fallon shrugged, focusing her attention back on the players who were starting to skate by on their way to the tunnel and the locker room beyond, and leaned closer to Tess. "So use your inside voice to tell me everything."

"There's nothing to tell." That was her story and she was sticking to it.

A tap on the glass pulled her attention away from looking at Fallon's not-buying-what-you're-selling expression. Cole stood on the other side of the glass. Her heart slowed down before speeding up to *Enterprise* at warp speed.

Fuck.

This should be illegal; he *should be illegal.* If she wasn't pregnant already, the look on his face would have knocked her up. Confident and cocky, the wink promised he was about to give her some live-action competence porn with a remember-how-those-solid-muscles-of-his-felt-underneath-her   chaser.

Then he turned and skated to the tunnel, disappearing inside.

"Yep, nothing to tell," Fallon said, sarcasm thick in her tone. "Totally just friends. Occasional fuck buddies." She shook her head. "Girl, you are a live-action version of that gif where the guy is standing in front of an explosion and says, *Nothing to see here*."

"It's just weird circumstances." Oh God, not even she believed that, but the words spilled out anyway.

Fallon snorted. "I don't buy it in the least. But it's a good reminder not to ignore what's happening whether you believe in it or not."

Tess made sure to keep her mouth shut—not because she was afraid of what would come out of Fallon's mouth next. It was more like she was afraid of what would come out of hers, because this thing with Cole was starting to feel like more than just temporary living arrangements.

. . .

Not even the shit talk of the Rage's star left forward, Elon Zarcheck, could knock the grin off Cole's face as Petrov took the face-off in the neutral zone five minutes into the second period.

Zarcheck snarled at Cole. "Just wait until I knock that smile off your pretty-boy face."

He lifted one shoulder and let it drop. "You can try, but it's not happening."

Shit, even going nose-first into the glass wouldn't shift his grin an inch. That was the power of seeing Tess in the front row staring at him like she couldn't look away even if someone had been offering her a twenty-million-dollar check.

"Finally got laid," Zarcheck said, one side of his nose lifting in a sneer.

"Yeah." Cole nodded, gaze focused on Petrov and the

puck about to drop from the ref's hand. "Your mom says hi."

The ref let go, Petrov won the face-off, and the half a second it took for Zarcheck's tiny brain to process the your-mom insult was all Cole needed to get a lead on the ice so he'd be in place for Petrov's pass. The move was one of the last that Zarcheck expected, in no small part because it wasn't one that Cole usually made. There was that benefit to Coach Peppers's new play system, even if it did feel like he was trying to eat peas while holding his fork in his left hand.

A deke here, a pass there, and Christensen shot the biscuit home right through the five hole. It was fucking beautiful when the goal light flashed. The crowd went nuts and all the players on the ice skated over to Christensen for a celly.

And for the first time since Coach had tossed that playbook into his lap, Cole thought he just might be able to make this work. His gaze landed on Tess, who was doing a high-five shimmy dance with Fallon in the front row.

She'd been avoiding him since the ultrasound and his failed attempt at seducing her by making bread. *Way to go, Phillips. You are the king of the have-no-game doughboys.* But here she was at his game. She wasn't in his jersey. She wasn't even wearing any Ice Knights gear. Still, she was here. He could get used to that change.

Cole was skating back to the neutral zone so they could hand it to the Rage one more time when his snarly little shadow reappeared at his elbow.

"That was your one time," Zarcheck bitched. "Next time you're kissing glass."

"Interesting nickname for your own mother." Was he being an asshole? Yes. Was it working to make the other winger go a little bananas and lose a step? Also yes.

"Fuck you, Phillips."

Cole shrugged. "I'm already taken."

They faced off to the right of the puck drop. The ref let

go of the rubber and it was on. Petrov continued to do his thing, scrapping until he got control of the puck and sending it flying down the ice to Christensen. The left winger did his dance, making it look like he'd been working the new play system since birth. Then he smacked the puck and sent it hurtling toward Cole.

A whisper of "oh fuck" breathed across the back of his neck, but he ignored it. This was hockey—almost every moment of a forty-second shift was an *oh fuck* situation. He didn't line up the puck and pass to Christensen according to the new system. Instead, that muscle memory of the old plays filled him, and he took his shot.

The puck was still blasting through toward the goal when his *oh fuck* turned into an *OH FUCK* and Lowell Moltan, a Rage defenseman, hit him hard with his shoulder, plowing into him hard enough to send him airborne. In a weird bit of life slowing down in the heat of the moment, Cole watched the puck ricochet off the pipes before he landed flat on his back. His sight dimmed for a second when his helmet hit the ice and every sound except for his own harsh breathing disappeared for a few heartbeats before everything roared back to normal. There was a second of quick assessment, and then fury propelled him up off his ass.

It was fucking bedlam.

Fans pounded on the glass. Players from both teams were getting chippy as they danced around each other. The team trainer was doing his awkward hurry skate to Cole. Blackburn had dropped his mitts and was having a go with Moltan that, judging by the arctic-cold, fuck-you snarl on the Ice Knights' captain's face, was not going to end well for the Rage defenseman.

"That was a late hit and you know it," Christensen told the ref.

An already bruising Moltan, thanks to Blackburn's fists,

got a five-minute major, and Cole got yanked off the ice for concussion protocol testing followed by an ass chewing from Peppers for not following the new system. He didn't get back on the ice until the third period, and by then, he was dying to touch the puck.

It took everything he had to ignore the moves that had been ingrained in him for as long as he'd played hockey and follow the new system. Change was a motherfucking bitch. But then he got the puck and let loose with a wrister that went top-shelf. The crowd erupted loud enough to almost drown out the goal-scored siren and he—because he was very much an asshole—did a slow skate by Zarcheck, who looked like he'd just eaten an entire handful of vomit-flavored jelly beans.

He didn't mean for his attention to move from Zarcheck's ugly mug to Tess, but it did, almost as if he couldn't help but glance over there and visually check in. While all the other fans were celebrating, she stood behind the glass with her hand splayed over her belly and a worried expression on her face.

· · ·

He didn't get hit after he took a shot on goal.

Not that time, at least.

Still, Tess's heart stayed in her throat as she stayed alert, watching for one of the Rage players to come tearing down the ice toward Cole.

This was hockey. Players got hit or checked or body-slammed or whatever the hell they called it. But she wasn't watching a player get smashed into—she was watching *Cole*, and she hadn't taken a proper breath since he'd gone down in the second period.

Fallon squeezed Tess's arm. "You okay?"

Nope. Not even a little bit.

"Athletes suffer from three hundred thousand concussions a year," Tess said, the words coming out stilted.

"Cole's fine. The trainer checked him out. They wouldn't let him back with a concussion."

Fallon was an ER nurse. She knew her shit. If she trusted the team trainer's two-second checkup—okay, it had lasted way longer and been more thorough than that, but that's what her head knew, not what the panic zooming through her acknowledged—then everything was fine. Fine. Everything was fine. Who in the hell ever said that when things really were fine?

No one, not a single person.

Tess sat back down in her seat, her jelly knees refusing to keep her upright. "Loss of consciousness only happens in ten percent of cases."

Fallon sat down in her seat, her sympathetic attention on Tess instead of the play on the ice. "The helmets and the game have both changed to help protect the players. Trust me, with what Zach goes through every game, I looked into this."

"You only get one brain," Tess said, her voice quiet compared to the roar of the rest of the fans.

Why did the inane words still keep coming out? Sure, it was true; there was totally a one-brain-per-person limit, but she really could just shut up right about now. Actually, five minutes ago would have been even better.

Fallon didn't roll her eyes, though, and she didn't edge over on her seat to put as much space between them as possible. Instead, she took Tess's hand and squeezed it.

"Do you want me to see if I can get you down to the players' tunnel after the game so you can see for yourself that he's fine?" Fallon asked.

Yes!

No.

What was she doing? This wasn't her. This gut-twisting, ass-clutching anxiousness about someone who wasn't part of her found family was definitely not what she did with 99.6 percent of people. Even worse, she was halfway to telling Fallon yes before she caught herself. That wasn't her place. That was for girlfriends like Fallon or expected-to-be wives someday like Marti, not accidental obligations like her. She was just temporary.

"No. That's not necessary," she said, clasping her hands together in her lap and turning so she was facing the ice again. "I don't want to impose."

"You're kidding, right?" Fallon snorted in total disbelief and disagreement. "He's the father of your baby, and you guys are..." Fallon waved her hands in the air as if she—the woman with no filter—couldn't find the words to explain what they were.

Tess understood. She was right there herself.

"The unexpected happened," she said, because the last thing in the world she was going to do was admit that she had no clue what was going on between them, either. "He took pity on me when my apartment flooded. That's it. That's all."

"But you two—"

Tess put her hand over Fallon's mouth before she could announce to the entire arena that she'd had sex with Cole. Again.

"Are friends. Sorta." Tess let out a sigh and slipped her hand from Fallon's mouth. "Look, I don't know what we are, but whatever it is, it's temporary, because we're most definitely not a couple—not while he's holding out hope for Marti to come back—and we're also forever because we're gonna have this baby together. It's complicated."

And as she watched the clock tick down on the game, she had to wonder how much time she still had and what kind of mark it was going to leave on her heart because even though she wouldn't admit it out loud, staying with Cole had changed everything.

And God help her, she was at a loss to figure out what to do about it or how to remember how to breathe when that goon of a Rage player started skating after Cole again. The best thing she could do was just ignore it all, use the old pretending trick like she had when she was little and her mom would tell her they were going for ice cream. Kid Tess would play along, hoping this time was different, that this time her mom wasn't going to end their ice-cream date with an announcement that Tess was going to be staying with this aunt or that uncle for a little while.

It never was different—not one single time.

So why would whatever was going on with Cole be anything other than the inevitable heartbreak she expected?

Chapter Fifteen

The media had been shuffled out to the post-game press conference room, AKA The Upchucker, and Cole was buttoning up his shirt when Peppers strolled by his locker.

"Phillips, my office," the coach said without even the slightest break in his stride as he headed out of the locker room to his office right outside.

Fuck. Coach only liked to have little chats when the shit was going down.

The game replay in his head started running at triple speed. It hadn't been his best game, but it hadn't been shit, either. Grabbing his jacket and heading out of the locker room, he went through every mistake, every missed pass, that fucking late hit, and tried to prep for whatever Coach was about to chew his ass about. After a quick tap on the doorframe, since the office door was open, he walked in. He was so preoccupied that he almost missed Marti being in there until he practically plowed into her.

On automatic, he reached out to steady her. "I'm sorry."

"No worries," she said, taking a step back, her smile as

huge as it was genuine. "How are you doing? That was a helluva hit."

His head could be hanging on by a string and he'd answer the same thing. "Fine, no problems."

A weird silence fell between them. Normally, this would have been where he took a step closer and the process of them getting back together for the millionth time would start, but he didn't have the urge. It was the weirdest thing, as if part of him had switched off and that thing that had always been between them was gone. He still cared—come on, they'd known each other for more than a decade, he always would—but it was different.

"Good." She nodded. "It's nice to see you again."

It had been weeks. Again, he couldn't believe he hadn't noticed.

"You too. Did Mr. Wall Street enjoy the game?" Look at him being all mature and shit, asking her about her boyfriend.

"Wouldn't know." She shrugged. "He's old news."

"That's too bad," he said—and he meant it.

She grinned at him, orneriness sparkling in her eyes. "Not really."

"I'll second that," Coach Peppers said as he sat down behind his desk. "He tried to give me coaching tips. Can you believe that shit? What an asshole."

Marti sighed and rolled her eyes. "Daddy."

"I know, I know," Peppers said, the conversation one they obviously had more times than not. "Your private life is your own."

"Exactly." She gave Cole a quick hug and headed around him toward the door. "See you later."

Cole was still trying to figure out his reaction—or more precisely his non-reaction—when Coach asked him to shut the door and sit down. Now, if there was a moment that struck fear in a professional athlete's life, it was that door-shutting thing. Nothing good happened after that. If a coach wanted to chew your ass, he did it in the locker room or on the bench. If he wanted to end your career with the team, he asked you to shut the door.

"I know you've been working on the new system," Peppers said, his tone measured. "I appreciate your efforts, but it hasn't been enough. You staying at the same level while everyone else continues to up their game isn't enough. I'm shaking up the lines to see if playing with a different winger and center helps."

Cole sat there like he'd been hit with a stun gun, his body frozen and his brain jumbled.

"What does that mean?" Sure, he knew what the individual words meant, but together it all sounded like a rocket train blasting through hell—impossible to imagine.

Coach didn't hesitate, just laid it out there. "You're moving to the second line."

If he hadn't already been sitting, that would have knocked his legs out from under him. He'd been first line since he'd been drafted.

"I know change is not your thing," Coach said before taking a sip from his sugar-milk-with-a-few-drops-of-coffee concoction. "However, if you tread water at this level, you can't compete. Everyone from the grinder to the future hall of famer is doing whatever it takes to get an extra tenth of a percentage of improvement. For you, that improvement needs to come in your ability to adapt to game changes."

A mix of frustration and desperation made Cole's palms clammy as he tried to unravel what was going on and figure out how in the hell he could fix it. "Give me another chance."

Coach dead-eyed him, laying it out there with a look. "I have."

"What do I need to do to get back?" There. A goal. He had one and he'd do whatever it took to reach it.

Peppers took another drink, eyeballing him over the top of the mug as if he was judging just how blunt to be—a first as far as Cole knew, and he'd known the man since juniors.

"Figure out how to work in the new systems," Peppers said after putting his mug down. "Get the plays to feel like ones you've been running forever. Stop being distracted. Yeah, I've noticed. Whatever is going on in your personal life, leave it outside the arena. When you step on that ice, it needs to be all hockey."

"I'll make it happen."

He would. There wouldn't be anything for him except for hockey for the rest of the season. He'd make this work. He had to.

"I have no doubt. Phillips, you're a hell of a player. You could be in the hall of fame if you buckle down and figure this shit out. The difference between NHL good and NHL great is in the sweat equity paired with talent and skill. You have to want it more than you want anything else. Do you?"

He nodded, ignoring the mental flash of Tess in that ultrasound room. "Yes."

"Then I want to see it in the next game and the one after that. Use the road trip we've got coming up to knock my fucking socks off."

Cole got up and said his goodbyes before heading to his car in the private parking lot and the short ride across the harbor that would probably feel like a million years. The worst had happened. Change had found him and cross-checked him hard into the boards.

He headed out to his car, his brain a fucking scattered mess. Hockey wasn't just his job; it was his life plan. Getting moved to the second line put everything he'd worked for into jeopardy—all because of a torn condom and a night he hadn't meant to have happen.

That's bullshit and you know it.

The voice in his head wasn't wrong. As Cole drove out of the player lot and onto the parkway that would lead him over the Harbor City bridge and home to Waterbury, he couldn't ignore the truth of it. Tess and the baby hadn't fucked his routine. He'd done it to himself. Well, he wouldn't be anymore.

From now on, he'd be shutting his bedroom door so that cat couldn't get in and mess with his morning schedule. He'd ignore the draw that tugged him toward Tess every time he got anywhere near her, thought about her, or—lately—even breathed. He'd get back to how his life had always been, and that's how he'd claw his way back up to the first line.

He'd never been surer of a plan in his life, right up until he pulled into his driveway and saw Tess's ridiculous car parked all cockeyed while still managing to look like it belonged there. Just like the woman who drove it, that car had become part of his every day, and he wasn't sure he was going to be able to turn it all off and keep his distance from her, no matter how much sense it made. Little by little, he'd started to rely on Tess as being part of his formerly well-planned-out existence.

Fuck. He was so screwed.

• • •

Tess was using every deflection skill she had to keep Kahn away from the two postgame chocolate cupcakes waiting for Cole on the kitchen island, but the kitten was determined and crafty. It was a dangerous combination. Still, she was a woman on a mission. She had to at least see him before she went to bed—alone—and make sure he was okay. Since she'd gotten home, her never-shuts-up brain had already worked through a million scenarios for how hurt he'd be when he got home.

Bandaged even though he hadn't bled once? Didn't

matter. She'd pictured it.

Hobbling a little, the way she did the day after a rare gym session when all her muscles spent the next day bitching her out? She'd totally imagined it.

Wincing with every intake of breath while holding his head with a goose egg protruding from the back? Oh yeah, she'd imagined that and more.

What kind of life was this for him? What kind of life would it be for the baby? She'd grown up in the eye of Hurricane Chaos. Nothing had been the same two days in a row. There was no one she could depend on to be there. Between Cole's game schedule with only a few days off a month during their nine-month season, when would he even have the time to see their child? Was she just sentencing her baby to having an unavailable parent like she'd had?

The only thing keeping her from pacing the length of Cole's kitchen while chewing her nails to the quick was the fact that Kahn hadn't given up on eating a cupcake.

"For the last time, Kahn," she said, picking him up and holding him so they were face-to-face, as if he could understand. "The chocolate will kill you, so stop trying to swipe one."

"Can you blame him, though? They're really good."

Tess whipped around at the sound of Cole's voice while Kahn leaped from her arms in that graceful way cats can do and landed on the island.

She was too slack-jawed at seeing Cole, searching his head for any signs of bruising and reminding herself that she couldn't rip his clothes off to do the same for his body, to react. Of course, that's where having a world-class athlete in the room helped. He blocked Kahn from the cupcake before Tess had even processed what was going on. In her defense, her brain was doing doubly duty taking him in and memorizing every line of him.

His hair was still damp, the blond a little darker for it, and tucked behind his ears. His white button-up was undone at the collar, his tie undone and hanging around his neck, and his sleeves were rolled up, exposing his thick forearms. On anyone else, the look would be disheveled. On him it was barely constrained. She had no idea what had happened to his suit jacket but damn, she wished the rest of his clothes would join it.

Simmer down, Tess. It's all just temporary. Don't get attached. You know the danger of that.

Discombobulated, she picked up one of the cupcakes and held it out to him. "The world record for eating the most cupcakes in the least amount of time is twenty-nine cupcakes in thirty seconds."

One side of his mouth lifted, and he stalked toward her, every movement with purpose. "There's a dirty joke in there somewhere."

"No there's not." Her chest tightened at the way his gaze traveled over her, hot and heady and hungry. "It's a cupcake. It's all frosting and sprinkles and goodness. They used to be called one, two, three, fours or numbers as an easy way to remember the ratio of ingredients."

She might be frozen to the spot, her nipples puckered and breasts heavy with need, but he kept striding toward her, everything about him taut and ready.

"It's also sometimes used as a euphemism," he said, his voice a low, deep rumble.

Her breath caught. "For what?"

He raised an eyebrow. "You really want me to tell you or show you?"

Both. Yes. Please. Oh my God.

She grabbed one of the cupcakes and all but shoved it at him, her arm outstretched. "Eat it."

"You're killing me, Tess." He accepted the cupcake and

took a bite. Correction. He licked off the top point of the frosting and then took a bite. "Aren't you going to have one? After all, it's just, how did you put it, frosting, sprinkles, and goodness."

The rat bastard. He had her and he knew it.

All she wanted to do was flee with her panties still attached, if not totally dry, and instead she was going to have to stay here and eat a cupcake while he continued to do indecent things with his tongue. When had eating the frosting from a cupcake become indecent? The moment Cole Phillips did it. And it shouldn't be! Food plus naked good times had never gone together in her mental wank bank. So watching Cole take a final bite of the cupcake and then suck the frosting off his fingertips should be a total and complete turnoff. But holy oh-my-God-cupcake-euphemism tingles, it was the hottest thing she'd seen since she'd gotten the full view of his naked body the other morning.

Now that mental image of him in his full professional-athlete-in-the-prime-of-his-life glory was all it took to send her brain into la-la land, and she stuffed her entire not-a-euphemism cupcake into her mouth at once without even thinking about the consequences. And this would be? Oh, the little things, like not being able to chew with her mouth closed and the coughing fit that came with having one barely chewed chunk go straight down her windpipe.

Very sexy.

Totally classy.

Without a doubt, 100 percent on brand for awk-weird Tess.

"Are you okay?" he asked, rushing to her side.

"Fine," she said, but even she could barely understand her answer because of the coughing and her hand over her mouth to keep the rest of it from flying everywhere because wouldn't spitting pieces of chocolate cupcake just be the sprinkles on the frosting?

Cole spun her around so she faced the sink. "Just spit the damn thing out before you choke on your pride." He thumped her on the back.

Chunks of cupcake landed in the sink and she sucked in a huge breath, lifting her arms into the air to open her lungs as much as possible.

"I'm okay," she managed to croak out, her throat raw and her cheeks burning from embarrassment.

Holding her gently by the upper arms, he gave her a searching look, as if he had to make sure for himself that she was okay. "Are you alright?"

Oh, how the tables had turned. "I'm not the one who went ass over end and landed on the ice tonight. I'll be fine."

"It looked worse than it was." His hands slid down her arms, his touch leaving a trail of awareness in its wake, and stopped at her hands, his fingers intertwining with hers.

"Really?" Tess tried squeezing his fingers, taking comfort in the touch after what had happened during the game. "Because even if it was only half as bad, it was fucking horrifying."

Cole pulled her in close so her cheek was pressed against his chest, the steady beat of his heart a reassuring rhythm. He dropped a kiss on the top of her head, the quick brush of his lips so soft that the lingering sense of anticipation made her entire body sizzle.

"I cleared the concussion protocol," he said. "And besides a few new bruises and sore spots—not on my head—it's all good."

"It scared me." Almost as much as admitting that bit of vulnerability to him.

He brushed another kiss across the top of her head. "I'm sorry."

"Show me how bad it is," she said, pulling back because

she needed the distance between them or she was afraid she'd give in to the feelings of maybe-this-time swirling around her like the scent of her favorite flowers. "I need to know what this baby is in for." And what she was, but she left that part unsaid.

He would have been within his rights to tell her to fuck straight off, but he didn't. Instead he took a step back and started to unbutton his shirt, making quick work of it, and opened it to reveal a narrow slice of his bare chest.

"Not a mark on me," he said, but his gaze didn't meet hers.

That wasn't how this could be. As a kid, she'd been able to pretend, to use her fact-filled brain to create distance, but she couldn't do that anymore. The baby would need more from her than that—the baby deserved a mom who would fight for him or her even when it was hard, even when it was uncomfortable.

She fixed her attention on Cole's face, looking him straight in the eye. "You said you had new bruises."

He sighed and shrugged off his shirt, revealing an ugly bruise starting to form on the left side of his chest. The size of a softball, it was already just about every color of the rainbow. Ignoring that part of her brain warning her of the danger, she reached out and brushed her fingertips across it. The moment she touched him, the air around them changed, grew heavier, became thick with possibility.

Was it pregnancy hormones? Pheromones? The absolutely natural reaction to being around someone so attractive that her panties had laughed at the idea of staying on?

Probably yes to all three, but none of it changed the fact that she wanted this man and had since the first time she'd set eyes on him at Lucy's rehearsal party. They hadn't gotten weddinged like she'd told him, she'd given in to the magic hopefulness inherent in those romantic events to believe that there could be someone who'd see her as more than an obligation or a temporary unwanted guest in their lives. She'd allowed herself to believe, if only for a few hours, that she could be wanted.

She lowered her hand, her fingers tingling as if she'd gotten some small electric shock. "Are you scared out there on the ice?"

"The other guys have my back." He stepped closer, picked up her hand, and put it back on his chest. "They do their job and I do mine, even if I'll be doing it from the second line now."

The frustrated fury in his tone twisted her up inside. And the look on his face? This was a man watching his dream, his plans for the rest of his life, try to walk away from him. It was agonizing for her; for him it had to be hell. But maybe she could help him forget, for tonight, what the world was like outside his front door.

"I'm sorry." She took a step closer so they were millimeters from whole-body touching—not because she needed to but because she had to.

Anticipation crackled in the air between them in that fraction of a second, some unexplainable understanding that he was going to kiss her or she was going to kiss him—either way, it was about to go down, and there would be no stopping it once it started.

"Do you want to talk about what's gonna happen?" Cole asked.

He could have been talking about the line switch or cupcakes or a million other things, but he wasn't, and they both knew it.

"What's there to say?" She rose up on her tiptoes so her lips were nearly pressed to his. "This is temporary."

"What if it's not?"

She didn't answer because the words "it always is" were almost too sad to say out loud. So instead, she decided to take comfort in the fleeting hope that maybe—*just maybe*—things would be different this time and kissed him.

Chapter Sixteen

After what went down in Coach's office, Cole had been absolutely 100 percent sure that the only thing he was going to be thinking about for the rest of the season was hockey. Nothing else would exist. Then he'd walked into his house and seen Tess trying to use logic on Kahn. The sight of her in a FLOWER POWER T-shirt that hung down almost to the hem of her tiny sleep shorts that barely covered her ass had short-circuited Cole's brain, and his cock had taken advantage.

She was the one sweet spot in his world right now. She wasn't supposed to be there, he had no plans for her, and yet Tess Gardner was there. He needed her, wanted her, had to have her, not just to block out his shit day but to remind himself that there was more if he just had the balls to go after it.

He wasn't complaining—not now when she was kissing him like a woman who'd found something she'd never realized she'd lost. He knew the feeling. His life had been planned out, organized, followed a set routine. It had been perfect—at least that's what he'd thought.

Then he'd seen Tess at Lucy's wedding answering every damn one of those trivia questions while pretending not to be listening to their game. There was a motherfucking pattern here, and it didn't take a genius to figure out what—or more correctly *who*—was at the center of it all. Tess always had him veering away from the expected into something so much better.

He glided his hands down to Tess's full hips, and he pulled her against him, desperate for the feel of her softness against every hard, aching part of himself. Fuck. Touching her was better than anything else, but he needed more and he needed it now. He hooked his thumbs into the waistband of those tiny shorts, the ones she probably didn't realize clung to her ass in a way that fried his brain.

"Can I take these off?" Cole asked, begged, prayed.

Her breath was warm against his ear as she whispered, "You're not sure?"

"Hell yes, but are you?" His fingertips practically vibrated being so close to her smooth skin, the middle knuckles of his thumbs being the only part of him touching her bare skin.

Looking up at him from beneath her thick lashes, she trailed her fingertips down his arms, her fingers like lightning against his bare skin, until her hands were on top of his. In that breath, the entire universe shrank until it was only him and Tess in this moment that stretched on for eternity; then she lowered her hands past his, sending her shorts down her legs, and time snapped back into motion.

"Yes, I'm very sure," she said, stepping out of the shorts pooled around her feet. "And if you don't do something more than just kiss me, I'm going to have to take care of it myself."

His breath hissed out at the image of watching her fingers slip between her legs to circle her clit. "If that's a threat, it's a really, really bad one."

She smiled up at him, a teasing curl of her lips, and he

was lost—if he hadn't been already. This give and take, the sense of unknown possibility of it all, grabbed him by the balls and tugged in the very best of ways.

"Why?" she asked and then whipped off her T-shirt and let it fall to the floor. "Do you want to watch?"

A blast of desire shot through him, hardening every part of him and taking him right to the edge of the breaking point. It wasn't about want, though; everything centered on his self-control. Could he be this close to her and not touch her, taste her, make her see that something more was happening between them? Could he watch her play with herself, see her face as she got close, look on as her fingers went faster and faster until she came? If that's what she wanted, he could—he would.

When it came to Tess, it wasn't about just getting off for either of them. There was more. And if she wanted to tease him, make him come without even stroking his cock once, then that's what would happen, because being with her wasn't routine and he still craved it, *craved her*, anyway.

"I want everything you'll allow," he said, gliding his fingertips upward over the roundness of her hips, the lessening dip of her waist, and to the curve of her tits, brushing his thumbs across the hard peaks of her nipples. "I want anything you're willing to give."

She narrowed her eyes at him, something shifting in the air around them. "Why?"

How did he put it into words to say out loud when he could barely manage to do it in his head? It was all too much, too new, too fresh and achy and needy. Why did he want Tess?

"Because being with you is like breathing; I just know I need to." His gut clenched. *Shit.* "That came out weird, creepy, stalkerish, but I'm not a word guy and it's just—"

She interrupted him. "People don't say things like that to me."

"If it's wrong to be glad about that, then I am beyond redemption because I don't want anyone else to say the things I want to say to you."

Yep. He was officially *that guy*. He had more than two brain cells to rub together and knew exactly how much of a dickhead he sounded like, but he couldn't help it. Standing here with her naked in his arms, everything about her from the splotchy red birthmark on her side to her different-colored eyes to the skeptical expression on her face was absolutely perfect.

She covered his hand on her breast, not pushing him aside but not allowing free motion, either. "Who gets to talk to me or touch me is not for you to decide."

"I know, but I want it anyway." He was fucking this all up, but the words—the truth—wouldn't stop. "I want all of you."

"Cole." She lifted her hand and pressed her fingers to his mouth. "If you want this to happen, you can't talk anymore. I'll start to believe and we both know that can't happen. It's just temporary, remember?"

"Temporary." The word left the taste of moldy gym socks in his mouth.

"Exactly." She nodded. "Now fuck me."

Tess may have thought he was agreeing about the whole temporary thing, but he wasn't. He also wasn't dumb enough to think that this was the time to argue, not when she'd made it crystal clear exactly what she wanted at the moment. As he lifted her up and sat her down on the edge of the island before spreading her legs wide, he decided the best course of action was to show her.

Watching her face as he kissed and licked his way up her inner thigh to her sweet, slick folds, he got the double treat of not only bringing her pleasure but watching her reaction to every move, letting him gauge when to slow down and when to speed up. The urge to rush in, get her off fast and hard, was like a river of lava in his veins, but he wouldn't—not yet. Forcing himself to slow down, to draw it out and make it better. He lingered and explored, her every blissed-out groan and reaction telling him exactly how much pressure to apply, how much suction to provide, and how to get right to the edge of orgasm before pulling back so the need built until the intensity of it was palpable.

Head tossed back, one blond curl caught in her open mouth, she told him exactly what she wanted with words and encouraging moans of "fuck yes." By the time he sucked on her clit as he circled her opening with his thumb, she was pleading with him for more.

"That's what you want?" he asked as he stroked her, teasing her and taking her higher, closer, but not quite pushing her over the edge. "More?"

"Cole, please." She tugged on his hair, pulling him close to her core. "Make me come."

Any thought of skating that thin line between too much and not enough disappeared at the sound of her voice. She wanted more. He'd always give her that. He'd give her everything if she'd only let him. He had no idea how he'd gotten to that place, that understanding, but as he pulsed his tongue against her clit until her thighs shook and she came against his lips, he knew there was nothing more real than the truth that Tess Gardner had changed everything.

• • •

Tess lay on the kitchen island, the granite cold against her naked back and her bare legs draped over Cole's shoulders, trying to catch her breath. She took off her glasses and laid them on the island next to her. How they'd stayed on while she was riding the wave set in motion by his mouth, she had no fucking idea. The man was going to kill her with orgasms like that. It would be days before her toes uncurled, and she was totally good with it.

Her legs shifted as he stood up, his mouth—*that mouth*—curled into a satisfied grin, but she wasn't fooled. The hunger in his eyes, the dark promise of more—*always more*—settled against her, firm as a touch and as solid as a promise she could take to the bank.

Sitting up, she let her gaze travel the length of him, taking in the shirt hanging open, revealing the broad muscular expanse of his chest, the rolled-up sleeves showing off his sinewy forearms, and the suit pants tailored to within a millimeter of perfection so that the outline of his hard cock was impossible to miss. Not that she did. No. She wanted all of it, all of him.

"You have too many clothes on," she said, reaching out for his belt and hesitating, her hold on the buckle loose and light. "Do you want to take them off?"

"That depends." He didn't move, just watched her, the heat in his eyes nearly burning her. "What happens after they're gone?"

"I have some ideas."

Some? More like a gazillion, in addition to the ones she could make happen tonight or tomorrow or the few days they had between now and her moving back into her apartment. Was that text she'd gotten tonight with a return date what pushed her into being here like this, demanding what she really wanted? Maybe. Life moved fast; she knew full well what happened when she blinked—everything changed and she'd be out of here for good. It would be her and the peanut but no Cole. Wasn't that forever her lot in life? It was always a temporary home, temporary family, temporary love. But not tonight. This she could pretend would last longer—or more likely that she just didn't care if it ended tomorrow.

"You still okay with this?" Cole asked, his hand cupping

her chin, tilting it upward so she looked him in the eyes. "You can say no at any point. You can walk away."

She undid his belt and immediately went to work on his pants. "I'm not going anywhere tonight." The second his button slipped free, she was lowering his zipper. "You wanna know what I want to do next?"

He let out a harsh hiss of breath. "Please tell me it involves my dick."

"It does." She slid down off the island and shoved his pants down over that high ass of his before wrapping her fingers around his hard cock. "And my mouth."

He swallowed visibly and worked his jaw back and forth as if it was taking everything not to move but to let her lead. "Fuck me, Tess."

"Yes," she said, already lowering herself to her knees. "But not yet."

Watching his face as she swirled her tongue around the head of his cock, licking up the salty evidence of his desire, she couldn't help but wonder just how far she could push this. Cole wasn't a man who let go of control easily; that's where there was the routine, the schedule, the way things had always been. He'd been white-knuckling life for so long that he had no idea the absolute fucking joy of letting go every once in a while.

Taking him deep, she let him fill her mouth as he fisted his hands at his sides, obviously fighting the urge to take over. There was a happy middle ground between taking and giving; he needed to see that. She reached out and took his hands, putting them on either side of her head. He let out a groan of surrender, tightening his grip on her curls, rocking his hips, and joining in on the give-and-take with her, meeting her halfway as she sucked him, stroked him with her tongue, wrapped her hand around the base of him and moved in sync with her mouth. No one was passive—for tonight, they were in it together.

"Tess." He held her head still, slowly withdrawing from her, and let her go. "This isn't what I had planned for tonight."

"You don't like blow jobs?" Sure, there was probably someone out there who didn't, but judging by his reaction, he wasn't one of them.

"That's definitely not it, but usually—"

"Cole," she said, stroking his cock to distract him from his love of routines. "Sex doesn't have to be P in the V. I can make you come with my mouth. I can jerk you off. You can jerk off. We could...well, we could do a million other things. There are so many ways to fucking come; are you really going to get caught up in the usual when you can let go and just let yourself enjoy the moment?"

He chuckled, the move making his abs tighten and showing off every definition line of his eight-pack. "Is this naked psychology?"

"Is it working?" She kissed the tip of his cock and then licked his pre-cum off her lips.

Letting out the groan of a man on the edge, he twisted one of her curls around his finger. "You might have convinced me."

"I'm willing to try harder." She had one hand wrapped around the base of his dick and raised the other to cradle his balls, tugging on them just hard enough to elicit a lusty moan from him. "Is that a yes?"

"It's a fuck yes." He thrust his hips forward, the slick head of his cock brushing against her mouth.

She didn't answer in words; instead she parted her lips and took him in until he hit the back of her throat. Moving forward and back, she kept pace with his hips as he fucked her mouth. God, having him like this, seeing him relinquish absolute control, was a kind of high in itself, like showing someone a sunrise for the first time or being there when an orchid bloomed. She couldn't have him forever, but this memory, it was going to stay, and that would just have to be good enough.

"Tess." Her name came out rough, pained. "I'm gonna come."

She tightened her hand, sucked him deeper, lapped at the sensitive underside of his cock with her tongue until he came, his entire body going stiff. Swallowing, she watched him come back to himself in small increments, one breath and heartbeat at a time until he was helping her up into a standing position and wrapping his arms around her to bring her close.

"Tonight was so much better than what I'd planned," he said, rubbing his palm in a circular motion on the small of her back.

"What exactly had you planned?"

"To say good night and then go hide in my room so I didn't fuck you six ways to Sunday."

She refused to look up at him, instead keeping her ear pressed to his chest as she tried to imagine a world in which they hadn't just done what they'd done. Her mind went blank and she shivered. "That was a horrible plan."

"Agreed."

There was a riddle of a promise in that one word that she wanted to untangle and solve, but she didn't trust herself for that. Things with Cole came too easy, too fast. The sixth sense of a kid who'd been shuffled from relative to relative should have been sounding in her ears. Instead, all she could hear was the steady, reassuring *thump-thump* of Cole's heart. Best not get used to that—she wanted it too badly already. For all she teased him about going beyond his comfort zone, she was perfectly happy to stay in her own, where disappointment wasn't a bug; it was a feature.

She took a step back, her hand automatically dropping to her belly as if to shield their baby from what she had to do. "I guess I'll head to bed now."

"As long as it's mine." He didn't move, but there was more than a hint of a possessive growl in his tone.

"That's not a great idea." Ignoring the way her pulse kicked up at the thought, she powered through the words coming out as neutrally as possible. "I'll be gone in a few days. The repairs to my apartment are almost done."

"That's then. Let's take now. Fuck the plans, remember?" he asked, holding out his hand. "If it's all I can get, I'll take it."

So would she, but as she took his hand and they walked together down the hallway to his room, she couldn't help but realize that it wouldn't be enough. It was too late for anything but forever to be enough—and there was no scarier realization than that.

Chapter Seventeen

For the first time since forever, Tess's voicemail box was full, and she couldn't bring herself to delete even a single one. That seemed to be what happened when Cole went on a road trip for a few days. Phone calls that she let turn into voicemails she could hoard for later.

"Did you know a dentist is the one who invented cotton candy? What kind of racket is that?" Cole asked in one message. The sound of a pilot telling everyone to buckle up because they were about to take off sounded in the background. "Gotta go. Call when I land. Miss you. Tell Peanut I said hi and don't think I didn't find that Bigfoot painting in the front bathroom. I put it in a more appropriate spot. I'm not telling where."

She'd already found it hanging on the wall in the back of the walk-in closet in her bedroom, complete with one of those gallery lights shining down on it. Cole was such a smart-ass. Of course, she'd made sure to hang it right above the sink in the kitchen where there was no way he'd miss it. Bigfoot would be there to greet him every morning when he made his hard-boiled eggs.

Then there were the voicemail messages that were longer, filled with the sound of raucous Ice Knights players in the background celebrating one victory after another. Others were just the sound of a tired Cole trying to stay awake long enough to reach her one last time. Tess couldn't explain why she didn't answer when Cole's number flashed on the screen and why she only called while she was watching him out on the ice. Was she a giant chicken? Yeah, pretty much. She needed that sense of distance, though, as a sort of moat of sanity, because she couldn't stop thinking about him, dreaming of him, wanting him home.

That was another problem. She wasn't thinking of the house as Cole's museum anymore. It was just home. Tess wasn't just entering dangerous territory, she was smack-dab in the middle of it and what was worse, she didn't want to leave.

All of which explained why she'd started spending so much time at her shop beyond business hours. That meant by midmorning today, though, she was yawning on repeat in her tiny office while doing all the admin work that came along with running a small business.

The cup of decaf coffee appeared on her desk while she was running the monthly profit-and-loss statement thanks to the world's best delivery driver who was now picking up a few extra hours manning the front a few days a week.

Ellis, who was so worth his weight in Gold of Kinabalu orchids, which went for six grand apiece, flashed her a shy smile. "There's a call for you on line two."

She thanked him and picked up the line after hitting print on the report. "Forever in Bloom, this is Tess."

"Two questions," Cole said, his warm honey voice doing things to her that probably weren't legal in at least a few states. "One, do you have plans for tonight? Two, do you have objections to being seen out in public with a man in a powder-blue tux with full-on shirt ruffles?"

By the time Cole was finished, she was smiling so hard, her cheeks hurt. "Well, to answer the first question, I was going to go shopping for my creepy porcelain doll collection and then hide them all over your house."

"Oh yeah, I'm foiling those plans for sure," he said. "How about the tux?"

She tried to picture him in a tux, but the only image she could muster was of him the morning he left for the latest road trip. He'd been naked in the shower and the water had been cascading down his back and over his hard ass. She must have made a noise—probably by not-so-whispering a "thank you, baby Jesus"—and he'd turned around, caught her looking, and tugged her inside with him.

Oh God. It was hot in her office. Really. Damn. Hot.

"Do I get to know why you're in a powder-blue tux with shirt ruffles?" she asked, sounding more than a little horny and out of sorts to her own ears.

"It's a charity fund-raiser costume party with a seventies theme the team is putting on," he said. "You should meet me there, be my date."

Shock made her almost drop her phone. A date? With Cole? Yeah, they'd skipped right past that part and had just embraced future co-parenting without any relationship strings attached. "I'm all out of tuxes."

Yes. That for sure seemed like the safest answer.

"Well, I just happen to have had the costume place deliver a disco diva outfit with bell-bottoms and sequins to our house."

Of course he did. He was Cole Phillips, Thor look-alike and professional athlete in a city that adored him. "You have everything."

"Not you," he said, managing to make it sound like the

truth instead of a pity pickup line. "Say yes."

"Public events aren't really my thing." That would be putting it mildly. Going to a costume party with a bunch of superstar athletes was enough to make her want to hide under her desk. "Remember what happened at Lucy's wedding?"

"You mean the screaming orgasms?" he asked, his tone roughening to a near growl. "I thought that was pretty awesome."

"No," she said, her cheeks burning. "The whole standing by myself and pretending to be on my phone so you didn't realize I was playing along with your trivia game like some loser who had no friends."

Oh God. Just thinking about how they'd met put her in a clammy-palmed tizzy.

Cole chuckled and somehow managed to make even that sound sexy. "Hate to break it to you, Tess, but the phone thing didn't work even if it was cute."

"That's not cute; it's awkward and weird." She let out a so-fucking-over-this huff and sank down in her chair. "I don't people well."

"I'll be with you the whole time," he said. "If you don't want to people anymore, we'll go home. No questions asked. Don't make me disco by myself. Say you'll come. Please."

Ugh. This wasn't fair. Not only did she miss him—and yes, she acknowledged being a total idiot for that, but she did—but he was using the voice on her, the one that made doing the totally awful sound completely reasonable. Plus the idea of seeing him in a powder-blue tux was enough to make her want to push past her usual reticence. Yeah, so what if Cole wasn't the only one with a spacious comfort zone?

"Fine," she said, giving in. "I'll be there."

What else could she say? Her brain had melted into goo and there weren't any other words left.

. . .

That evening, when she walked into the Harbor City Hotel grand ballroom, the words wouldn't stop swirling around in her head, keeping time with the light-speed thumping of her heart and the rushing in her ears. Hanging back in the doorway, Tess searched the crowd for Cole, the awkward building with each butterfly-collar shirt, bell-bottom-pants-wearing guy who wasn't Cole. She recognized a few faces, guys from the trivia game at the wedding whose names had been replaced in her head with completely useless information such as the literal Greek translation for "utopia" is "no place" and "eisoptrophobia" is the fear of mirrors.

Sweat began to make her hair frizz, and her lungs tightened as she scanned the crowd for Cole. Sure, it was a costume party, but how hard was it to miss Thor's twin? Pretty damn difficult.

She scanned the room again and again and one more time before that all-too-familiar feeling of being alone settled in the pit of her stomach like sour milk and getting the hell out of there became more important than finding him. Head down, she turned and rushed toward escape and right into the hard chest of a man in a dark wig wearing a polyester baby-blue tux opened that showed off the gold medallion nestled in his too-plentiful-to-be-anything-but-fake chest hair.

"Oh my God, I'm so sorr—" Something in the teasing glint of his blue eyes stopped her mid-word and recognition flooded her. "Cole?"

He grinned down at her. "You weren't about to ditch me, were you?"

She totally was, but instead of a quick affirmative, her mouth did that nervous thing. "Did you know the name Milt is also the zoological term for fish semen?"

Yes, because that was exactly what this already nerve-racking and awkward moment needed—fish jizz.

One side of his mouth tilted upward. "We definitely won't name the baby Milt, then."

She tensed, looking around at the crowd of strangers. "Have you told anyone on the team?"

"Only Petrov and Christensen, who are here somewhere." He scanned the crowd, obviously looking for the men. "They're idiots, but they're family and—" He let out a harsh groan and a mumbled curse. "They brought their karaoke machine. This is not going to end well."

"Why?" Following his gaze, she spotted the two hockey players carrying a seriously big karaoke set up the steps leading to the DJ booth on the stage.

"They both have this nasal twang whistle thing when they sing," Cole said. "I mean, with one person it's bad enough, but with two people who sound like mirror images of each other, it's just… Oh God, we gotta cut this off or everyone will run away before this thing really starts and the charity won't raise any money."

He slipped his hand into hers and pulled her forward into the crowd, acting as the point of the arrow as they zipped around groups and hustled through the ebbs and flows of people packed into the ballroom—the whole time Cole offering hellos and how ya doings to every other person until they got to the stage. Normally, this many strangers—to be honest, this many opportunities to do a speed round of did-you-know random facts and general weirdo knee-jerk responses to having to be around new people—would have overwhelmed her, especially without the added backup of having her girls with her. None of it seemed to matter when she was with Cole, though; it was like she was safe at home.

Of course, that realization hit right as he let go of her hand and made a leap up onto the stage, startling the DJ and cutting off his friends before they could get to their target.

Her jaw dropped as she tried to figure out if she was in too deep with him to get away in one piece. Short answer? Nope. Long answer? What in the fuck had she been thinking? This was a fucking disaster.

And proof of the truth of it just walked in the ballroom. Tall, easy smile on her face, and her attention focused on the men on the stage, Marti Peppers looked like she belonged here. No doubt because she did, unlike Tess.

So while he did the quick maneuvering needed to save the DJ the unenviable task of telling Ian Petrov and Alex Christensen that they couldn't karaoke sing their way through the entire ABBA greatest hits album, she took a few quick breaths and tried to imagine if tonight had been for real in a forever kind of way as opposed to a just-for-now temporary truth. Hand on her belly, rubbing soft circles over the spot where their baby was, she let that sense of belonging, of permanence fill her from her toes to her probably-need-to-be-waxed eyebrows. It was more intoxicating than a shot of tequila on an empty stomach.

"You doing okay?" Ian asked, hopping down from the stage while Cole walked Alex and the karaoke machine down the stairs leading from the DJ to the dance floor. "Do you need to sit down? Water?"

"Thanks, but I'm okay," she said, grateful for the kindness but unable to look away from Cole.

"He's a good guy, you know," Ian said, jerking his chin toward Cole. "Always takes care of his responsibilities. You don't have to worry."

Responsibilities. That was the reminder she needed of the reality of the situation. It's all she was to him, an accidental obligation. She'd been here before, too many times, with one drop-off at a relative's home or another. That creeping demon who told her that she'd always just exist on the fringes of a family but never actually be a part of one crawled right up her spine and whispered in her ear. That asshole never let her just enjoy the moment. And when Cole stopped at the bottom of the steps to talk to Marti, it got louder. Then, when Cole smiled at the other woman like she was the most fascinating person in the world, that demon started shouting one word over and over. "Temporary."

. . .

In the usual way of Cole's world, talking with Marti would have taken priority over nearly anything that didn't involve hockey skates. Those short conversations a few months after a breakup were always what led to getting back together again until the next breakup. It was their pattern. It wasn't the healthiest, sure, but it was the way Cole's life worked until Tess had gotten him to throw that trivia game.

Now, all he could do was keep sneaking peeks over Marti's shoulders at Tess, who was talking with Petrov—a man he used to like a helluva lot more than he did at that moment, when just seeing the other man smile at Tess was enough to make Cole's stomach churn.

Testosterone caveman much, Phillips?

Yeah, he was an asshole. This was a now well-established fact.

"Good call on saving all of us from having to hear a Petrov and Christensen duet. I think I'll make an extra donation in your name as a thank-you." Marti grinned at him, looking him over from head to toe with an appraising but not hey-baby gleam in her eyes. "How have you been, anyway? It's been forever."

For them it had been. He'd spent most of the past ten years talking to Marti even when they were broken up, a habit started when they became friends while Coach Peppers taught Cole's juniors team.

Usually, there was a tangible sense of unease that crawled like ants across his skin when they didn't, but this time that hadn't happened. It was like being weddinged with Tess had been a shock to the system that had jerked him off the usual beaten path.

Still, he waited for that nearly overwhelming anxious sensation that left his entire body buzzing—but it never appeared. Instead, it was a little hum, barely noticeable and more like a memory.

"I'm good," he said, meaning it. "How about you?"

"I've been working on a few things here and there." Marti glanced over at a guy with dark hair who looked like he bench-pressed Volvos and her cheeks flushed.

Cole gave the other guy a harder look, not out of jealousy but because despite everything, Marti was still his friend and always would be. The big guy looked like trouble.

"You aren't going to end up in jail, are you?" he asked, turning back to Marti.

She gave him a wicked grin and winked. "Only if I get caught."

Cole couldn't hold it in anymore. The laugh escaped from him like a dam breaking, pulling the attention of people around them. It was just too ridiculous. The Marti he'd known for years was more likely to turn into Martha Stewart with a killer softball pitching arm than even think about jaywalking, let alone anything really illegal.

"It's kind of crazy how things have turned out for us, huh?" she asked with a sentimental sigh. "Who would have thought? But I'm glad, though. Everything works out the way it needs to when we just open ourselves up to change. So tell me everything about the situation with your adorable date tonight."

How in the world was he supposed to answer that when he wasn't sure himself? "It's complicated."

Marti shrugged a shoulder. "So unravel it."

"You of all people know how difficult that can be. I had my whole life planned out. Play hockey, get drafted, be with you. Now? That seems completely ridiculous—no offense."

She threw back her head and laughed. "None taken—we were each other's mac and cheese. We were comfort food."

It wasn't the analogy he'd have made, but he got where she was coming from. They were used to each other. That was all. "Everything has changed. I'm on the second line, struggling, and Tess is like an entire fireball of change that makes the rest of it look unimportant. She's everything I never expected and definitely never planned for and I don't know how I feel about that."

"Bullshit." Marti jabbed him in the chest with one of her long fingers. "And shame on you if you can't admit that a little shock to the system is exactly what you needed."

Fuck. Why did everyone seem to have a better handle on the situation than he did? "I guess things don't always work out the way we expect."

"Yeah, sometimes they're even better." She glanced back at the big guy who did a very unsubtle chin nod toward the door. "I gotta go, but take some advice from an old friend and put it all out there with this one. Don't miss your chance just because change wasn't part of your daily routine."

But missing his chance was exactly what he did for the rest of the evening. It seemed like the fates were conspiring against him, sending every other player on the Ice Knights to dance with Tess while he ended up taking an endless number of selfies with fans who had donated warm coats to the city's homeless shelters. Normally he didn't mind that part of his job—especially when they were all there to help such a great charity—but it took what seemed like forever for him to get back to Tess.

She was on the dance floor with Christensen of all

people, who was holding her a little too close. The other man's fingertips resting just above the curve of Tess's ass had Cole tensing, and he was on the dance floor tapping on the forward's shoulder before he could even process the thought that he needed to get over there.

"No cuts, Phillips," Christensen said with a smirk. "You left your girl alone, and I'm entertaining her with stories of my many daring exploits."

Tess snorted and shook her head. "He's telling me how he got caught stealing women's underwear when he was twelve."

"I was dared to do it!" Christensen said. "It wasn't like some perv move. Plus, I got caught and they called my mom." He shook his head. "There is nothing scarier than having my pissed-off single mom having to cut out of work early to come to store security and pick my scrawny self up for being a dumb-ass."

Cole looked over at Tess. Her cheeks had turned a little pink and she was gnawing on her bottom lip. Shit. Adding to her worries about impending motherhood was very much not on his to-do list. Fucking Christensen. Acting purely on the need to turn her thoughts back to a better place, he all but hip-checked Christensen out of the way and led Tess farther onto the dance floor.

He pulled her against him so they fit perfectly, his hand resting lightly on the small of her back, and dipped his head down to her ear. "You won't have to do it on your own."

She let out a sigh. "I know you feel obligated, but—"

"That's not how I'd describe it." Obligation was pretty much at the bottom of his list at the moment. At the top? Wanting to make life as good for her as possible. Of course, getting her out of this disco outfit was pretty close to the top, too. What could he say? He was an asshole.

"Oh really?" She rolled her eyes. "A baby just fit perfectly into your ready-made plans?"

She had him there, but his plans were changing, evolving, becoming more flexible. "No, but—"

"Okay, folks," the DJ interrupted. "It's time for the disco dance-off. Who is ready to get their Bee Gees on?"

Tess's gaze skittered from one part of the room to another without landing on him. She was ready to make a break for it and damn his selfish soul, he couldn't let her go.

Cole raised his hand and hollered out, "We are."

"No way," she said, her eyes huge behind her glasses.

"Come on, be spontaneous with me." Sure, it felt weird, kinda like putting on someone else's skates or using the wrong color tape on his stick, but he was willing to push out of his mac and cheese comfort zone for her.

Tess narrowed her eyes and gave him a hard look. "Who are you and what have you done with Cole Phillips?"

"Dance with me and find out."

She hesitated, but only for the first two beats of the song. "Did you know the Bee Gees tried to change their name to Rupert's World?"

He released the breath he hadn't realized he was holding. "That is a trash band name. You ready to do this?"

She nodded, and that was all the encouragement he needed. They hustled and did the pointy-finger-up-in-the-air move and he spun her around—all of it as if they'd been dancing together for years. And when Coach Peppers came around with the charity CEO and handed Cole and Tess the trophy that looked like a disco ball, Tess's smile was back in place and her two-colored eyes were bright and sparkly. He hadn't made that change happen, but he'd helped, and he'd never felt more like he'd conquered the world—not even when the Ice Knights won the cup.

Tess and the baby had never played into his well-thought-out plans before, but now he couldn't imagine home without them. And it wasn't just making them part of his normal routine. It was more. He was falling for her. Hard.

He was still riding high when they walked into the house and found what looked like an explosion of toilet paper in the otherwise perfectly clean and organized hallway. Kahn sped by in the middle of having the zoomies with a streamer of toilet paper stuck to the claws on one of his back paws, jumped onto a console table, and—while maintaining perfect eye contact with them—took a swipe at the playbook. It slid over the side and hit the floor in just the right way that the clasps holding the pages opened and paper went everywhere.

"Oh my God, I'm so sorry." Tess hurried over and grabbed Kahn before the pissed-off kitty could make a break for it. "I guess the good news is that we'll be out of your hair soon. I can move back into my apartment."

A kick in the balls would have felt better. An illegal check from behind that sent him sprawling into the boards would have been less of a shock to his system. Everything stopped for him—his heart, his breath, his fucking world—and for once he had no plan, no spin move, no guidance on what to do when he'd embraced change and the change told him she was moving out.

"And you want to do that?" he asked, wishing like hell that her answer would be no.

"Of course—this was just temporary." Her hand went to her belly as she magically managed to hold onto the squirming kitten in her other arm. "Let me get Kahn locked up in my room, and then I'll get this mess cleaned up."

"Don't worry about it. I got it. I want to take care of things and put them back in order." For her. He wanted to do that for her, but he couldn't let that part out, not with her leaving.

Her bottom lip trembled and Kahn let out a meow of protest as if her grip had tightened. "Of course." Her lips curled upward, but it wasn't a smile so much as it was a faulty mask. "I'll just get out of your way. Good night."

His gut dropped and he clenched his fists. He'd said the wrong thing. "Tess…"

But nothing came out after her name, and he had no idea what should, so when her steps didn't falter but actually sped up, he shut his mouth and watched her walk away.

Chapter Eighteen

"I shouldn't have come," Tess said as she looked around the Ice Knights family suite at the arena between the first and second period during the next day's afternoon home game. It was filled with the people who had actual ties to the players, wives, girlfriends, boyfriends, family members. There was even a three-year-old running around with a giant glob of jelly doughnut on her chin. "I don't belong here."

"Why not?" Fallon asked as she handed Tess a bottled water and then popped the top off her own beer.

"This is for families," she said. "That's not me."

Fallon shot her a smile. "It will be."

"Cole and I aren't together." And he didn't want them to be. He'd made that perfectly clear last night when he said he just wanted to get everything back in order.

Message sent. Message received.

Her best friend gave her a you're-so-full-of-it look of disbelief. "So you keep saying."

She was saved from having to respond by the puck drop. The first line was on the ice, a guy by the name of Hedrick taking Cole's usual spot against the hated Cajun Rage. The Ice Knights were down by one when the coach called for a line switch and Cole hopped over the boards.

Tess's chest clenched the moment his skates touched the ice.

God, he was amazing out there, skating and weaving through the other team's players like he didn't just see them but as if he could anticipate where they were going to be. It was the new plays. He was running them as if he'd always been doing so.

And if she could breathe while she watched, she would have been able to appreciate the beauty of getting to watch a man at peak physical condition do the one thing he'd trained for all his life.

She jumped up from her seat, the unopened water bottle clutched close to her chest as he zoomed toward the goal, all dangerous grace and feral determination. He pulled back his stick to send the puck flying toward the net and right before he made contact, a Rage defenseman came practically out of nowhere and slammed into Cole, sending him straight into the boards.

In an instant, everyone in the family box was on their feet screaming for a penalty, but Tess couldn't get any sound out. Cole was still facedown on the ice, unmoving. Each thump of her heart was like a battering ram against her ribs as she watched the other players skate over to him, circling him. A heavy silence slammed down when the team doctor rushed onto the ice, as if the rest of the world had stopped existing. Hand on her belly, Tess stood there watching, helpless as a sickening dread seeped into her, making it hard to stand, or breathe, or do anything except stare at the man she loved despite knowing she shouldn't as he lay still on the ice.

Fallon slid her arm around Tess's waist, anchoring her as she watched Cole on the Jumbotron waiting for any hand motion or jerk of his foot—anything to show he was going to be okay. There was nothing.

Her lungs ached from not taking in any air. Her entire body was shaking. Everything, her entire world, collapsed down to one man.

"Tess," Fallon said, her voice sounding distant even though she was right next to her. "Are you okay?"

"Garden worms have five pairs of hearts," she said, the words tumbling out as she stared at that giant screen. "A rhino horn is made of keratin." Her voice was getting louder, higher pitched as the panic roared through her while a gurney was rolled out onto the ice. "There are twenty-two bones in the human skull." She sucked in a ragged breath, trying to bury the howl just under the surface as Cole lay on the cold ice as still as death. "Cumulonimbus clouds can form tornadoes."

And one was building in her, violently whirling around and shrieking, slamming against every part of her as her attention remained glued to the image of an unresponsive Cole as panic screamed through her.

Temporary. Everything was temporary.

Fallon jerked Tess around so she couldn't see the Jumbotron and yanked her close. Tess didn't cry, she didn't let loose with the scream building inside her, she just stood there shaking and praying as Fallon held her tight.

Please God, let him be okay. Just let him be okay.

She could have stood there for another minute or ten or a million listening to the blood rushing in her ears and praying but finally, clap by clap, the cheers of the Ice Knights fans in the arena broke through. Turning her head back to the ice, she watched as they wheeled Cole off the ice and he lifted his arm and gave the crowd a thumbs-up. The other Ice Knights players whacked their sticks on the boards in front of their bench and even some of the Rage players, too, as he disappeared down the tunnel leading to the locker room.

"It's gonna be okay," Fallon said, taking a step back. "He's hard as nails. He'll be just fine."

Tess collapsed into her chair, suddenly so weary that even holding her head up was a epic challenge.

"Speak to me, Tess."

Unclenching her body, muscle by muscle, like she'd done during that nap with Cole, she took in a deep breath before letting it out. "Inanna is the Sumerian goddess of love, fertility, and war. It's kind of appropriate that they put those three things together, don't you think?"

"Why's that?" Fallon asked.

"Because they're all scary as shit." And that was the God's honest truth.

Temporary had always been her mantra, her constant in a swirling world. She was ready for the rest of the world to come and go but not Cole—and that hit her square in the face, a hard slap of reality. She loved him.

"Come on." Fallon held out her hands. "Let's go down to the locker room. You need to see him."

"He's fine," Tess said, her voice strained and tight as the possibilities of what could have happened to him out on the ice continued to ripple through her. "He'll be fine. You said so yourself."

"Tess." Fallon held out her hand. "Let's go."

A security guard waiting outside the suite walked them through the twisting back tunnels leading from the upper-level suites down to the locker room. Every once in a while, the cheers of the crowd could be heard as the game went on, but the sound barely penetrated for Tess. It was all a numb haze.

When they got to the locker room, Fallon pointed to the treatment room beyond the coach's office. "Do you want me to go with you?"

Tess shook her head. "I need to go myself."

This was a new world, uncharted territory. She needed to see him, touch him, talk to him, and make sure the man she'd fallen in love with was okay. By the time she quietly opened the glass door to the treatment room, Cole was sitting up on the table. His helmet and gloves were off and his mouth twisted into a grimace as the doctor flashed a light into his eyes. The moment she saw him, all the numbness faded away and the tears she hadn't realized she'd been holding back came cascading down her cheeks, hot and unwanted.

He was okay.

"I was only out for a second," he grumbled. "You were the one who told me not to move. I'll be fine, Doc."

The sound of his voice, even as raw and full of pain as it was, was like a cool breeze on a humid August day—a total and unexpected relief, and she sank against the doorframe to catch her breath, relief seeping through her. Three deep breaths and she'd have herself under control and ready to go out there, wrap her arms around him, and tell him she was there for him. Tonight. Always.

Marti burst into the room from another door, rushing over to him and taking his hand in hers and lifting it to her mouth for a quick brush of her lips across his knuckles. "Oh my God, are you okay, Cole?"

"It's nothing." Cole practically growled out the words.

The doctor let out a snort of disgust. "That is a different way to pronounce minor concussion, but I just went to the best medical school in the country, so what would I know?"

Marti reached out and took Cole's hand while the doctor continued his exam, the fact that they cared for each other was obvious as the smell of Icy Hot in the air. Tess took a step back, letting the door fall shut in silence, unable to look away but unable to move forward, either.

How many times growing up had she watched from the outside as a similar intimate scene played out? Her aunt Suzy bandaging up her cousin's knee and then giving it a kiss. Her uncle Arnie sharing a knowing look with Aunt Zoe after an inside joke. Her younger cousin Sherice curling up on her mom's lap even though at ten, she barely fit anymore.

Observing those moments while standing around the corner just out of sight had hurt, but nothing like this. Those times had been like a mosquito bite compared to the bone-deep pain of seeing Cole with Marti. This was true intimacy, a connection, something more than a sense of responsibility or obligation. This was what she'd always wanted and had never had. Her love wasn't temporary, but it also wasn't returned. He'd never promised her forever, but like a fool, she'd let herself start to imagine it anyway. Taking a step back and then another and another until she couldn't see Cole anymore, she broke inside all over again.

The hurt, too raw and fresh to cover, must have shined off her face because the second she turned the corner and found Fallon standing in the hall outside the locker room, her friend rushed over.

"Oh my God," Fallon said, grabbing her by both shoulders and pulling her in close. "Is he okay? What can I do? What do you need?"

What did she need? She needed Cole, but that wasn't going to happen. They'd been weddinged, had one amazing night together and a few weeks of playing pretend. It wasn't real. It was just temporary. How many times had she told him that? If only she'd listened to her own words. She returned Fallon's hug, took a deep breath, and stepped back, every primal instinct telling her one thing and one thing only—run before she got hurt worse.

"I have to get out of here," she said, holding on to her control by a frayed thread. "Now. I need to go pack up my things."

Fallon cocked her head. "But why? I don't under—"

Tess held up her hand, silencing her friend who she knew only meant well, but each question sliced open a different part of her soft underbelly. "Please."

No doubt there was more Fallon wanted to say, questions she wanted to ask, but she didn't, and Tess let out a relieved sigh as they made their way through the back halls and out of the arena. She'd been on borrowed time with Cole and she'd pretended that wasn't the case. It was past time she stopped.

. . .

Cole had been an asshole for thinking Tess would show up to check on him. Really, it had been better that she hadn't. Nothing proved that his routine and standard operating procedures were superior like the double tap of "hey stupid" he'd taken tonight.

First the hit that sent him flying into the boards and out cold because instead of listening to his on-ice awareness warnings that a freight train was coming, he'd stuck to the new plays Coach Peppers had been pushing. And what had it gotten him? A slight concussion and the news that he wouldn't even get to sit on the bench again until the doc had cleared him.

That had been bad, but the second blow had hit harder because it was delivered via ghosting. After she'd peeked in on him, he'd sent Marti looking for Tess because there was no one he needed to see, to hold onto and remind himself he was still all there than the woman who'd shaken his world right down to its seven-hundred-and-sixty-mile-radius iron core. It was security who told him that she'd left the building. She hadn't stopped in to check on him first. She hadn't left a message with the others in the family box. She hadn't even texted or left a voicemail. Everything—his head, his shoulder, the fucking hole in his chest—had stopped hurting after that because he stopped feeling anything.

"You sure you're going to be okay?" Marti asked as she stopped her car in front of his house. "You're not supposed to be alone tonight."

He glanced over at the VW Beetle in his driveway, the cheerfulness of the long eyelashes on the headlights seeming to mock him. "I'll be fine."

"Do you want me to come in?" she asked. "Get you settled?"

Marti was trying to be nice, he knew, but it didn't change the bone-deep frustration making every one of his words come out like a punch. "I said, I'm fine."

So why was he still standing on his front porch, door half open when the security gate clicked shut behind Marti's car? Because he was a giant liar. He wasn't fine—he wasn't even close—and it had nothing to do with the concussion.

Man the fuck up, Phillips, and go inside your own damn house.

He took a deep breath and followed his own advice, walking inside and stopping in front of the ugly-ass Bigfoot painting hanging above the table where he always left his keys. Despite everything, the stupid thing made him smile. It always did. There was so much sparkly ridiculousness painted onto the twenty-by-twenty-four-inch canvas that it was nearly impossible not to grin. He'd have to find a new spot for it, somewhere Tess wouldn't be expecting it, and maybe it would make her smile, too.

"Kahn, here kitty, kitty." Tess walked out from the kitchen into the hallway, spotted him, and jerked to a stop. "You're here."

"It *is* my house." And up until she'd told him in his driveway that he was going to be a dad, it had been his refuge. The one place where things always stayed the same and made sense. Chaos ended at his front door—at least it used to.

She clasped her hands, her knuckles turning white as she clamped her jaws together hard enough that it squared the shape of her face. "I thought they'd make you stay overnight at a hospital for observation."

"I declined." Which had gone over about as well as expected, but he needed to see Tess more than he needed to be looked after by a nurse.

And now that he had? The gaping invisible hole in his chest was still there, still screaming in agony.

She didn't move, could barely look at him. "You shouldn't be alone."

The fact that she wasn't offering hit him square in the kidneys. "You going somewhere?"

At that question, she did look up, her eyes bright behind her glasses and her chin angled up a few degrees higher than necessary. "Home."

"And I take it that's not here." Where she'd been living. Where he wanted her to stay living.

"No." She shook her head, her gold curls swaying with the movement drawing his attention even as the rest of her all but shouted for him to stay away. "This was only—"

"Temporary," he finished for her, the single word like razor blades on his tongue.

Silence as solid and subtle as concrete landed between them. God, it hurt. It fucking wrecked him, scraping him raw. This was what happened with change? With leaving behind his usual process? Well, fuck that. He didn't need it, not any of it. He'd be better on his own at home and making the same plays on the ice as he always had. It's what he knew.

"You should get off your feet," Tess said, breaking the unnatural quiet. "Do you need water? Aspirin? What can I do to help?"

A day ago, that list would have been miles long and all consisted of the same damn thing: stay. Now? There wasn't a damn thing she could do for him besides wreck the sense of settled certainty he'd built his life around.

"I don't suppose you can magically make it so that I'm back on the first line and get Coach to can his ridiculous idea that I need to learn how to play differently?" he asked, not even bothering to try to keep the skate-sharp edge out of his tone.

Tess took a step forward, arms outstretched toward him, before seeming to realize what she was doing, coming to a halt, and lowering her arms awkwardly. "I'm sure he's only trying to make you a better player. I know it's hard, but—"

"You know?" He let out a bark of a laugh filled with the icy anger surging through him. "How in the hell would you know that when all you fucking do is run away? That is what you're doing right now, isn't it? Running?"

Her cheeks flushed. "You're full of shit."

"If believing that helps you sleep at night, then who am I to dissuade you?"

"That's rich coming from a man who can't accept that things move on, that change is inevitable."

"I'm not an idiot," he snarled. "I know that. I also know that when things are working, you don't fuck with them. My routines work. They've gotten me this far."

"Where's that?" she shot back, stalking forward, her moves jerky and stiff with fury. "On the second line with a coach breathing down your neck that you need to improve your game and still in love with the same on-again, off-again girlfriend who you've been dating since the dawn of time?"

It was a good shot—fuck that, it was a great shot, one that slid right between the pipes so fast and hard that he'd barely had time to see it coming before the red goal light was flashing. "You don't know a damn thing about what you're saying."

"It's a good thing I'm out of here, then, as soon as I find

Kahn," Tess said.

Her words were final but there was a shake to them, a tremble that sliced through all the anger to the vulnerable center of him. But he didn't call out to her when she whirled around and marched through the house, but she didn't find the kitten. No matter how much she called or where she looked as Cole sat on the couch and watched, Satan's little fur ball never showed his fuzzy butt.

Standing in the doorway between the living room and the hall, a duffel bag slung over one shoulder and a suitcase at her feet, she looked at him and sighed. "I can stay tonight so you're not alone, make sure you're okay."

"I'll be fine." Something in the sympathetic look in her eyes now that all her anger seemed to have burned away made his gut twist, and he lashed out. "All I really need in my life is to go back to what it was. Anyway, Marti is coming back in a few minutes." The lie came out smooth and easy. "She just needed to grab a few things from her house before she could spend the night. What's between her and me? It's anything but temporary."

Tess flinched, his shot landing with a force he immediately regretted. Fuck, he was an asshole. He shouldn't have said it, but he was still flush with an angry heat, his head pounding and his chest aching. He was in fucking agony and he wasn't going to be the only one in it.

Pursing her lips together, she closed her eyes for a beat before opening them and staring at him with a cool neutrality. "When Kahn comes out of whatever hiding spot he's in, please let me know and I'll come get him."

He nodded, not trusting himself to say anything at this point because if he opened his mouth, all that would come out would be him begging her to stay, and he'd be damned if he did that. She wanted to go? Good.

Tess nodded, more to herself than to him. "I'll text you

about the next doctor's appointment if you want to go." She looked around, her bottom lip quivering. "Until then."

Then she walked out of his living room, his house, and his life. And he let her go because it was past time he got back to his usual routine, the way he'd always planned for his life to work out.

And finally everything was perfect, so fucking perfect that he was grinding his teeth to powder as her taillights disappeared into the night.

Chapter Nineteen

That damn kitten was somewhere in his house. The clues were all there the next morning. The shredded paper towels in the kitchen, the scattered Xbox games on the coffee table, and the sad little mewling from the end of the hallway where the evil fur ball sat in front of Tess's bedroom door and glared at Cole as if all of this was his fault.

"I didn't tell her to go. She didn't want to be here," he said, keeping his words soft and steady as he inched toward Kahn. "Now, stay right there and I'll take you to her."

The kitten watched Cole approach, his tail flicking with impatience and annoyance.

Oh yeah, you're put out, are you, devil cat? You're not the one tiptoeing like a cartoon villain down your own stupid hallway.

Kahn tilted his head to the side as if he could understand Cole's thoughts.

"That's right. Stay right there."

He reached out. The kitten started. And the closest he ended up to catching the cat was a brush of silky fur across his fingertips before Kahn scurried down the hallway as if Satan himself was on his tail.

"Kahn," he hollered, the name a cry in the otherwise silent house, but the kitten was gone.

Like Tess, the kitten didn't want to have a damn thing to do with him.

Cole sank down onto his ass and leaned his back against Tess's door, making sure to use extra caution when it came to resting his head against the wood and letting his eyelids drift downward. God, he was exhausted, like bone-deep-weary, triple-overtime exhausted. He'd set his alarms last night so he'd woken up every hour on the hour and then, at the doctor's insistence, he'd texted the doc. Of course, the doctor thought that it was Tess texting him, not Cole.

It wasn't just the fucked-up sleep schedule that had him feeling as if he was part zombie, though. It wasn't even a small part of it. The real reason was because of the woman who wasn't behind the door, the one who'd jostled his entire world—shaking it like a snow globe—and then had walked out.

"What do you get for changing things up?" He let out a sigh and opened his eyes, his gaze falling on Tess's Bigfoot painting. "Kicked down to the second line, a concussion, and a gaping empty space in your chest."

God. He sounded like an angsty emo teenager drunk for the first time on wine spritzers.

Someone pounded on his front door. "Hey, Phillips," Petrov yelled. "Open up, you dumb-ass."

Great. Visitors (and he knew Christensen had to be there, too) were pretty much the last thing he wanted when he was having a fucking amazing time sitting in his hall feeling sorry for himself. The center continued to hammer away on the door because fate just loved to tell him that he was wrong. Cole got up and ambled over to it, mumbling a string of curses to himself.

"We know you're alone," Christensen hollered. "You better not be fucking dead or unconscious."

Cole flipped the dead bolt and opened the door. "And if I was, would I be opening the door?"

"Coach is going to have your ass if he finds out you stayed by yourself last night," Christensen said, giving him an assessing once-over before barging inside without asking if he could come in and heading straight for the kitchen—of course.

"How in the hell did you two knuckleheads know?" Was his damn house bugged?

"Tess told Fallon who told Blackburn that Marti was staying with you. He knew that was bullshit because unlike you, he's not a total idiot. He called me and said to come over and find out if you were still breathing or if we needed to kill you ourselves," Petrov said as he strolled in, his attention on the ugly painting. "What in the hell is that?"

Cole's gut twisted. "Tess painted it."

Petrov lifted an eyebrow. "And you hung it here where everyone could see it?"

"She did. It was a..." Fuck, how in the hell did he explain flirting via moving a painting to Petrov and Christensen without sounding like a total idiot? *You don't, you moron.* "It doesn't matter."

"When did you get a cat?" Christensen yelled from the kitchen. "And why is it looking at me like it's plotting my death?"

"Obviously it has good taste," Petrov shot back.

For the first time since his head smacked down on the ice, Cole cracked a smile. He did more than that—he laughed loud, like a man who'd just remembered he could.

"Oh fuck," Christensen said, poking his head out of the kitchen and eyeballing Cole warily. "Your brain's totally broken. You're laughing."

He flipped off the other man and walked into the kitchen, which looked exactly like it should—except for the two uninvited hockey players lounging against his counters like they owned the place.

"It happens. I laugh." He stopped in front of the fridge and stared up at Kahn, who had situated himself on top of it so close to the edge, he looked like a fuzzy gargoyle. "Now, help me get Tess's kitten down so I can take him to her apartment."

"She isn't coming back?" Petrov asked.

Cole's jaw tightened and some invisible force squeezed his lungs tight. "Why would she?" He tried for a nonchalant shrug that felt stiff and awkward. "The repairs on her apartment are done. This arrangement was just temporary."

Christensen and Petrov exchanged a who-in-the-fuck-does-he-think-he's-fooling look as if he wasn't there to see it.

"And you're okay with that?" Christensen asked.

"Why wouldn't I be?" Another shrug, this one a little smoother. "Now, help me get this damn kitten."

He reached up toward the top of the fridge only to have Kahn gracefully leap up to the top of the cabinets, where he sat down and sent a hiss Cole's way before starting to clean his paws.

"You're fine with Tess leaving, huh?" Petrov rolled his eyes. "There is a motherfucking painting of Bigfoot hanging in your hall." He kept his focus on the kitten as he moved to the right of the cabinets, automatically taking a zone defense position. "It's the only thing in this whole place that isn't light brownish tan or whatever they call that color your decorator approved."

Cole took a step forward, and Kahn started toward the opposite end of the cabinets. "It was a joke."

"Oh yeah?" Christensen kept his position as the kitten approached, hands at the ready to swipe the cat out of midair when it jumped, but his gaze cut to Cole. "So you don't care if one of us takes it down and trashes it?"

Cole flinched. It was small, barely noticeable, but he'd done it. Why? Because he would tear apart whoever touched that damn painting to the fucking bone marrow unless it was Tess.

"Go ahead." He moved forward, closing the circle of open space around the cat so that he, Petrov, and Christensen formed a tight triangle. "I don't care."

Without a word, Petrov broke ranks, turned, and started toward the hall.

Panic shot through Cole with breakaway speed. "Leave it be."

The center turned, a knowing smirk on his face. "Again, why isn't she coming back?"

Cole looked from one of the men to the other, his stomach sinking like he'd just caused the mother of all turnovers on the blue line that resulted in an overtime loss. Neither Petrov nor Christensen looked away. There would be no squirming out of this, no brushing them off. They were here to call him on his shit.

He let out a sigh. "I said some stuff. I mean she said stuff first, but…" His words trailed off, the excuse sounding lame even to his own ears. "I told her Marti was coming over to watch me last night because I knew she wanted to go and just needed an excuse to do it because of the concussion. I wasn't going to have pity keep her here."

"When did this happen?" Petrov asked, getting back into cat-catching position.

"Last night." He shoved his fingers through his hair, the tangles making his fingers catch. "Right out of the blue. Everything had been going great."

"You mean it happened right after she saw you sprawled out on the ice looking like a dead man in skates and pads?" Christensen asked, giving him an are-you-really-that-stupid shake of his head.

"What does that have to do with it?" He was fine. Sure, it had probably looked like he was ready for a pine box, but he'd been alert—for most of it—and he was a little dinged up but otherwise fine.

Petrov inched closer to the cat. "Well, what did she say to you in the locker room?"

"Nothing." He readied himself as Kahn flicked his tail and surveyed the escape possibilities. "She never came down."

Christensen snorted. "That's not what I heard."

Cole was trying to process that when Kahn made his move, leaping off the wall cabinets with a perfect trajectory for the kitchen island. The cat, however, hadn't been expecting the quick reflexes of a professional athlete. Cole swiped the cat out of midair, catching him like a puck that had shot up from the ice. Kahn was about as happy at the results as a pissed-off opposing defenseman. Of course, hockey players rarely sank their claws into someone like Kahn did to Cole as soon as he tucked the ticked-off kitty close to his chest.

"Now, can you interfering assholes drop me off at Tess's place so I can hand over Kahn?" he asked, glaring at the other men.

For once, the pair of them didn't argue or make any smart remarks. Sure, they gave each other that stupid he's-a-moron look as if he wasn't standing right there again, but what the fuck did he care? They hustled out of the house as Kahn's caterwauling protests echoed in the near-empty hall. He didn't stop until they were all packed into Petrov's truck.

"Want us to wait for you there?" Petrov asked as he started the engine.

"Nah." He grimaced as Kahn found a new place on his arm to play pincushion. "I'll Uber back."

"Hoping to swing a little come-home-baby move?" Christensen asked, sounding less like the player he was and more like a guy who had his fingers crossed.

"Not in the least." The words came out strong and fast, confident, as if he meant them—which he did. Really. Mostly. Almost. "We're going to be parents together, nothing more. It's all there ever was."

And he'd been an asshole to think there ever could be a different outcome.

"As much as I hate to agree with Christensen, I think he's right," Petrov said, disgust thick in his tone. "Your brain is broken."

Kahn sank his claws into a fresh slice of flesh.

"Just shut up and drive before Satan's fuzziest demon scars me for life," Cole snarled.

Tess had been more than clear about what she wanted (her cat) and didn't want (him). Fine. Good. Perfect. He had had enough of his usual routine being messed with, and he was done trying new things. It was past time he went back to being the man he had been before that wedding—and he didn't need to have his brain bounce against his skull again to figure that out.

• • •

Tess wasn't moping. She wasn't. She was very determinedly staring at the slapdash patching of her ceiling and trying to figure out what to do today, since the flower shop was closed, her friends were with their significant others, and her kitten had abandoned her.

No, she wasn't thinking about Cole.

She wasn't wondering how he was feeling, or whether he needed help, or if he just wanted someone to crawl in bed with him and tell him made-up stories about Bigfoot. That kind of thinking would get her nowhere and she knew it. Whenever leaving a house that had been a temporary home, the best thing was just to put it behind her and never think about how it had felt to be part of a real family.

Chin wobbly, she dropped her hand to her belly and circled her palm softly over that spot that would be getting bigger and bigger during the next few months. It was fine. She'd create her own family and would do everything she could to make sure the little peanut growing inside her would never wonder if she or he was wanted. They would just grow up knowing it.

The knock on the door startled her out of her thoughts, and she roused herself off the bed and went to answer it. Cole stood on the other side, a large fresh scratch across his cheek and a squirming Kahn in his arms. The kitten took one look at her, let out a mournful mewling sound, did the magic liquid trick cats do to free themselves, then sprang free and sprinted into her apartment where he curled up on the couch and started to purr.

They stood there just staring at each other. The silence should have felt weird. It didn't. It was more of a prelude than a pause. It gave her time to take him in, look for any kind of fuzziness in his gaze or evidence from the concussion. All that she saw, though, was the angry scratch that had to be from Kahn and a man who made her heart stutter stop. It wasn't just the Not-Thor broad-shouldered hotness of him, it was more. It was everything.

He worked his jaw back and forth for a second, his gaze going up to the ceiling for a beat before landing back on her. "We never got to have that bar trivia night."

Was there a German word for nostalgia for something that hadn't happened? There should be, because that's exactly what was coursing through her right now. Loss for what could have been, but she was going to handle it like a grown-up. Suck it up. Be an adult.

Swallowing past the emotion—fucking hormones and

heartbreak—she managed to curl her lips in what she hoped looked like a smile. "We would have killed it."

"Yeah."

"Do you want to come in?"

Damn. She hadn't meant to ask that. It came out as automatically as her awk-weird fact verbal explosion. And when he clamped his lips together, the muscles of his jaw tightening, it took everything she had not to just shut the door on Cole and pretend he wasn't standing on the other side of the threshold.

"Sure." He nodded. "Let me check out the new ceiling."

He came in, seemingly at ease in her brightly decorated apartment with its plethora of knickknacks, pillows, and snarky tea towels hanging from almost every drawer pull in her kitchen nook. While she was an internal wreck of emotions and pheromones popping up everywhere inside her like wildflowers, he was as cool and unbothered as he always was. It wasn't fair. Then again, when was life ever fair?

They walked into her bedroom, the bed still unmade and her clothes from last night in a pile by the open closet door. If he noticed, he didn't say anything. Instead, he walked right up to the edge of her bed and looked up at the ceiling.

"Are they coming back to finish fixing it?" he asked.

"The cosmetic stuff?" She snorted. "Not likely."

"Your landlord is an asshole."

Yeah, that was putting it mildly. "Well, he is my mom's brother, so that makes sense."

He looked back at her, his focus going to her belly. "Have you told your mom yet?"

"I might include it on the annual Christmas card." Or not. Really, was the woman who couldn't be a mom suddenly going to become the world's best grandma? Did she even want to take the chance when the outcome would probably only be silence?

He shoved his hands in his pockets, suddenly looking a bit lost. "I'm sorry."

So was she, but not for what he was talking about. The ache in her chest had nothing to do with her mom or the state of her ceiling or the fact that she seemed to always be looking for her place in this world. It was because of him— correction, it was because she was for all intents and purposes saying goodbye to the man she'd fallen for. Sure, there'd be parenting discussions and custody exchanges but nothing else, and that left a burning hole in her heart. And she'd been such a bitch last night, all because he had his forever constant and it wasn't her.

The muscle in Cole's jaw flexed while he looked at her, really looked at her, and he let out a long breath. "I better get going."

She nodded, watching him turn and start back out of her bedroom. Heat made her cheeks burn as her pulse quickened while she forgot how to breath or think or make her heart beat, the whole world seeming to be balanced on the tip of this moment. He got almost to the door before she couldn't hold it in anymore.

"Baskin Robbins used to sell ketchup-flavored ice cream," she said, the words coming out in a rush.

He paused and turned. "Lois Lane had a younger sister named Lucy."

Tears pricked at the back of her eyes, and she quickly blinked to keep them from falling—not yet, anyway. She could make it until the door closed behind him. She *would* make it that long.

After what seemed like a zillion years but was probably two seconds, she managed to find the ability to speak again. "We really would have been amazing at bar trivia."

"Yeah." He nodded, his entire body tense. "We would have."

Then he was gone, moving at a fast clip out of her

bedroom and into the living room. Before she even had a minute to process it, she heard her front door open and then the final click of it closing behind him.

The urge to collapse back on her bed and let out the sob bubbling up inside her was nearly overwhelming, but she refused to give in. She knew what this was like. She'd been here before. That moment every time when her mom dropped her off at some relative's house with her clothes in a battered rolling suitcase that had been used too often to have ever seen better days.

She'd survived that.

She'd survive this.

Inhaling a deep breath as she stared up at the patchwork mess of her ceiling, she counted to ten slow and steady. Then she let it out and walked into her living room, coming to a dead stop as soon as she entered the room. Cole stood in front of her closed door, his hands clenched, his jaw squared, and a look of yearning so palpable on his face that she almost took a step back.

"I couldn't go," he said, the words coming out harsh and hard. "Not yet."

She rushed forward, looking for signs he was hurt worse than she realized, not stopping until the only thing separating them was an inch of electrified air. "Are you okay?"

"I can't just walk out of here without a goodbye." He reached out, cupping her face with his hand and running the rough pad of his thumb across the line of her jaw.

"You need me to say it?" Her voice shook even as she tried to remain neutral to the heady sparks of want and bittersweet lust that his touch set off. "Goodbye?"

Something dark and desperate flashed in his eyes. "No."

And his mouth was on hers in a demanding kiss that stole her breath and her self-preservation, and she kissed him back like a woman getting her last glimpse of forever.

Chapter Twenty

Cole shouldn't be kissing Tess. It wasn't part of his plan when he'd shown up on her doorstep. It wasn't even close. Yet here he was, trying to tell her everything he couldn't put into words and hoping she'd hear the meaning anyway.

Trailing his lips down her neck, he memorized every soft moan of pleasure she made, the feel of her fingers threaded in his hair holding him close, the way she fit perfectly against him as if they were made for this. It was the sweetest agony and he wanted more but he was only temporary.

Forcing himself to stop, he lifted his head and stared into her eyes, searching for a sign—anything—to let him know what she was thinking. "Tess, do you want me to stop?"

The right side of her mouth lifted up in the smallest of half smiles. "One last time."

It wasn't enough. He wanted more. He wanted forever. But if this was all she was willing to give, he'd take it. He'd remember it all, every breath and move, and lock it away somewhere safe. And when he returned to his usual routine in his house that seemed so empty without her, he'd remember and it would be enough. It would have to be.

He brought his mouth back to hers, pulled her close, and let his palms glide down over her curves to her ass. They were close enough that even daylight couldn't penetrate, but it wasn't enough. There were too many layers between them. He snuck his fingers under the hem of her T-shirt and lifted it inch by inch until it was off.

God, she was beautiful, standing in her jeans and a bra, her glasses askew and desire giving her pale skin a pink flush. He licked and kissed his way across the full roundness of her tits encased in a pale-pink bra. The need to rip it off, play with her nipples, roll them between his fingers, nearly laid him low, but if this was the last time, he planned to take it slow.

Lowering himself to his knees in front of her, he caressed and tasted his way over her growing belly while his hands were busy with the button of her jeans.

"When I get these off you, I want you to spread your legs as wide as you can and brace yourself against the wall."

The pulse point in her throat went into overdrive. "We can go into the bedroom if you want."

"I can't wait that long." He tugged her jeans over her hips and down her legs, desperate need running hot through him. "I need to taste you, lick the sweet, slick folds of your pussy and feel you come on my tongue. Then I'm going to fuck you against the wall, good and hard, until you come again, hard enough to make you remember this for the rest of your life."

He took her by the hips and turned her so her back was to the wall. Then, while kissing his way up her inner thighs, getting oh so close to the apex but never actually reaching it, he lifted one leg and then the other, freeing her from the jeans that had been pooled around her ankles. Down on one knee in front of her and gliding his hands over her smooth skin as she adjusted her position, he took in her belly starting to round, the full heft of her tits, the way she tugged her full bottom lip between her teeth as her eyes closed and her head tilted back whenever he got close to brushing his fingers near her slick folds.

"You're killing me, Cole," she said after one almost touch.

"Do you want me to stop?" He dipped his head down, kissing his way across the soft skin above her tight curls, taking in the heady fragrance of her and the soft lilting sigh of pleasure she made. "Or do you want me to take my fill?"

She let out a shaky groan. "Definitely not the first."

Raising his hands, he used his thumbs to spread her folds open, holding them taut and blowing a teasing breath against her swollen clit. "So say it. Tell me what you want."

"You." She slid her fingers through his hair, cupping his head and urging him closer with the slightest pressure. "Your tongue on me." She tilted her hips toward him. "Your fingers in me. Your cock. All of it." She closed her eyes and let her head fall back against the wall as if it was too much to admit to herself, let alone out loud. "I want all of it."

Every game-sharpened instinct screamed at him to do it, to dive in and feast on her until she came, but he fought it off, needing to give her another chance to turn him away, to change the pace. "Sure you don't want me to take it slow?"

Her eyes snapped open and she looked down at him, her glasses askew on her nose, her curly hair going every which way, and a lazy smile on her lips. "When have we ever done that?"

She was right.

The die had been cast the minute he'd spotted her at that wedding. Her glasses had been smudged and had kept sliding down her nose. It had taken him a minute to realize that she hadn't been talking to herself there on the edge of the dance floor but had been getting every single trivia question right.

Then, there was the way she'd looked at him and dared him to even try to tell her no to throwing the game so the rookies wouldn't have to foot a bar tab that would take a far bigger percentage of their bank account than it would his. He'd fallen for her the minute she'd thrown him under the bus by saying he'd given her the wrong answer.

His world had changed so hard and so fast, he hadn't even realized it. Who the fuck believed that could happen? It certainly hadn't been on his schedule for that day. But then Tess happened and everything changed. And now? Well, he had now, and whatever she wanted, he was going to give her.

Eventually.

First, he kissed her belly, her natural roundness soft under his lips, and then he went lower, taking his time and teasing her with every touch and taste until he was circling his tongue around her swollen, sensitive clit. She shivered in his arms, her grip on his head tightening as he lavished his attention on that one spot, tormenting her with slow pleasures that left her squirming against him, begging for more with her needy moans.

God, was there anything better than having her like this, happy, wild, totally and completely in the moment? He'd won the cup before. He'd had his dreams come true when he was drafted. He'd thrilled at hard-fought victories. This was better because it mattered more, Tess mattered more than the plans he'd made for himself, the schedules he kept, the routines he followed.

He glided the tips of two fingers along her folds as he tongued her, keeping his attention focused on her responses, learning when to go faster, slower, harder, softer. Giving her what she needed so that when he finally slid his fingers inside her, she let out a groan of pleasure and tightened around him.

"Please, Cole," she panted. "Please."

He didn't answer in words—his mouth was busy—but he

did so in actions, pushing her higher and closer to the edge she was so desperate to fall over. And when he sucked her clit and then lapped at it with his tongue while he brushed the sensitive bundle of nerves just inside her opening, her thighs tensed on either side of his head.

"Don't stop," she cried out, rocking her hips and arching her back to change the angle just the slightest bit. "That's it."

As if he would when she was so close, he could feel it in the tension of her body and the desperation in her voice. He rolled his thumb over her clit while still using his tongue, and she went still, a tightness locking her body, and then she came with a harsh moan that made his dick ache with the need to be inside her.

Rolling back on his heels, he kept his hands on her hips, keeping her steady as she slid down the wall until they were eye to eye, catching their breath.

"You turned my legs to jelly," she said, a satisfied smile on her face. "I'm not sure I can stand for the next part."

"Don't worry." He picked her up, drawing her close to his body as he stood and relished the feel of her legs as she tightened them around his waist. "I've got you."

And I always will stayed silent on the tip of his tongue because the truth of it was that he wouldn't—she didn't want that—but he'd have today and he'd have to make that be enough, because he knew there wouldn't be any more. He couldn't stay. If he could have, he would tell Tess everything. He would beg her to come home. He would fuck up everything for her even more than he had already.

She deserved better than that, but if this was all she wanted from him, then he'd give it to her without any regrets.

• • •

Tess's knees were wobbly, her heart sluggish, her brain

buzzing with post-orgasm bliss, and melting into the ground seemed like a distinct possibility—but then she looked at Cole, and the whole world righted itself and everything fell into alignment. Damn the man for making it so easy to love him because that's exactly what this was.

She tightened her legs around his waist and curled her arms around his neck, letting them rest easily on top of his shoulders. "Where are you planning on taking me?"

"Nowhere," he said, his hands cupping her ass and pulling her against him. "I'm not sure I could even wait until I'm across the room to bury myself inside you."

"We've got a slight problem, then."

"Oh yeah?" Cole asked, the blue of his eyes turning dark with desire. "What's that?"

She dipped her gaze down from his face. "You still have all your clothes on."

Laughing during sexy times wasn't always appreciated, but when Cole's face went from baby-I'm-gonna-do-you-right-here to are-you-fucking-kidding-me in a heartbeat, she couldn't help herself. She threw back her head and laughed.

"I guess I got distracted by the crazy-hot naked woman," he said, joining in on her amusement.

"So you're going to have to put me down to fix this."

He raised an eyebrow. "Is that a challenge?" He adjusted his stance so his left leg held their combined weight and flicked off one shoe, repositioned, and then did the same with the other. "Hold tight."

She clutched his shoulders and hooked her ankles together. "You're not gonna…"

"Yes I am." He let go of her.

A few heartbeats and a few body shifts later and she heard the unmistakable sound of a zipper lowering. Then he shoved his jeans down and kicked them off.

"You doing okay?"

She glanced down his back to his high and round naked ass. "More than okay."

"Then keep holding on."

He reached behind his head and grabbed the neck of his T-shirt, pulling it upward so it went over his head and hung between them, his arms still in it.

Wrapping a strong arm around her waist, he dipped his head and nipped at her earlobe. "Let go."

She didn't think about it, didn't wonder what would happen next, she just trusted him and unwrapped her arms from his neck. He held onto her with one arm while freeing the other from his sleeve and then used his newly shirt-free arm to hold onto her while he repeated the process on the other side.

"Practice that often?" she asked as he dropped his shirt to the ground.

He winked. "Never before you."

Because all she wanted to say after that was everything, she kissed him instead, teasing him with her tongue, tasting him, talking without words but putting everything out there. It was like there was a ticking clock only she could hear reminding her that her time with Cole was limited. Before all of that could sink in, though, and pull her down, he carried her over to the wall until her back was against the cool blue paint.

"Put your feet down," he said.

Without hesitation, she did. He lifted her arms, wrapped one hand around her wrists, and let the other glide over her skin. He cupped her breast, lifting it, squeezing it, and rolling her nipple between his fingers before tugging it tight. Sensation sparking throughout her body, she let out a shaky moan of pleasure.

"I love hearing you make that sound," he said, his lips hot against the upper swell of her breasts, tracing the curves with a reverence that left her breathless. He let her arms go and dropped his hand to her core. "Still so wet and tight for me. Are you gonna come again all over my dick like I want?"

"So cocky." Reaching between them, she wrapped her fingers around his cock, the tips nearly touching, and stroked him firm and sure. "What if I change things up? Jerk you off until you come all over my belly?"

He hissed out a harsh breath and shuddered. "Another time. Right now, I want to be inside you, fill you up, make you mine."

Another time? Make you mine? Her hand stilled. It wasn't role-playing so much as it was not denying the fantasy. That was okay. She could take that even if his words did hit her like the sharp slap of an icy breeze in December.

"Tess?" He stilled. "We can stop whenever you want."

"It's not that." She resumed the leisurely rhythm of her hand on his dick, being sure to circle the head with her thumb and spread out the pre-cum pooling there. "I want you in me right now, too."

"Are you sure?"

She slid down to her knees and licked her lips as she looked up at him. "Why don't you let me show you just how sure I am."

Then she took his cock in her mouth, taking him deep, nearly all the way to the base, and gliding her hands over his lean hips to the curve of his ass and pulling him closer, taking him until his length knocked against the back of her throat.

"Fucking hell, Tess." He pressed his palms against the wall above her and began to thrust his hips forward, pushing and withdrawing from her mouth as she rolled his balls and gripped his ass. "That feels so damn good."

She swirled her tongue around his dick, lapping against the pulsing vein on the bottom, as her only response. One, two, three more times he pushed into her mouth before pulling away and taking a step back. Before she could anticipate what would happen next, he changed up on her, grabbing her by the shoulders and yanking her up and into the air. Again her back was against the wall, her legs were wrapped around him, and his hands cupped her ass. Anticipation had the air crackling around them, and her heart was beating faster than she'd ever thought possible.

Cole lifted her up another few inches and then pulled her down on his cock, sheathing himself inside her. They both let out a desperate groan of satisfaction. It felt good, but it wasn't enough. Then he moved and she rotated her hips in time with each stroke and she lost track of anything else except how it felt to be with Cole right now and right here.

Leaning forward, she captured his mouth and let her hands roam over his sinewy shoulders and back, needing to touch him and feel him everywhere. His muscles moved under her fingertips as he thrust into her, one hand on her ass to hold her in place and the other behind her head to protect her.

"Tess." Her name came out half plea, half demand. "I'm so close."

"Then fuck me hard." She lifted her hips, circling them and arching against him, changing the angle and urging him to go faster. "Right there—right fucking there."

A ball of energy inside her tightened, flared outward, collapsed in on itself and then built back up as she rode him, holding on to his slick shoulders as she kissed him like a woman who knew she wouldn't get to again. And then, before she was ready, before she had a chance to realize it was coming, her orgasm hit, washing over her and taking away everything but her and Cole and this single moment.

"Tess, I—" But before he could finish whatever he was going to say, his entire body stiffened and he came, clutching her close to him.

Body ravaged by the force of it all and trying to catch her breath, she laid her cheek against his chest and listened to the wild beating of his heart as he came back to himself.

"Holy hell," he said, his tone nothing but wonder and awe.

She chuckled. "Pretty much." She let out a long sigh, not wanting to let go but knowing she couldn't force him to hold her like this any longer. "You better let me go."

He didn't say anything, but after she unwound her legs from his waist, he lowered her to the ground.

She scooped up her clothes. "I have to go to the bathroom real quick."

He nodded, running his hands through his hair and keeping his gaze lowered. "I'll just wait out here."

And in that breath, the reality of all of that hit her. She loved him. He would still be getting back together with Marti, hell, she was probably still at his house after watching him last night. What had just happened had been a mistake.

"You don't have to stay," she said, holding her clothes tight to her chest.

He stiffened and looked up at her, his expression hard. "Why, because everything you touch is temporary?"

Her breath caught, his words slapping her. "That's not on me."

"Bullshit." He jerked on his underwear and jeans. "You've been waiting to walk out on me since the day you walked into my house."

That wasn't true. She was just realistic. They'd barely known each other. She knew better than to think walking into a new-to-her house would mean she'd become family. But Cole? Even with all his moves, he'd been the one leaving, not the one being left.

"Fuck you," she said, her entire body aching with a bone-deep misery. "You don't know what it's like. I have to protect the baby from disappointment."

The color drained from his face, and then the words roared out of him, "Is that what I am to you? A disappointment?" He pulled on his shirt, the movements stiff and angry. "You think you're an obligation and I'm a disappointment. Ever think that people don't stick around because you make it impossible to? Even with your friends, you're probably just waiting for them to ditch you, aren't you?" He paused, sucking in a ragged breath as he watched her. "Oh my God, you are. You're something else, you know that?"

Every word landed like a punch, and she was breathing hard by the time he got to the end of it. Weary, hurt, and frustrated that she couldn't deny a single true word of it, she stood there staring at him as he shoved his feet in his shoes while she was still naked and clutching her clothes in a tight ball in front of her. There wasn't a part of her that didn't ache.

"All of that is just amazing coming from someone who has spent his entire life swimming in circles." It all came rushing out of her in clipped words as sharp as knives. "Always the same plays at home and on the ice. Always the same Marti, who couldn't get to the locker room fast enough the other night. Always the same everything. Maybe it's time you grew some fucking balls and learned to stop hiding behind all that routine."

He crossed his arms over his chest and glared at her. "Don't bring Marti into this."

"Why not?" Tess's chest burned and emotion nearly choked her. "She's always been there anyway."

His upper lip curled in a snarl. "Tell me how you really feel."

"I don't feel anything about you. You said it yourself—you're just temporary," she said, her shaky voice barely above a whisper as the lie fell out. "Just go, Cole."

"Oh, don't worry. I'll be sure to live down to your

expectations." He started for the door but stopped, turned, and glared at her. "But if you think I'm going to sit by and watch you instill this chickenshit attitude about the world into our child, then you couldn't be more wrong. There is more to life than expecting the worst from people and fixating on the shitheads who did you wrong. Your ghosts will not live rent-free in our kid's head. You got that?"

She flinched, taking a few steps back. "I'd never do that."

He let out a harsh, cold laugh. "That's funny because I thought I'd never leave, but look what I'm doing."

Then he walked out the door just like she'd been expecting since the beginning.

She threw her clothes down, squeezed her eyes shut, and clamped her mouth shut so hard, her teeth hurt, but she didn't cry. Not a single tear.

Not.

One.

It was for the best. Really. She'd gone into this whole arrangement knowing it was temporary. That's how things always worked out. She was so used to it that it barely hurt. She bit the inside of her cheek to keep her lips from trembling and to distract from the sob building up inside her.

"But don't worry." She rubbed her belly. "You're wanted. You're loved. You'll always have me."

Chapter Twenty-One

Cole's kitchen looked like a bomb of bad cooking had gone off. Flour covered almost every surface. There was a grapefruit-size pool of brown liquid that smelled a little like vanilla and a lot more like bourbon on the island. The carcasses of half a dozen burned cakes, flattened soufflés, and charcoal briskets masquerading as chocolate chip cookies littered every available flat surface. Not even a bite of it was edible.

Still, he couldn't stop. He'd been trying since he'd left Tess's house for one single, solitary moment of baking stress relief, and all he'd had was days of shit cooking that had depleted his flour and his liquor without offering any release. He wasn't giving up, though; this had always worked. It would this time. He just had to go at it harder.

The timer went off, and he pulled open the oven door. The cold oven door. Cole closed his eyes and groaned. He hadn't turned it on. He grabbed the towel over his shoulder and whipped it across the kitchen. It landed in the sink on top of the pile of unwashed, crusty dishes.

"Fuck. This." His yell of frustration filled the room but

not enough to banish Tess's ghost.

She was everywhere. He looked at the couch and saw her snuggled up under his Ice Knights blanket. He walked by the guest room and could still smell her flowery perfume. He lay down in his bed at night, closed his eyes, and the weight of her not being in bed with him nearly flattened him. Then he woke up in the morning and did it all over again. Added to that hell was the fact that he had another two days in a row off, and he was ready to hurl the muffin tin across the disaster zone of a kitchen.

Fury—at himself, at her, at the world in general—ate at him, poisoning everything he looked at or touched until he couldn't take it anymore. He stormed out onto his patio. Every fucking lounge chair was turned so it faced the pool, each one exactly two feet from the other. Just like they'd always been. Just like they were supposed to be. Just like he motherfucking hated seeing them.

He marched over to the closest one, grabbed it, and spun in around so it faced the house. As he let out a laugh that was more than likely at least 50 percent completely unhinged, some of the pent-up shittiness stringing him tight unraveled—not much, but more than enough to power him forward. He tore through the area around his pool, his muscles unwinding with each step forward. He turned the next chair so it, too, faced the lawn, then the one past that he rearranged so it wasn't aimed at anything, and then he took the last one on the west side of the pool and flung it away like a shot put, the explosion of energy still doing nothing to sate his anger.

"Hell yeah," he yelled as he surveyed the disarray.

Holy shit. He felt good. Sucking in the cold winter air in harsh, quick breaths that burned his lungs, he sprinted to the other side of the pool and went to town creating chaos where there had only been rigid order. God, he was on fire, he was—

"Fucking A, Phillips," Petrov said, his voice cutting

through the euphoria of the moment. "Please tell me you haven't cracked, because I am not equipped to talk your ass down."

Cole whirled around, adrenaline rushing through him, making it feel like he had lightning in his veins. Petrov stood in the open french doors leading into the kitchen, his arms crossed and a wary expression on his face. Christensen stood behind him, his mouth hanging open and his eyes as big as hockey pucks. They were looking at him like he'd lost it. Well, maybe he had, and maybe that was exactly what he needed.

"You two are just the people I'm looking for," he said as he shoved a chair with his foot so it was cockeyed.

Christensen looked over at Petrov and raised his eyebrows before turning back to Cole. "That doesn't sound creepy at all, considering how your house looks."

"We're not going in there." And he wasn't thinking about how gross his kitchen was at the moment. "Come on."

He took off around the house, jogging toward the wide curved driveway. It wasn't rink size, but he'd make it work. By the time he got out front, Christensen and Petrov had backtracked through the house and were on his porch.

Cole jerked his chin toward the middle of the drive. "Let's work on those new plays. We're going to do it again and again until I finally have it. She's not right."

"Who's not right?" Christensen asked, his head cocked to one side. "Tess?"

"Tess, Coach, whoever the fuck else has been bitching about me," Cole snarled. "Let's do this."

Petrov snorted and rolled his eyes. "You hate those plays. Plus, we're in your driveway and we don't even have roller blades."

"Loosen the fuck up, Petrov." Cole acted out a deke to the left and then sprinted to the center of the driveway. "Live a little."

"Who are you and what have you done with Cole Phillips?" Christensen asked.

"I broke him." Yeah, as if he could make a transformation like this on his own. "No. She broke him." Closer but still not quite right. "Correction. Tess leaving broke me, but I figured it out." That was it; that was exactly why he had this energy revving him up, opening his field of vision, letting him see the world in a whole new way. "Just run the plays with me," Cole said. "I am going to make this work. I'm not stuck. I'm not moving in circles. I'm going forward."

And he would. He had to.

"Enthusiastic" was pretty much the farthest thing from a descriptor of Christensen and Petrov, but they rallied and set up with him as if it was puck drop. "Fluid" wasn't the right word for it. He was definitely choppy, a little stiff, still holding onto the old way, but then on the fifth run-through, when he was on the edge of thinking all of this had just been a pipe dream, it happened.

Then the light bulb went off and he got it, felt his muscles moving as if he'd been making this play his entire life, and he saw it, what Coach had been talking about—this was the thing he'd been missing. This was something new, something fresh, something as unexpected as getting weddinged with the wrong woman who turned out to be right in every single way. That was it. That was the truth he'd never scheduled time to consider. He stopped dead in the middle of the play, sucking in air and feeling like his spine had just been ripped out of him.

"I fucked it up," he said, looking from Petrov to Christensen. "All of it. Hockey. Tess. The baby. I ruined it all."

And just like that, all the energy blasting through him disappeared without warning. His entire life, he'd been able to fight back the chaos by controlling the game. This time, however, he saw what a lie that had been. He hadn't been in charge of anything; he'd been hiding from everything, and it was too late now to do anything about it.

· · ·

The flower shop had always been Tess's refuge. The oxygen levels were higher thanks to all that photosynthesis, it was colorful and cheery, plus there was the fact that everyone—with the exceptions of when it came to funerals—was buying flowers as a happy occasion. It was hard to be down in that kind of environment, yet somehow she was managing to be a moping, sighing, eyes-watering-up-for-absolutely-no-reason sad sack today.

It sure wasn't because of Cole. She didn't need him—or anyone.

Yeah. Keep telling yourself that and maybe you'll stop tearing up.

Obviously she had developed some kind of pregnancy-related allergy, and it had nothing to do with the fact that she was listening to her voicemails on loop as the soundtrack to her heartbreak.

"Hey, Tess, we just landed in Denver," started one message.

Another began with, "How are you and the peanut doing? Did you manage to talk anyone with shit taste out of buying roses today?"

The voicemail after that started with the sound of men yelling and singing in the locker room after a win as Cole ineffectually tried to get them to "let me make this damn phone call already."

If she wasn't crying so hard, that one would have made her laugh. Instead she was reordering roses because she'd failed to talk a single person out of buying at least a half dozen of the damn things. For some reason, her customers seemed opposed to taking the advice of a woman who couldn't stop sniffling or wiping her cheeks with the back of her hand.

The bell attached to the shop door ding-a-linged a second before the unmistakable sound of her girls filled the shop. She set her phone down—yeah, she'd been listening to Cole's voicemails one after the other on loop for most of the afternoon. What could she say? She wanted even if she couldn't have.

"You can't just go straight at it, Fallon," Gina said, her voice carrying across the shop's showroom floor and to the back room where Tess was. "Some things take a little gentle touch."

"I'm still gonna cut off his balls," Fallon said.

The smack of two people high-fiving sounded and Lucy said, "He better hope I don't see him at the practice rink tomorrow or he's in for a world of hurt. I spent most of last night awake staring at my ceiling and imagining the shitty stories I could plant about him."

Gina gasped. "That's unethical."

Tess peeked her head out of the back room at her trio of best friends who stood next to the stand of orchids and next to the cooler filled with every shade of roses it was possible to get. They were here even though she hadn't called them and had actively been avoiding them since everything happened with Cole. She'd sent one text of explanation and then ignored every one of their follow-ups. She had to. Her heart hurt too much already. She couldn't take any more walking away. This time, she needed to be the one to leave.

"It's Tess," Lucy said, giving the other women a who-are-we-kidding face. "Who wouldn't cross a few lines for her? It's not like I'm saying we stuff him in my trunk and take a drive out to the swamps outside Waterbury."

"I think that's the perfect plan." Fallon's grin looked like she had completely forgotten that as a nurse, her duty was to help people, not whack them.

"Okay," Gina said, smoothing her palm over her pink skirt. "You might have converted me. I can reach out to a cousin of mine who knows a guy—just to give Cole a scare."

Whatever battle Tess had been waging to keep her cheeks dry ended with a rush of tears that immediately stuffed up her nose. Despite everything she'd done over the past few days to push them away, her girls, the very people she'd been worrying about for months that she was losing, were plotting to avenge her. They weren't going anywhere. They were *her* girls, and she had been being too much of a paranoid weirdo to realize it.

She walked out of the back room, wiping her hands across her cheeks and trying desperately for a sense of cool. "Did you know the highest bail amount ever set was $100 million for a guy accused in a $20 million insider trading scheme?" Tess gave her girls a wobbly smile. "I love you guys, but none of us has bail money tucked aside."

"We really should," Lucy said, as always thinking six steps ahead. "It seems prudent."

"Are you okay?" Gina rushed over to her and enveloped her in a solid hug. "You wouldn't return any of my calls, and I was so worried about you."

"I'm fine," she said, squeezing her friend back. "Why wouldn't I be?"

Okay, that almost sounded normal. She hadn't sniffled, her voice hadn't quivered, and her cheeks barely felt hot from the bald-faced lie. Sure, her eyes were bloodshot, her cheeks wet, and her chin wobbly, but her friends would ignore that.

Yeah, right.

She stepped out of the hug and gazed at her friends, the women who knew her almost as well as they knew themselves. They didn't look like they'd spent even a penny buying her nonchalant pronouncement.

"Lucy told us all about the fight and how Cole left," Fallon said.

And yeah, she hadn't exactly told Lucy the whole story, but even the awk-weird liked to guard their vulnerable underbellies. "There was no expectation that it was ever anything more than just sex. I knew all along it was temporary."

"Really?" Gina, the sweet wedding planner who always managed to see the good in people no matter what, scoffed.

Her girls knew her history. They knew how she'd grown up, the middle-of-the-night surprise drop-offs and the uncertainty of when, if ever, her mom would swing back to pick her up. They *knew* all of that, but unless a person had lived it, it was really hard to explain that gut-level sense of vigilance that never went away.

That sense of perpetual disappointment was the one thing her mother had given her that hadn't been temporary.

"Look," she said with a sigh, trying to keep her chin from trembling and clasping her hands together so they wouldn't shake. "I've spent my whole life watching the signs, reading people, waiting for the moment that always comes when I know my time is up. This isn't anything new."

But God, it hurt so much worse than anything that had come before. It was like walking around with a broken rib; every breath hurt and there wasn't a damn thing she could do about it but wait for the pain to go away. That should happen in about a million years.

"He's an idiot," Fallon said, summing up her support in three words.

Lucy nodded. "A shithead."

"A weasel-brained numb-nutter," Gina finished.

Tess, Lucy, and Fallon all turned to look at Gina, who was blushing furiously.

"What does that even mean?" Tess asked.

Gina shrugged. "No clue, but I've never been as good at the insults as those two."

"Well, there's no reason for them when it comes to Cole." Tess backpedaled a few steps, needing the space as her stomach clenched and tears pricked her eyelids again. It wasn't fair. She knew better than this. She knew better than to believe. And if he'd really wanted to stay, he would have fought to instead of walking out. "This really is a case of it's not him, it's me. I'm just not built for that."

Fallon cocked her head to the side. "For what?"

"Forever." Tess spread her arms wide, the one word encompassing the whole world, the sense of inevitability about it sinking like a stone in her gut.

"Bullshit," Gina said.

Tess looked at her friends, the ones she knew loved her and wanted to be there with her, but she couldn't shake the truth that had proven itself time and time again. Like the flowers she surrounded herself with, their friendship was beautiful and filled the room with absolute joy, but in the end they would wither. Things changed. Lives got busy. People who she thought loved her left.

"Are you sure?" Tess said, her voice shaking. "Everything is so different; our lives are changing so much. It's just that you're all moving on with your lives, falling in love, getting married, and it's only a matter of time before we drift apart."

The last word hung in the sweet-scented air among them, the weight of it pressing down on her even as she couldn't deny the relief of finally saying it out loud.

Gina shook her head and strode over to Tess, wrapping her in another hug. "We're forever family. Temporary doesn't apply to us."

"We're here for you," Fallon said, joining in on the hug.

Lucy wrapped her arms around Tess. "Always."

Standing in the middle of her shop, her arms pinned to her sides because her girls were hugging her that hard and with tears running down her cheeks, Tess loosened her hold on the fear she'd lived with her entire life. She'd always figured that if she held onto that knowledge that abandonment was right around the corner, that no one really wanted her, it would make life easier. But she'd been wrong. It had almost lost her the three most important women in her life, her family, because she'd been too scared to admit her own vulnerabilities.

The fact that hugs released oxytocin was about to fly out of her mouth, driven to the forefront by the emotion and fear battling it out in her heart, but she pulled it back. There'd be other times for her favorites. She didn't have to distance herself from her family.

"I love you guys," she said.

They answered in unison, "We love you, too."

"So what about Cole?" Fallon asked when the group hug finally broke up. "Do I need to go get my shovel?"

"It doesn't matter. I knew going in what the situation was." And no matter how much she wished it wasn't, she needed to accept it and be glad that someone as amazing as the baby had resulted from it. "We got weddinged, I got knocked up, and then I was an idiot and fell for him even though he was up-front from the beginning that he was just trying to be a good guy."

Telling them all the hurtful shit they'd hurled at each other wouldn't change anything, so she kept her mouth shut about that. The truth was that it never would have worked. Everything she touched—even her flowers—was temporary. That her girls weren't was just the exception that proved the rule.

"Does the fact that I brought dill-flavored ice cream help?" Gina pulled a grocery bag out of her huge tote.

"Oh my God, that sounds disgusting." Her stomach growled. "Okay, maybe it's worth trying at least."

"It's your taste buds' funeral," Lucy said.

"I have the pizza guy's number on speed dial," Fallon added, "because we need to order something before Paint and Sip, since there's no way I'm eating that ice cream."

"Come on," Tess said, shaking her head at her friends' antics. "I've got spoons in my office."

They followed her to the back. It wasn't until they walked through the door and the sound of Cole's voice hit her ears, though, that she remembered what she'd been doing before her friends had shown up.

"I have got to take you to this place in Minneapolis," Cole said. "They have this cheese-stuffed hamburger called a Juicy Lucy here. I'm already dying for another one, as if I'm the one with the pregnancy cravings. How's our little peanut doing today? I'm about to crash out but I'll sleep with the phone under my pillow so I'll wake up if you call."

"Peanut?" Gina asked, swerving around to Tess, who stood frozen in the doorway to get inside the office.

Tess let out a shaky breath. "That's what we call the baby."

"And did you call him that night?" Lucy asked as she nudged Tess into the small room where they all crowded around her desk, looking at the phone as if it was the Rosetta Stone.

"No, just left voicemails for each other. It's dumb. I should erase them." She reached for the phone, but Gina snatched it away before Tess could.

Before she could protest, the next message started.

"We didn't get to stop, but the team bus drove by the mother of all baking supply shops on the way to the rink this morning. The damage I could do in there," Cole said, his smile obvious in his voice. "I bet I could even find some rainbow glitter sprinkles in the shape of unicorns for the next time we make cupcakes together. I dreamed about baking with you last night. Of course you were naked. It was a very good dream. Still, though, I'd rather be home."

Tess's chest ached. Listening to the messages and knowing she would never get any more was like sticking a rusty nail into an open wound—pure torture. Emotion filled her throat as she fought to keep it together. Falling apart wouldn't help anything.

Gina hit pause and pressed the phone to her chest above her heart and let out a dreamy sigh. "He's in love with you."

"No." Tess couldn't—wouldn't—pretend. That way only led to heartache. Look at what a mess she was already. "It was just sex."

"And baking," Lucy said, you're-full-of-shit plain in her tone.

"And making plans to go across the country to experience heaven in hamburger form," Gina said.

"Is this the part where we pretend you're not being a stubborn idiot?" Fallon asked. "Because that was not a man only interested in banging. That's a guy in love."

Tess's gut twisted as she ran through every interaction with Cole without the drumbeat of "everyone always leaves" pounding in her heart. The voicemails. The dance. The cupcakes. Him cuddling Kahn. Almost everything with her right up to that last final fight when every truth he'd hurled at her burned like a brand. But wait. That didn't take into account the third person always with them.

"What about Marti?" Her voice broke on the other woman's name.

Lucy cocked her head to the side. "What do you mean?"

"Cole loves her." They'd been the ones to tell her all about it the morning of Lucy's wedding.

Fallon scoffed. "Is that what you think?"

Tess set her shoulders and looked at each of her friends. They loved her, but they were wrong about this. "She went down to the locker room right after he got hurt, and she stayed overnight with him. It's only a matter of time until they get back together. It's what they do. Fallon and Lucy said so themselves at the wedding."

"Marti is head over heels for some tech guy." Lucy gave her a sympathetic look laced with more than a little regret. "I should have told you. I didn't think it was even an issue. I'm sorry. Plus, she never stayed with him. He spent the night alone."

"No, he told me she was staying with him and that's why I left him alone that night." Guilt knocked Tess's knees out, and she sank into the guest chair in front of her desk. "That he would want her there told me everything I needed to know about the impossibility of us being more. We were just temporary. We both said it."

The floor tilted for a second as she tried to process it all. Had they both said it—or had she been the only one? She wasn't sure anymore about anything.

"Tess, we love you, but you are so stuck in a rut of constantly thinking everything is temporary." Gina rounded the desk and squatted down in front of Tess's chair so they were eye to eye. "I hate to tell you, but *everything* is temporary, just like those flowers you sell. Does that mean people should stop loving flowers or is it that we should appreciate them more while we have them?"

Tess's chest was tight, and she couldn't get enough air. Palms flat on her desk, she tried to fill her lungs. Here she was, in the middle of her flower shop, surrounded by so many plants and flowers turning carbon dioxide into oxygen, and she still couldn't breathe.

She didn't have what she needed. She didn't have Cole.

She'd been such an asshole.

Was she projecting everything onto him? Maybe, but her world was off-kilter and not in the Mom-just-dumped-me-at-another-relative's-house way but something else, something worse. It was as if she was living in that half second between dropping a glass vase and it hitting the floor, that moment when she knew something bad was going to happen and she couldn't do anything to stop it. But what if she could? What if it wasn't too late?

"I have to fix this," she said, never so sure of something in her life.

All three of them gave her knowing looks. They should—they'd been in this exact same spot before. "Tell us what you need," they said as a unit.

If she knew, she would have asked, but the truth of it was that she had absolutely no idea.

• • •

Cole took the ice at practice and got to work. Over the past few days, he'd spent every waking minute walking through the new offensive system and going through the movements on his driveway until his muscle memory kicked in and everything flowed like it should have months ago. Now all of that was paying off as they took the ice in their practice jerseys and got to work.

His playing was clean.

His moves unhesitating.

His insides burned and roiled as the one person he'd been practicing to forget stayed with him on every stride, pass, and check.

No matter how hard he pushed himself, no matter how exhausted he was when he crashed at night, he hadn't been able to forget Tess, and it was eating away at him.

"Phillips!" Coach hollered from the bench. "Come see

me when you get changed out."

Cole finished his practice shift and made his way off the ice, ditched his skates in the locker room, and walked into Coach's office still in his pads.

"You wanted to see me?" Cole asked, his gut doing spins even though he knew he'd had a great practice and that the new plays had finally clicked.

"You were looking good out there," Coach said, standing up in front of his bookshelves and putting one of the many trophies back on the shelf.

Cole let out the breath he'd been holding. "I've been working."

"Good." Coach nodded, mumbling something to himself under his breath that sounded a little like *at least you're doing something.* "I'm glad you put the past few days to good use. I'm moving you back up to the first line for the next game. That gives you forty-eight hours to work out whatever kinks are left. Don't make me regret it."

It took some work, but Cole managed not to shout out a loud holler of celebration right then. "You won't, Coach."

He was on a high all the way back to the locker room, right until he realized that the person he most wanted to tell wasn't there. And she didn't want to see him.

Guilt about the shitty things he'd said to her and the crappy way they'd left things sucked all the joy out of what should have been his best moment in months. By the time he walked into the locker room, he was spoiling for a fight.

Blackburn was waiting by Cole's locker, standing with his arms crossed and his usual perma-glare on his face.

"I talked with Fallon, and she told me Tess is back at her place," Blackburn said, an almost smile of approval curling up one side of his mouth. "You probably made the right call there, judging by what you've been showing on the ice. I shouldn't have pushed you to let Tess move in. Now that she's gone, you have your life the way you want it again. Everything is in its place. Your schedule is yours, and you don't have to worry about anyone else. Sure, you'll see your kid on the weekends and holidays, you'll be involved, but it won't change anything. It's not like Tess is actually important to you."

"Could you imagine?" Petrov asked with an exaggerated shiver. "I mean, she's not like a puck bunny who rolled the dice and hit the jackpot, but you still dodged a bullet."

Heat blasted through Cole, and he was across the locker room before he realized it, pressing a forearm against Petrov's chest and backing him up against the wall. "Don't talk about Tess that way."

Petrov snorted, seemingly totally unperturbed by Cole's move. Blackburn didn't even flinch, just watched with a look of genuine amusement on his face.

"What way?" Petrov asked. "The truth?"

"That's not the truth." Pulse pounding in his ears, red seeping into his vision, Cole held down on the last thread of his control like a man who knew he was about to lose it. "You don't know what the fuck you're talking about. Tess is amazing and smart and determined and she's going to be the greatest mom."

"What makes you say that?" Snark. Derision. Cynicism. It was all there in Petrov's tone, laid on as thick as mayo on a BLT. "Do you really know her?"

Images of Tess flashed in his head. The way she'd protected the rookie players she barely knew. How she was with Kahn. The way she managed to get moving forward when life had dealt her enough body blows to take most people down. And the way she looked at him in her apartment the other day when she came, it had filled him with such hope, such optimism for what could be that he almost couldn't handle it. All he wanted to do was stay down on his knees and beg her to come home, but he couldn't because he was afraid—of rejection, of change, of all the things that would shake up his very orderly world.

Did he know her? He sure as fuck did.

Petrov snorted. "I can tell by your face going all soft and goofy that you finally figured out you need to remove your head from up your own ass." He cleared his throat and gave Cole a back-the-fuck-up-now look that was just this side of slasher-movie scary. "Now, how about you take this opportunity to take two steps back before I remind you that I may be a center, but I'll still kick your ass."

Cole dropped his arm and stepped back, his hands shaking and his mind racing. "I'm sorry, I don't know what I was thinking."

"That seems to apply to a lot of things lately," Blackburn said. "So what are you going to do about Tess?"

Shit. That was the question. "I don't know."

Blackburn shook his head and grumbled something quietly that sounded like *dumb-ass*. "You better figure it out and quick—the plane for Montreal is wheels up at ten in the morning on Monday."

Something shifted in his chest, and he took his first deep breath since she'd walked out of his house. "It's too late." The truth of it burned like a shot of straight grain alcohol all the way down to his gut. "I fucked it up too badly."

The team captain narrowed his eyes and practically snarled at him. "Well, if you're giving up that easily, then I guess she's lucky to have avoided being tied down to some kind of chickenshit chump anyway."

Guilt smacked into Cole, nearly knocking him back a few feet, but shame reacted first, dropping the gloves and coming out swinging. "Screw you, Blackburn."

The captain took a step forward, his stance loose. Cole went to meet him in the middle, ready to let the frustration out even if that meant getting his ass kicked.

"Boys," Petrov hollered, stopping Cole and Blackburn. "Cut the shit."

Still sucking metaphorical wind after the sucker punch Blackburn landed, Cole took a few steps back, his pads weighing a million pounds. The laughter and the shit talk filtering out from the training room and the showers was the same as almost every post-practice skate, but it grated against his skin, scratching down to the bone and then going in for the marrow. Christensen walked into the room, air-drying instead of using a towel like a normal human and checking the messages on his phone.

"I fucked up," Cole said.

Christensen didn't look up from the messages on his screen. "Is this where I'm supposed to have a shocked face?"

Usually, he would have just walked away here, stuck with his plan to live his life like he always had, but it was time to act like he played football instead of hockey and call an audible.

"I've got to get Tess back," he told his line mates.

Petrov let his head drop back and released a groan. "Fucking A, Phillips." He straightened and stared right at Cole. "I had another three days to go in the team pool for how long it would take you to stop being a moron."

"Meanwhile, I guessed right on the money," Christensen said with a grin. "However, you've got one big problem, Phillips." He finally slid on his joggers. "Tess thinks you're still in love with Marti and that's why you blasted out of her apartment without an *I love you* after giving her the good D."

Cole's gut dropped the three floors to the subbasement. "How do you know that?"

"He was playing Xbox at my house and Fallon unloaded on him—guilt by association," Blackburn said with a grin, showing absolutely no sympathy. "You might not want to get within swinging distance of Fallon for a while."

"Shit," Cole muttered and rammed his hands through his hair, scrambling for a solution.

In the movies, this was where the plan finally came together. In reality? His brain was a giant blank and he was so very, very fucked in the worst way possible.

Chapter Twenty-Two

Tess was still trying to figure out what in the world to do hours later when she and her girls had taken off for Paint and Sip. Hoping the creative atmosphere would clear her brain, since studies had shown that ideas needed space to percolate, she'd drank her organic grape juice. Finally, Tess put the finishing touches on the pastel-colored painting of a smiling baby—who happened to have two rows of shark teeth on full display—and sat back in her chair, still waiting for inspiration to strike.

"I hope you're going to hang that in a place of honor in the baby's room," Larry said with a smile as he shoved a wrapped package her way.

Tess managed to keep her mouth shut because it seemed cruel to tell their eccentric painting instructor that all the bizarre Paint and Sip night paintings went into a closet—well, except for the Bigfoot one at Cole's house that she wasn't going to think about because it would only make her think of him, and damn it she was emotional enough lately without doing that. God, she missed him. Kahn did, too. The little beastie liked to prowl through the house as if he was looking for Cole and his tail flicked with frustration every time he made his rounds and didn't find him.

"Oh, you didn't have to get me a present," she said as she accepted the tiny gift. "That's very sweet of you."

His pale cheeks flushed pink and his gaze dropped to his shoes that looked suspiciously like he'd swiped them from a bowling alley. "Well, you four are here almost every week, and despite your tendency to talk more than paint, we're kinda family. Congrats on the baby."

Her throat tightened, and she blinked back tears that lately always seemed to be searching for an excuse to escape as she tore the wrapping paper. Inside were two teeny tiny white socks with little paintbrushes on them. They were adorable and sweet and just... She let out a shaky breath, trying her hardest not to cry.

"I know they're pretty basic, but the things they sell at the baby stores are so lame. Someone really needs to start a business that has some badass baby gear with a message, you know? The babies are the ones inheriting this planet we've managed to fuck up so thoroughly," he said. "I left the receipt in there in case you wanted to take them back because they're not what you want."

Giving up on the whole dry-eyed thing, she threw her arms around Larry and hugged him tight. "They are perfect and exactly what I want. Thank you."

He went stock-still before awkwardly patting her with three solid thumps. "You did take the grape juice, right?"

"Yes," she said, chuckling as she let him go. "I just, well, I guess I hadn't realized until now how lucky I am in the family I've found."

"Dude, that's modern living; we create the world we want to inhabit." Larry gathered up all the paintbrushes and unused canvases from the painting session. "Anyway, have a good night and I'll see you next week." He started to walk away but stopped mid-stride. "By the way, my cousin is looking for a few hours of volunteer work, too, so after the baby comes, maybe we can have her come by during the painting session to look after your baby while you paint."

And with that little bit of kindness, he turned and walked toward the back of Paint and Sip where all the supplies were kept.

Tess stayed frozen, processing everything that had just happened. Larry wasn't wrong; people did create the worlds they wanted to inhabit. Sure, it didn't always work out the way they intended, but that was the beauty of life—it was always possible to start again. Looking around at her girls who were putting on their coats and getting ready to brave the weather on the short drive to Moretti's Bar and Grill for the traditional post-painting wine (and now seltzer), it dawned on her just how lucky she was. She'd been waiting for someone to make the world she wanted without realizing that she'd already done that.

There was only one person missing, and it was beyond time she did something about it.

"I'm gonna have to skip out on Moretti's," she said, brain already spinning as she tried to formulate what she'd say to Cole as soon as she saw him, how she'd explain that the temporary thing wasn't working for her and that together just made so much more sense than separate because she loved him and hoped he could maybe start to love her, too. "There's someone I need to go talk to."

"At nine on a Saturday night?" Lucy asked, doubt pouring off her. "Who?"

"We don't have to be in Tess's business all the time," Gina said, rolling her eyes at their workaholic bestie. "If she wants to go meet up with a mystery stranger, then it's no business of ours even though we, of course, will always be here for her to hear what was said and how the happily ever after happened."

Tess cocked her head and gave her friends a good scan. They looked clueless—a little too clueless—about her plans. Did they have her brain bugged? "You forgot the part about who I'm meeting."

"Like we don't know that already," Fallon said as she zipped up her parka. "Why do you think I'm trying to get you to Moretti's? I told you guys just being up front would be so much easier."

"Not all of us are blunt like the business end of a hammer," Gina said.

Lucy looked at Fallon and grinned. "Well, two of us definitely are."

"You guys are totally confusing me." Tess looked from one of her friends to the other. "Who is going to be at Moretti's?"

"Cole Phillips," all three said together.

Okay, that was not the answer she was expecting. And why did they look so happy about it? Earlier all three of them were deciding the best ways to hide his body. "I thought you guys were planning his painful demise."

The three of them exchanged knowing grins.

"Let's just say we had a feeling you might change your mind about him," Gina said.

"My shovel's still in the trunk, though," Lucy added in a tone that promised it was not an exaggeration and that Harbor City's scariest crisis communication guru was indeed in possession of a possible murder weapon.

Tess laughed, a big, loud sound that filled the Paint and Sip and earned them all a shushing from Larry as he prepped for the next class that was starting to filter in.

She gave her girls a quick group hug, her eyes doing that whole tearing-up-because-pregnancy-hormones-are-a-bitch thing again. "You guys are the absolute best friends I could ever have."

"Friends?" Gina let out an exaggerated gasp. "I'll have you know, we're sisters."

"Come on before it gets all sappy again," Fallon said, steering them toward the door. "Let's go see your man."

Her man. It was as much of a strange concept as having sisters, but both fit. Her grin couldn't have been pried off with a crowbar when she got into Lucy's car with the ever-present Mountain Dew in the cupholder and took off toward downtown Waterbury and Moretti's Bar and Grill. She had no idea what was going to happen next, but she was positive she was going to make sure it ended the way it should.

• • •

Cole had played in sixteen playoff games, ten game sevens, and two Stanley Cup finals, and none of them had been as nerve-racking as walking into Tess's neighborhood bar and grill, Moretti's, with Blackburn, Christensen, and Petrov. It wasn't until they walked through the door that he realized it was karaoke night. The man caterwauling up onstage was bad enough that Cole's head was hangover aching and he hadn't even had a beer yet.

"This is a bad idea," he said, looking around, his gaze lingering on every blonde in the room, half hoping it would be Tess. "I'm leaving."

Blackburn's giant hand landed on Cole's shoulder. "Simmer the fuck down and have a beer. She's not gonna be here."

"How do you know?" It wasn't like Tess kept to a certain schedule, and this was her neighborhood bar and grill.

"Do you really think she's knocking back shots in her condition?" Petrov shook his head in disgust as he sat down at the bar, holding up four fingers to let the bartender know their order.

Cole claimed the next seat, his gut churning at both the idea that he might run into Tess before he had figured out how to get her back and that he wouldn't. "So this is really just a planning meeting?"

"Yeah," Christensen said while scanning the bar, no doubt for hot chicks. "We're starting a new club called Phillips Is a Pussy."

"Watch your stupidity, Christiansen," Fallon said, sliding up beside them at the bar before anyone had even realized she was approaching from behind. "A woman's vagina is stronger than a pair of balls any day." She leaned into Blackburn and gave him a quick kiss before turning to glare at Cole. "Speaking of balls, you've got some, showing up here."

It wasn't a shiv to the neck, but it wasn't friendly, either. He couldn't blame her. He was the one who knocked up her friend. And what was he gonna do about it?

"Is Tess here?" Was it possible for him to equally want the answer to be yes and no? Because he definitely did.

Before Fallon could answer, the world's worst karaoke singer finished his song and handed the mic over to Tess, who walked onstage, her hands shaking and her cheeks flushed pink.

Cole couldn't look away. How in the hell had he let her get away? He'd been an idiot, a total moron.

"Oh my God. This is awful," she said, her eyes wide. "There are so many of you. I know they say to picture everyone naked and you won't be as nervous, but oh my God, I am visualizing that and not only has it made me extremely uncomfortable, but I am still freaking out." The crowd chuckled, but if Tess noticed, she didn't let on. Instead, she used her hand to shield her eyes from the spotlight and looked out into the bar.

If he could have moved, he would have stood up or

waved to her, but there was just no way. He was frozen to his barstool, afraid that if he even blinked, she'd disappear and he'd miss his chance to get her back.

"And if I'm doing this and Cole isn't even out there, I might just die of embarrassment," she continued, her words coming out faster than Christensen on a breakaway. "Lucy and Gina promised he was here and Fallon said she'd work her magic to make sure he stayed, so that means she could have kneecapped him or something."

Another laugh from the crowd as Tess started to pace the small stage, so obviously nervous, it was a miracle she didn't spin herself up into the air.

"So why am I crashing karaoke night? Because I fell in love with a guy and, well, that's never been something I'd ever expected to happen—especially not with someone like him. He's smart and sexy and could be mistaken for Thor, minus the accent of course, because he doesn't have one." Everything started coming out in a rush. "He grew up all over, his dad's job had them moving a lot but not because he's a hit man. His dad has specialized skills but not that kind and oh my God, this is why I should never be given a microphone. Also, I have no idea what to do with my hands. Anyway, Cole, are you here?"

He got up and started toward the stage, his heart processing her words before his head had managed to do so. "Yes."

She looked this way and that into the crowd, the spotlight obviously too bright for her to see him. "To be honest, I'm not sure if that's good or bad because I am about to pass out from being in front of all these people."

"Do you want to come down?"

"No, I have to do this, and it has to be like this."

"Why?"

"Because you have to know what you're in for if you say

yes." She let out a deep breath and pushed up her glasses. "I know we got weddinged and that you never had plans for us in your life, but I love you, Cole Phillips, and I'm really hoping you can give me a second chance. So I know I said some horrible things. I'd take it all back if I could because you were right. I never gave us a chance and I should have. There are a million other people out there who—"

He jumped up on the stage. "Stop talking, Tess."

Her chin trembled. "Why?"

Unable to go another second without touching her, Cole pulled her into his arms, relishing the just-right feel of her against him. "Because I love you, too."

"Even though I'm the weirdest person in the room?" she asked with a sniffle.

"Especially because of that." And he'd never meant something more.

Tess went still, except for the smile beginning to tug at the corner of her mouth, and his breath caught. God, she was beautiful. Her hair was piled up on top of her head, but several strands had escaped, the curly lengths framing her face and tangling in her glasses.

"I love you, Tess Gardner." He dipped his head lower, quieting his voice because the rest was meant only for her ears. "I want you and the baby in my life however you want. This isn't temporary for me; it hasn't been since the first time I saw you. You changed everything, and I'm so lucky you did."

And there it was—everything he had to give her was out there in the open. Being vulnerable was new and scary and he fucking hated it, but it was worth it if Tess saw something in him like this that she could fall in love with. He dropped his hands and took a step back, not wanting to make her feel like he was forcing her into a decision.

"Well," she said, stepping forward so that there was barely a hint of space between their bodies. "Kahn has been missing you, and you do have a very valuable piece of art that I would love to see."

He hadn't moved that ugly Bigfoot painting since she'd left, and as far as he was concerned, it should always be displayed. "Does that mean you'll come home?"

She nodded, raising herself up on her tiptoes and brushing a kiss across his lips. "Permanently."

He couldn't imagine a better life than the new one he was about to embark on with her. Whatever changes there would be, they'd face them together, and there was absolutely nothing that would stop them.

They'd been weddinged good and proper.

Epilogue

Many months later…

The epidural hadn't kicked in yet. There was no way it could have because Tess's body hurt from the contractions like she was about to have an *Alien*-style baby. She had definitely not signed up for that. But here she was in the hospital room, Cole on one side of her trying not to show that he was six seconds away from hyperventilating, nurses on the other side looking like it was just another day in the office, and the doctor sitting on a stool between her feet that were up in stirrups and eating Cracker Jacks and spicy Cheetos for all she knew, since she could only see the top of his bald head.

"You're doing great, honey," Cole said, the tension in his voice and the slightly panicked look in his blue eyes giving away that he was just as overwhelmed and freaked out as she was. "Amazing."

"You're never touching me again." Of that she was certain. How did women do this on a frequent enough basis to populate the planet? "Not a single time."

"Ice chip?" Cole held up a cup full of frozen shards.

She was about to tell him where he could shove that ice chip when another contraction hit and hit her with enough force that it felt like the U.S.S. *Enterprise* had run her over, backed up, and plowed over her again for good measure. Somewhere in the back of her head, she got that the analogy of a spaceship running someone over was ridiculous, but she was in pain and her poor brain was doing the best it could.

"I can see the head; only another couple more pushes," the doctor said from between her legs.

The contraction eased, and she took a deep breath, already feeling the next one starting to build at a rapid clip. She reached out and grabbed Cole's hand, holding onto him as her body revved up for another go.

"We should get married," he said, his words coming out faster than the *beep-beep* of her heart rate on the monitor. "I spotted a minister right outside in the waiting room. His niece is giving birth, too."

"Cole," she groaned through clenched teeth. "I love you but I'm gonna kill you if you try and drag a stranger into this room so we can get married while I'm in the middle of having a baby."

"So no change in plans? No adjustments to the schedule?" he asked.

God love him, the man had taken to change and had become Mr. Spontaneity.

He went on, "Although I've been reading up in my *1001 Rules For Baby Scheduling* and some routine is necessary."

The change in him showed up in different ways. At home he'd learned to vary his routine—finally putting off the dumpster-diving raccoon that had been stalking his regular trash removal—and on the ice he'd become unstoppable with he and Coach Peppers seemingly trying to one up each other in the creative new plays department. The result? The

Ice Knights finished the year with a record-setting winning streak and the Stanley Cup—which just happened to be in the hospital room with them right at this moment. And now he wanted to get married? The man needed to slow down just for a second.

"I've created a monster," she said as her muscles started to tense in anticipation of the upcoming contraction.

He squeezed her hand. "The baby is gonna be great."

Despite everything going on, she giggled. "I was talking about you."

"What can I say, I learned from the best." He leaned down and brushed his lips across her forehead. "And you're doing great."

She was about to tell the guy who was feeling none of the pain exactly what he could do with his coaching when another contraction struck and all she could do was follow her body's orders. She bore down, giving the push her everything, Then all the pain was gone—or at least the epidural had finally kicked in—and an angry cry filled the air.

The doctor chuckled. "Never met a baby yet who wasn't pissed off about being shoved out into the world. Welcome to the world, little girl."

A girl.

Her girl.

Their girl.

Happiness flooded her as she looked up at the wiggling baby the doctor held. She looked over at Cole, who looked dumbstruck, with his jaw hanging open.

"You want to cut your little girl's cord?" the doctor asked Cole.

He gulped and nodded, walked over near the baby, reached for the scissors, and fainted, falling back and collapsing into a nearby chair.

Tess shot straight up into a sitting position, the beeps on

the heart monitor going nuts. "Cole!"

"Don't worry," one of the nurses said, hustling over to him. "He's not the first. Daddies tend to get a little overwhelmed. There's a reason why that chair is positioned exactly where it is."

Cole blinked his eyes open and was back almost as quickly as he went out. "What happened?"

"Parenthood," the doctor said as he snipped the umbilical cord. "And this is just the beginning."

He handed the baby to the nurse, who cleaned her up and took measurements before wrapping her up and bringing her back to the bed and placing her on Tess's chest. Everything in her entire body seemed to still. She counted ten fingers and ten toes. The baby's bald round head was covered with a little blue, pink, and white cap and she stared up at Tess like she was the entire world. The happiest tears she'd ever cried wet her cheeks as she looked over at Cole. He was gazing at her and the baby with the exact same expression, as if nothing outside of their little bubble existed, as if the universe had granted every one of his wishes and this was the result.

"Feeling okay, Dad?" the nurse asked. "Can I get you anything?"

Cole shook his head. "Everything I could ever want is already in this room." He glanced down at their girl, a perma-grin on his face. "So what are we going to name her?"

They'd been talking names for the past month, but picking one without meeting their baby didn't sit right with her, so they'd waited. Now, looking down at the baby's long-limbed body and sweet, gentle face, the perfect name popped into Tess's head.

"What do you think about Willow?" She smiled down at the baby, unable to imagine how she'd gotten so lucky, become so wanted. "It's a tree known for its flexibility and resilience."

Cole nodded, running his palm over Willow's cap, his

face soft with awe. "Sounds like the perfect mix of the new me and the always amazing you." He turned his focus to Tess, his eyes a little watery with emotion. "I love you."

Her head didn't fill with random factoids, and only the truth came out. "I love you, too."

And with their little girl's finger wrapped around hers, Tess leaned over and brushed her lips across Cole's in a soft kiss, absolutely certain for the first time in her life that she'd truly found her forever family and her always home.

Keep reading for a sneak peek at the next book in the Ice Knights series, *Loud Mouth*!

Loud Mouth

Chapter One

Shelby Blanton was never going to sleep again.

She should have known better than to watch a double feature about possessed houses while staying alone in a rented cabin out in the middle of the snowdrift-covered nowhere. Yeah, that had definitely been mistake number one. The other big, bad move had been her after-dinner espresso. She was a green tea drinker, but the cabin came with an espresso maker and it seemed fancy and fun and oh my God she could practically hear her heart beating from all the caffeine in her system and her eyes were all, "Blinking? It's for the weak!"

So now here she was, starfished on a king-size bed, practically vibrating from caffeine, and wondering if every creak and groan of the cabin in the dark was actually a malevolent force waiting for her to fall asleep so it could steal her soul. The *tick, tick* had to be the huge grandfather clock—complete with antlers—in the living room. The intermittent hum was the heat kicking on and going off. The shuffle of steps had to be— Shelby jackknifed into a sitting position, one corner of the thick down comforter clutched to her chest, and told herself it wasn't an ax murderer.

Steps? It was her imagination. Or the wind. Or the pipes. Or—holy fuckballs, there it was again.

The noise was coming from downstairs. All of a sudden, the back-to-nature thrill of being in a cell phone dead zone without a landline became a cold blanket of dread that covered her from her chin to the little hairs on her toes. Focus glued to the bedroom door that was open—of course—she reached over to her purse on the nightstand and fished around in it until her fingers brushed by the cool metal of her flashlight stun gun. It wasn't a rock salt safety circle and a blowtorch, but it would at least give her a running start as long as the intruder was human and not a one-eyed ghoul with a grudge.

Okay, she knew the whole haunted thing was just in her head, but tell that to the lizard part of her brain that was doing the ultimate freak-out right now. That was it. She was never watching another scary movie again. Ever.

Slipping out of the bed, stun gun in her tight grip, she held her breath, straining to hear something over the sound of blood rushing in her ears as she tiptoed to the door. Taking up a spot just to the left of the open door, she flattened her back against the wall.

One of the stairs creaked and then another as someone who sounded very un-ghostlike let out a long sigh that under other circumstances would have sounded tired as hell, but considering it was made by a house burglar serial killer, she wasn't about to give him any sympathy.

A nervous giggle started working its way up from her belly. Gritting her teeth, Shelby tightened her abs, hoping to stave off the very inopportune timing of her most hated reflex.

Fuck.

This was not the time for making noise—especially not the high-pitched sound that had resulted in her having the nickname The Squeaker growing up. Okay, it hadn't just been the giggle. She'd never gotten rid of her little-girl voice—no matter how many voice lessons she'd had—and now it was that sound that had telemarketers asking if her mommy was home when she answered the phone that was going to get her straight-up murdered.

Focus, Shelby. Be the badass your tats promise you are.

She had several, but her biggest was a detailed leaf tattoo the length of her forearm. It wasn't exactly a skull and crossbones with a bloody dagger tough, but getting it had hurt like a bitch and she'd survived. That meant she could live through this.

The steps got closer, and she pictured a Goliath of a guy, maybe with a little drool stuck to the corner of his mouth and wild black eyes, walking toward the open bedroom door. She adjusted her sweat-slick grip on the flashlight stun gun—thank you, nerves, for adding that to the mix. Letting out a deep breath, she put her thumb on the switch that would turn on the super-bright light and her finger on the button that would turn on the arc of electricity.

According to the self-defense course she'd taken after the threats got more than the usual you're-a-real-bitch-and-I-hope-you-get-raped variety of being female on the internet, the light would momentarily startle her attacker so she could get in close enough to jab the electric arc into a sensitive spot. The jolt wouldn't be enough to knock him out, but it would incapacitate him long enough for her to run down the stairs, grab her car keys, and get the hell out of this Stephen King book in the making.

He walked through the door, pausing just inside, presumably looking at the tumble of sheets and blankets on the empty bed.

Too bad, asshole, I'm not waiting for you to attack.

Shelby let out a banshee shriek—okay, squeak. The

man whirled around, hands curled into fists. She flipped on the flashlight on the inhale as he reared back, and then she shoved the arcing end into his stomach. Technically, she was supposed to hold it there for three seconds. She got maybe half of one before her grip slipped and she lost contact. He stumbled back, letting out a low rumbly yowl of pain.

That's when she was supposed to run, sprinting away from death and danger. But she didn't, not once her flashlight's beam landed on the man's face and her stomach dropped down to the cabin's wine cellar.

Ian Petrov. Hockey player. Curly haired, bearded sex god. The one person in the world who hated her more than anyone else in the world.

"What the hell," Ian yelled, holding a protective arm over his gut as he advanced toward her. "You better get the fuck out of here before the cops show up."

"Did you follow me?" Brilliant question? No, but her brain was a little shell-shocked at the moment.

"Why in the hell would I do th—" The word died on his lips as recognition and something that looked a lot like disgust crossed his way-too-ruggedly-handsome face. He stopped walking and groaned, letting his head drop back as he mumbled curses at the ceiling. "You have got to be fucking kidding me. You? Here? What are you, stalking me? Haven't you fucked up my life enough?"

Shelby winced. It had been an accident, but the result was the same. *She* was the reason why everyone in Harbor City now knew that Ian's best friend and fellow Ice Knights hockey player Alex Christensen was actually Ian's secret half brother.

When it came out that Alex had known the truth for years without telling Ian, the two men had stopped speaking to each other. Now, the Ice Knights had been torn in two just as the playoffs were starting. It was an unmitigated mess.

Ian may not be a friendly neighborhood murderer, but he might just kill her—metaphorically. All the same, still looked like he wouldn't mind tossing her out into the snow and leaving her to freeze in the night. And part of her couldn't even blame him.

• • •

Ian Petrov had been in some weird situations with women before.

There was the date who showed up in head-to-toe Ice Knights gear and asked if he wanted to see the tattoo of his face on her ass. He'd declined.

One woman had pledged daily blow jobs in exchange for helping her hook up with stern brunch daddy Coach Peppers. Ian still had no idea what a stern brunch daddy was, but if it was a guy who walked around the locker room drinking coffee that was more sugar and milk than caffeine, the team coach would qualify.

His favorite, though, was Clarissa, who had brought both her parents and her little sister along on their date. He'd had a blast at the amusement park with them, but a second date hadn't been a priority for either of them.

Never—not one single time—though, had he ever been stun gunned in his rented AirBNB by the woman who'd ruined his life with her big mouth and who'd managed not just to figure out where he was staying for the next two weeks but to get there early. He had to admit that before he'd Googled her, he'd never pictured the woman behind Harbor City's favorite hockey blog, The Biscuit, to have a Jessica Jones tough-chick look, but now it was made all the more jarring by her high-pitched pipsqueak voice.

"Look, I can give you a head start," he said, turning on the lamp by the bed. "But I'm calling the cops."

"To turn yourself in?" She crossed her arms and snorted in disbelief. "Perfect."

Shelby Blanton—yeah, he'd made it a point to find out her name after what she'd done—was deranged. Sure, she was hot, but definitely one crazy bitch if she thought showing up at his rental cabin was the way to get an exclusive interview or to make an apology for what she'd done. Standing his ground, he did a quick appraisal. Her dark hair was short and wavy, with one side of her scalp shaved down to such a short length, it would have made a Marine recruit envious. She couldn't be more than five foot six, but even in her one-piece black thermal underwear, she managed to look tough. Maybe it was the tattoos or the nose ring—wait, it was definitely the eyes, big and dark and all but shooting laser beams of fury at him.

"Why would I call the cops on myself?" Ian asked, rubbing his abs that still ached from the quick jolt from her stun gun. Fuck, he was wearing a leather jacket and a thick sweater, and it still hurt like hell. If she'd actually managed to get him for longer, his ass would be down on the ground. He probably would have pissed himself just to add to the humiliation of being held at stun-gunpoint in his own rental.

"This is my cabin," she said.

"Nice try, but I have a signed contract for this place." Check and mate.

"Big whoop, so do I, but mine is legit."

He reached for his phone and she leveled that mean little flashlight on steroids at him again.

His gut tensed, which made his stomach hurt even more, and held up a hand. "Whoa, I'm already nursing an injury— don't shoot me with that thing again."

Getting his ass kicked by a stun-gun-wielding emo Goldilocks who sounded like a ten-year-old while standing in the middle of the AirBNB he'd rented specifically because it was in a communications black hole was not something he wanted to have happen. Once Shelby gave him a curt nod, he pulled his phone out and brought up the email confirmation of the booking.

"See?" He turned the phone so the screen faced his attacker.

She rolled her eyes but eventually looked at it. He doubted it was an accident that she kept her stun gun at the ready even as she stayed out of arm's reach. If it wasn't for the fact that she'd showed up uninvited *and armed* at his cabin when all he'd wanted was to be alone and drinking a bottle of scotch, he might have been attracted. He wasn't going to think about that now, though.

Nor would he be dwelling on his dickhead dad with a wandering dick and former friend who'd spent years lying to him. Or contemplating how several of his teammates didn't see what the big deal was. Or bemoaning the fact that he was off the ice for two weeks because he'd fallen over his own damn feet at a team dinner, gone down like a klutz without any athletic ability, and had messed up his thumb enough to need surgery.

"This is bullshit," the woman declared, but she lowered her stun gun. "I have the same confirmation." She stomped past him to the nightstand and picked up her phone. A quick scroll later, she shoved it in his face. "See?"

A fast scan confirmed it was an exact copy of his confirmation from the rental management company for the cabin. "How'd you get this?"

"A sort of friend arranged it for me." She tossed her phone onto the bed but held on to the stun gun even though it was held loose in her grip. "Who pranked you with this confirmation?"

"One, it's not a prank." The only person he knew who would find this kind of joke hilarious was Christensen, and they might share half their DNA but that was it. They weren't friends anymore, let alone the kind who would set something like this up. "Two, it was our team PR person Lucy—"

"Kavanagh," she finished for him.

No. Lucy wouldn't. Okay, she might have helped set up his teammate Stuckey and his now-live-in girlfriend, Zara, plus Ice Knight right winger Phillips and Tess had met and hooked up at Lucy's wedding, but she wouldn't do something like this—not with him, not now, and definitely not with Shelby Blanton. It had to be a mistake.

"Just look at this." She grabbed her phone off the bed and brought up the email that had accompanied her confirmation, and there it was in black and white.

Shelby,

I know just the place. Peaceful with gorgeous views. It's already booked. Plenty of space because the cabin is huge so you can have enough "me time" as you need without being totally alone, which you really don't want to do, considering. It's just what you need. This is actually perfect. Two solitary birds, one fabulous rental cabin. You in?

Lucy

"I thought it was a joke," she said. "Why would I think it was a bird?"

The muscle in his jaw went into hyperactive twitching mode. "Because we're both a pair of dodos for not seeing this coming." So much for not messing with a man when he was down. "She did this on purpose."

Shelby paled. "Why would she do that?"

"Have you met Lucy?" He shook his head, trying to wrap his brain around this mess. "She's all about controlling the situation and the spin. No doubt she thinks this will fix things."

"I can't stay here." Shelby backpedaled a few steps, clutching her phone and the stun gun to her chest.

Ian didn't need to look at his phone to confirm that it was way too late for that. When he'd pulled off the highway and onto the mile-long dirt road to the cabin, the guy on the local radio had just announced it was ten o'clock and warned everyone to get home before the snow got any worse. Anyway, the cabin was miles away from anything even slightly resembling a town.

"Yeah, good luck with that. It's already snowing sideways out; you don't want to be driving in the dark in that," he said because he had enough shit to deal with without worrying about her stuck in a snowbank because he kicked her out. "You can have this room. We'll figure it out in the morning."

Shelby screwed up her mouth like she'd just sucked on a lemon and glared at him as if he controlled the weather or the Ice Knights' PR queen Lucy Kavanagh. Finally, she let out a very unhappy huff. "Fine."

Okay, one battle won. He'd take it. God knew he needed it.

He started toward the door, giving her—and her stun gun—a wide birth. "Hope you don't talk in your sleep. I'd hate for you to go spilling any more life-ruining secrets."

He could have sworn he heard her mumble something along the lines of "fuck you, asshole; it was an accident" as she slammed the door shut in his face. He definitely heard the lock being turned. He couldn't blame her. The whole situation was a mess. First thing tomorrow, he'd find another cabin to sit and drink scotch in and growl at anyone who dared to cross his path. He'd rather go find a frozen hedge maze to wander until he turned into an icicle than to stay here with her. Glancing at the window, he saw the snow piling up fast on the drive. As long as it stopped by dawn, he'd be out of here before breakfast.

It was a great plan, and when he woke up the next morning to bright sunshine spilling in through the huge window looking out onto the front drive, he let out a contented sigh. This was what he'd wanted, fucking serenity now. Then he made the mistake of getting up from bed, walking over to the window, and glancing out.

There wasn't a driveway anymore. The road back down the mountain to the highway was gone. Everything was covered in enough snow to obliterate any hope of an escape.

The unmistakable, might-just-break-glass pitch of Shelby's voice forced its way past his closed door. "Have you seen all the stupid snow? Neither of us is going anywhere."

The sound jabbed him right in the eardrum and he winced.

His life was so fucked right now that he couldn't even manage to be alone so he could contemplate the dark pit of his existence while nursing a scotch and his misery. Instead, he was trapped here—with the woman who'd turned his life into a hellscape.

Things couldn't possibly get any worse.

Author's Note

Trivia facts taken from randomtriviagenerator.com, healthymummy.com, Centers for Disease Control, The Dodo, The Catnip Times, Wikipedia, Science Daily, The Knot, Ava's Flowers, Lifehacker, Supply Time, Love Your Drapery, Visit Denver, Huffpost, History.com, Mental Floss, Smithsonian, DoSomething.org, mobilecusine.com, neatorama.com, NASA, ExpertBail.com.

Acknowledgments

I made this entire book happen all by myself. Only me. No one else. Ha! Yeah, that would be such a nightmare. Y'all don't want to know how badly I abuse the poor comma or overindulge in the word "just." A big thank-you hug to my partner in crime Liz for her editing genius. The entire team at Entangled works magic behind the scenes and does their absolute best not to let me go off the rails. They try, they really try. Thank you so much, Stacy, Curtis, Jessica, and the rest of the team! As always, I would never be able to function without the solid advice and stop-whining tough love from Robin Covington and Kimberly Kincaid. They really are the best friends I could have. They have to put up with so much and yet they still talk to me. AMAZING! And a huge thank-you for my family; I have no idea what I'd do without you. I love you 3,000.

About the Author

Avery Flynn has three slightly wild children, loves a hockey-addicted husband, and is desperately hoping someone invents the coffee IV drip. Find out more about Avery on her website, follow her on Twitter, like her on her Facebook page, or friend her on her Facebook profile. Join her street team, The Flynnbots, on Facebook. Also, if you figure out how to send Oreos through the internet, she'll be your best friend for life.

Don't miss the Ice Knights series...

PARENTAL GUIDANCE

Also by Avery Flynn...

BUTTERFACE

MUFFIN TOP

TOMBOY

THE NEGOTIATOR

THE CHARMER

THE SCHEMER

KILLER TEMPTATION

KILLER CHARM

KILLER ATTRACTION

KILLER SEDUCTION

BETTING ON THE BILLIONAIRE

ENEMIES ON TAP

DODGING TEMPTATION

HIS UNDERCOVER PRINCESS

HER ENEMY PROTECTOR

DADDY DILEMMA

Discover more Amara titles...

THE TROUBLE WITH CHRISTMAS
a *Credence, Colorado* novel by Victoria James

When Suzanne St. Michelle's hoity-toity parents insist she come home for Christmas, she blurts out that her sexy landlord is actually her boyfriend and she can't leave him. Rancher Joshua Grady does not love Christmas. Unfortunately for him, the chattiest woman ever has rented the cottage on his ranch, invited her rich, art-scene parents, and now insists he play "fake rancher boyfriend" in a production of the Hokiest Christmas Ever. And somehow...she gets him to agree. But in the midst of all the production, he's starting to want what he lost when he was a kid—a family. Too bad it's with a woman heading back to New York before the ball drops...

JUST ONE OF THE GROOMSMEN
a *Getting Hitched in Dixie* novel by Cindi Madsen

Addison Murphy is the girl you grab a beer with—and now that one of her best guy friends is getting married, she'll add "groomsman" to that list, too. When Tucker Crawford returns to his small hometown, he doesn't expect to see the nice pair of bare legs sticking out from under the hood of a broken-down car. Certainly doesn't expect to feel his heart beat faster when he realizes they belong to one of his best friends. Hiding the way he feels from the guys through bachelor parties, cake tastings, and rehearsals is one thing. But he's going to need to do a lot of compromising if he's going to convince her to take a shot at forever with him—on her terms this time.

CPSIA information can be obtained
at www.ICGtesting.com
Printed in the USA
BVHW031810201019
561583BV00001B/20/P